ONCE UPON A STAR

THE ADVENTURES OF MANNING DRACO, VOLUME 1

Kendell F. Crossen

ONCE UPON A STAR

THE ADVENTURES OF MANNING DRACO, VOLUME 1

KENDELL FOSTER CROSSEN

ILLUSTRATIONS BY PAUL ORBAN & ALEX SCHOMBURG

FOREWORD BY KENDRA CROSSEN BURROUGHS

ALTUS PRESS • 2013

Published by Altus Press

EDITED AND DESIGNED BY
Matthew Moring
Visit altuspress.com for more books like this.

This edition is based on *Once Upon a Star: A Novel of the Future* (1953), edited for this publication by Kendra Crossen Burroughs.

PUBLISHING HISTORY
The Prolog and Glossary originally appeared in *Once Upon a Star: A Novel of the Future* (New York: Henry Holt & Co., 1953).
The featured stories were originally published as follows:
"The Merakian Miracle," *Thrilling Wonder Stories*, vol. 39, no. 1 (October 1951). Illustrated by Paul Orban.
"The Regal Rigelian," *Thrilling Wonder Stories*, vol. 39, no. 3 (February 1952). Illustrated by Paul Orban.
"The Polluxian Pretender," *Thrilling Wonder Stories*, vol. 41, no. 1 (October 1952). Illustrated by Alex Schomburg.
"The Caphian Caper," *Thrilling Wonder Stories*, vol. 41, no. 2 (December 1952). Illustrated by Alex Schomburg.

Printed in the United States of America.

ISBN: 978-1-61827-102-0

For

STEPHEN, KAREN, KENDRA, AND DAVID

The Terran Miracle
in four acts

CONTENTS

FOREWORD

ONCE UPON A STAR is a quartet of science fiction detective tales that first appeared in *Thrilling Wonder Stories* and were then combined into "A Novel of the Future" (the book's original subtitle). Within its pages, Ken Crossen populated a 35th-century federation of some one hundred planets with an array of weird-looking species evolved by a Mother Nature gone berserk: The Caphians are descended from bats… the Polluxians are reptoids… the Merakians have "psycho-adaptable" flesh… and the Terrans are the ancient race of humankind, with their brief snouts and inadequate teeth. If Charles Darwin were alive today, he'd turn over in his grave.

Before there were the Men in Black, Crossen designed the black-clad Galactic Police with their paralyzers at the ready. Before there was *The Hitchhiker's Guide to the Galaxy*, he envisioned a genderless hitchhiker hanging in space—an Ohio University freshman named Nar Oysnarn from the planet Kholem, whose inhabitants have geometric bodies of changing hues.

Our Terran snoop, Manning Draco, zips through space in his private cruiser, on official business for the Greater Solarian Insurance Company, Monopolated. If some of the techno-wonders of Manning's era—miniature computer, audio-reader, demagnetizer, geoscope, robosmith, and a puny little energy gun—seem a bit lame by today's standards, recall Ursula K. Le Guin's observation that "science fiction is not predictive; it is descriptive." We are transported to another time and place, but it's strangely familiar—a multicultural universe of beings of many colors, where one must respect even the most bizarre customs. As Manning discovers, one culture's fraud is another's bylaw, and you can even make money by dying.

Manning Draco is a master of many talents. He recites Martian love poems, competes in four-dimensional chess and telepathic games, and boasts greater mind-reading abilities than any other human being. And though he would prefer spending his time in romantic dalliance with a curvy humanoid in a blue-feathered hairdo, he ably matches wits and locks minds with con men and scammers both human and alien.

In something of a variation on Le Guin's comment, blogger Dave Maleckar wrote, "Science fiction is whatever we're worried about now, spray-painted silver." But there are no worries between these pages. It's all cheery satire, snappy repartee, dry witticisms, and good-natured fun for all.

A word about the editing. In a Letter to the Editor of *Thrilling Wonder Stories* (April 1953), Ken Crossen wrote that "when I was a mere barefoot schoolboy in Southern Ohio I was accustomed to writing the exam-answers on my otherwise bare feet and this is why I am still so addicted to footnotes." I hope readers won't be too disappointed that I incorporated some of my father's most cumbersome algebraic footnotes into the glossary, for reasons of typographical taste.

Other changes to the text, though minor, make this edition distinct from both the *TWS* stories and the 1953 novel. I am grateful to Matt Moring of Altus Press for giving this vintage classic a new life.

Kendra Crossen Burroughs

PROLOG

Like leaves on trees the race of man is found,
Now green in youth, now withering on the ground:
Another race the following spring supplies,
They fall successive and successive rise.

Homer—*Iliad (VI)*

GALAXY I, sometimes known as the Milky Way Universe, contains almost one million planets known to be inhabited by intelligent beings. Many of these possess ancient and honorable histories, yet to the modern student the most interesting planet of all is the third one in the system of Sol. Once known as Earth, or *the* world, beginning with the twenty-second century it became known as Terra.[1]

In many respects the Terrans advanced far more rapidly than any other race in the galaxy. In an incredible span of about three thousand years, the planet raced through primitive dictatorships, primitive and advanced monarchy, republics, and democracies, totalitarian rules of the Left, Right, and Middle, and finally

---

1 History is vague on why this name was taken. It is known that the ancient Romans on that planet worshiped a goddess named Terra. She was considered the daughter of Chaos and was the goddess of fertility. She was always invoked in the most solemn oaths as Mother Earth *(tellus mater)* and as the common grave of all things. Long after this goddess vanished from religion, the inhabitants of this planet continued to observe a great variety of fertility rites (some of them quite bizarre) and it is believed that Terra may be the one goddess which continued to this day to exert a great influence.

achieved an equalitarian one-world government in 2164 following a two-hundred-year war that almost destroyed the planet.

Terra first achieved space flight (as opposed to simple rocket flight which enabled them to reach their satellite in 1987) by 2200. This was about the same time that space flights were being made by the inhabitants of five other star systems in the galaxy. The first contacts between the strange planets were tentative and marked by considerable hesitation on the part of everyone. Concealed by this diffidence, however, each planet was planning how to conquer the others. As a natural result, interplanetary war broke out in the spring of 2306 between Terra, Mars, Vega I, Rigel IV, and Dubhe III.

Those early ships were slow and cumbersome and there was little damage done in the first fifty years of the war. But progress was rapid and as the galactic battle went into its second century, fifteen other planets declared war on one side or the other. For six hundred years the battle raged across the galaxy and the damage and loss of life stagger the imagination. Finally, in the year 3014, the war was suddenly ended following a secret agreement between Terra, Mars, Vega, Sirius, and Procyon.

Shortly after peace was restored, Terra, once more backed by Mars, Vega, Sirius, and Procyon, formed the Galactic Federation which they have dominated since that time.

In the early years the Federation was what might be described as a loose democracy and during that time it grew to include almost a hundred planets. Then the Terran bloc pulled the coup of 3453 and the first monopolist government came into power.

For our purpose, it is significant to notice that a young man named J. Barnaby Cruikshank played an important role in the shift of political power and received the first monopoly charter to be granted by the new government. He was only twenty-three years of age at the time.

The year that J. Barnaby Cruikshank achieved the status of a federation monopolist, Manning Draco had just entered Solar University on Rigel Kentaurus, and Dzanku, the Rigelian, had only picked his first pocket.

The brave new universe was just around the corner....

ACT ONE / SUMMER 3472

THE MERKIAN MIRACLE

CHAPTER ONE

MANNING DRACO leaned over the railing in the outer offices of the Greater Solarian Insurance Company, Monopolated, and studied the Martian receptionist. She had been working in the home office on Earth for only a week, but she was showing the influence of the Nyork stylists. Her reddish head fur had been given a henna rinse, bringing out the burnished copper tints, and arranged in the Nebulae Upsweep that was the rage that summer of 3472. Skillful makeup had enhanced the copper of her skin and played up the slight slant of her eyes. Her figure was unusually voluptuous for a Martian and a new Earth-style dress brought out the best of her humanoid points.

All in all, the improvement was so great that Manning Draco had stopped for a second look. He moved nearer to her desk and waited until she glanced up.

"My mind is open to you," he said. It was a formal Martian greeting, but he managed to give it undertones never dreamed of by the original Martian semanticists.

"And mine to you," she responded, looking at him with one eye, and lowering the other two demurely.

"What's your name, honey?" It was more polite to ask than to probe mentally for it. Besides, he knew by experience that it was difficult to slip by the mind shields of Martians.

"Lhana Xano—Mr. Draco."

"You know my name," he said in delight. "Well, then, you must know that I work here, too, and that we are all, as J. Barnaby Cruikshank is so fond of saying, one big happy family—so why don't you have dinner with me tonight?"

"Thank you, Mr. Draco, but I'm afraid not." A slight lisp was the only trace of her Martian accent.

"Give me one good reason why you won't," he challenged. He tried a swift probe to see if she was being coy, but it bounced off her mind shield.

"I'll give you three reasons," she said promptly. She surveyed him swiftly with all three eyes. "It's true that you are tall for a Terran—perhaps three inches over six feet—but you are still seven inches shorter than I am. I dislike being conspicuous when I go out."

"I'll rush right out," Manning said with a grin, "and buy a pair of shoes with a Galactic-lift. You know the ones they advertise on the Martian video for the tourist trade, with the slogan: 'Now you can be as tall as your Martian dream girl.'"

"My second reason," Lhana said seriously, "is that when I first came to work here, I was warned about you by every girl in the office, including that little file clerk who comes from Upper Seginus and isn't even remotely humanoid."

"It was a dull evening," he said defensively.

"And my third reason," she continued, "is that when you were watching me a few minutes ago your secondary mind shield relaxed for a second and I caught what you were thinking."

HE GRINNED ruefully. "Every time I get to feeling smug about being the only Terran to develop a secondary mind shield, I run into one of you Martians and get taken down a parsec or two," he said. "But now that you know my intentions, how about having dinner with me?"

Before she could answer, the visiplate on her desk glowed redly. She flipped a switch and a section of the desk swung up to shield the visiplate and the voice which would come from it from anyone standing before the receptionist.

"Yes, sir," the Martian girl said. She listened a moment and then added, "Yes, sir. I'll tell him." She cut the circuit and the visiplate, now gray and empty, swung into view again.

Manning Draco had never discovered a sense of humor in a Martian, but he could have sworn there was a hint of laughter in her third eye as she looked up at him.

"Mr. Cruikshank would like to see you in his office immediately," she said. "I'm afraid you're not going to be free for dinner, Mr. Draco. But it's been nice meeting you."

"Not so fast, honey. I'll be back and we'll resume our discussion of that dinner date." He turned and strode through the offices.

Outside the private office of the president, he waited until the door-scanner recognized him and the door swung open. He stepped inside and faced the head of the monopoly.

At forty, J. Barnaby Cruikshank was the president and chief stockholder of a company that spanned two galaxies. It was true that he had inherited the original company from his grandfather, but up to that time it had been a small company insuring only humans and confining its operations to Earth. Under the direction of J. Barnaby, policies had been issued to cover all forms of life on every planet. Since J. Barnaby was also influential in Federation politics, the Earth corporation had soon achieved an intergalactic monopoly charter and Manning Draco, as his chief investigator, was accorded limited police powers throughout the galaxies.

The urbanity of J. Barnaby Cruikshank was at low ebb as Manning Draco entered. His hair was rumpled and his plastic sport coat, guaranteed not to wrinkle, was wrinkled.

"What were you doing at the reception desk?" he growled as soon as he saw Manning.

"Trying to date the receptionist," Manning said frankly. He dropped into one of the comfortable chairs. "It's amazing how soon those girls lose their provincial look when they get to Nyork."

"I hired that Martian girl," said J. Barnaby, glaring at his investigator, "partly in the hope that you'd stay away from the reception desk. Don't you draw the line anywhere?"

"Well, you know the old saying—all stars look the same when you're cruising in space.... Did you call me in to discuss the moral tone of the office or do I detect the air of the worried business man?" Manning spoke quietly.

J. Barnaby shuffled through some papers on his desk, but it was obvious from his manner that he already knew what they contained. "What do you know about Merak II?" he asked.

"Obviously it's the second planet in the system of Merak," Manning said with an easy grin, "but outside of that I'm afraid I know nothing. Are we selling policies there now?"

"You'd know we were if you were doing your job instead of doing your best to undermine what you call the moral tone of this office. "The planet was opened for intergalactic trade two months ago."

"Okay. So I'll run over to the main library tonight and take a hypno-course on the planet. Then if anything comes up—"

"It already has," J. Barnaby snapped, "and you'll be on your way to Merak II tonight. I'll give you all the information I can and you can pick up the rest when you get there."

MANNING LEANED back in the chair and prepared to fix the information in his memory. "Okay," he murmured.

"When the planet was opened," J. Barnaby said, "the new territory was requested by two of our men. Since they had done an excellent job on Sirius III, we gave it to them."

"Sirius III," mused Manning, triggering his memory file. "That would be Sam Warren, a Terran, and Dzanku Dzanku, from Rigel IV. They're the two characters who sold insurance as a team. I think I warned you that they would steal the gilt off the seal on the policies if they could find a market for it. What have they done now?"

"Nothing," snapped J. Barnaby. "At least, I don't think they have. They're just good high-pressure salesmen, that's all. The trouble isn't with them at all."

"But I'll bet they're mixed up in it some way. Go on."

"The Merakians," said J. Barnaby, "are non-humanoids. I am told that their bodies are globular in shape and that they have no necks and heads in the humanoid sense. Their mouths, noses, eyes and ears appear as needed and when these organs are not in use, all that can be seen is the smooth surface of a globe. They usually have two arms and two legs, but these are retractable and extensional, so that a Merakian maybe three feet tall when you first meet him and eight feet tall the next time you see him."

"A perfect solution to the problem of Martian girls who are taller than you are," Manning murmured.

J. Barnaby suppressed his irritation, for he had learned that the surface levity never interfered with the working of one of the best developed brains in the galaxy.

"Culturally, and socially," he said, "the Merakians are a Class D people. Their interests are on a primitive level, but they seem to have a boundless enthusiasm for everything new and it is expected that they will soon become Class C, perhaps even Class B, but it is doubtful if they will ever progress beyond that point. They have already learned English, Rigelian, and Vegan, the three official galactic languages, and have taken up most civilized sports.

"Two things will illustrate how childish they are. Although they do not eat at all, drawing their energy directly from their sun, they have bought two million dish-washing robots since trade was opened, and ten million dishes for the robots to wash. They have also adopted with great enthusiasm the one childish holiday which our American state has insisted on maintaining. A billion credits' worth of atomicworks were imported to Merak II so that they could celebrate the Fourth of July last week."

"The trouble with you," said Manning, "is that you begrudge people the simple pleasures of life. Who sold them the fireworks—you?"

"No. Warren and Dzanku did it on their own. You know, we allow our agents to carry on a certain amount of private business as long as it doesn't interfere with selling our policies."

"And I gather this didn't?"

"I'll say it didn't." For a minute, J. Barnaby's face brightened. "In less than six weeks, Warren and Dzanku sold straight life insurance policies on Merak II totaling four billion, seventeen million credits." The happiness faded from his face. "Although each policy holder was in excellent health, and none of them was more than two hundred and fifty years old while the average life span there is four hundred years, the majority of our insured on Merak dropped dead last week. We are being asked to pay out four billion, six million credits in benefits, after having received only one premium on each policy."

"Ah-ha," said Manning. "J. Barnaby has been struck where it hurts. Straight life insurance, too, which means there probably isn't a loophole even if you have been taken."

THE PRESIDENT bobbed his head. "That's what I thought until today," he said. "But we have heard from a very reliable source that two of the insured who died last week were seen alive yesterday. So it begins to look like a straight fraud case."

"Wait a minute," said Manning Draco. "If the Merakians look as you described them, how do you tell one policy holder from another?"

"They have a strange pattern of whorls, not too different from our fingerprints, on their stomachs. Apparently these can't be altered, and the pattern is different with each Merakian."

"What is the population of Merak II?" Manning asked with a grin.

"About seventy-five million, I believe. What's so funny about it?" he added irritably as Manning burst into laughter.

"I was just picturing the Intergalactic Patrol making seventy-five million Merakians belly up to an ink pad."

"I suggest," J. Barnaby said coldly, "that you spend more time picturing our four billion credits—unless you want to lose your job." His voice softened. "Manning, my boy, you've got to find some way of saving us on this."

"I'll blast off sometime tonight," Manning said, getting up, and be there to take it up the first thing in the morning. Relax, J, Barnaby."

"You might as well forget about the Martian receptionist," J. Barnaby said. "You're blasting off this afternoon, not tonight. I ordered your ship serviced, and it will be ready by the time you can reach the spaceport. I ordered an encyclotape on Merak II loaded on your ship and you can pick up what little is known about the planet while you're on your way. By the way, your first stop is Muphrid VIII, in Boötes."

"Muphrid VIII?" Manning said. "Why?"

For a moment he thought that J. Barnaby looked embarrassed but then he dismissed the idea. Later, he was to remember it.

"Our newest branch office," J. Barnaby explained, "has just been opened on Muphrid VIII. Technically, Merak II falls in their territory, so I thought you might stop off there and meet the vice-president just as a formality."

"Muphrid VIII—Class A planet inhabited by a humanoid race," muttered Manning. He ran over the rest of the information on the planet mentally and could see nothing to indicate more than the formality mentioned.

"That's right," J. Barnaby said eagerly. "The vice-president in charge of the branch office is a native Muphridian—comes friom one of the oldest families there. I don't want him thinking that we're by-passing him completely, but you don't have to stay there long. The vice-president's name is Schmendrik Korshay."

"Okay, I'll look him up," Manning said. "And don't transfer that new receptionist before I get back." He grinned and left.

CHAPTER TWO

A T THE SPACEPORT, Draco's ship was already on the launching level. He cleared with the tower, fed the position of Muphrid VIII into the automatic pilot, and pushed the panel button that hooked the ship into magnetic power.

As the ship blasted off, he found the encyclotape and fed it into the audio-reader. Then he leaned back to listen.

"Merak II," said a pleasant voice from the concealed speaker, "is a Class D planet In Ursa Major. Although discovered and charted in 3160 by Galactic Commander Daniel Horlan, there has been little contact with the planet until this year when it was admitted to the Federation and trading agreements were signed. The planet is a mean distance from its sun, Merak, of ninety-two million miles. Its mass is 0.9 in relation to that of Earth, its volume 0.976; its density is 5.16 times that of water; its diameter, six thousand nine hundred miles; orbital velocity, 17.8 miles per second; escape velocity 6.9 miles per second; period of rotation, twenty-five hours, six minutes; eccentricity, 0.0157—"

Manning Draco reached over and punched a button. The tape skipped a few inches and the voice took up its story again.

"—gravity at surface, 0.97. The dominant race on Merak II are technically known as Deetahs. The main trunk of their bodies is globe-shaped and also serves as a head. Their flesh is highly psycho-adaptable, the various organs of senses appearing only when needed. They have at least two arms and two legs, somewhat humanoid in general shape, but these limbs are re-tractable and extensional. The Merakians are non-eaters, drawing their energy directly from their sun, but they do consume liquids, mostly water. There is some evidence of intoxicants also being used.

"There is as yet no definite information concerning reproduc-tion among the Merakians, but it is believed that it takes place by fission. Although it seems that the members of this race are all of one sex, they do marry and carry on primitive domestic relations. Our information shows that normally three members of the race will marry, one of them—usually chosen by some form of crude lottery—will reproduce while the other two take over the task of raising the young.

"The Merakians are ruled by what seems to be a benevolent dictatorship. There is a hereditary Council of Selectors, which might be compared to royalty among human races, but they do no ruling at all. They do, however, choose one individual from the inhabitants who is trained to become the ruler, or Dukar. His rule is then absolute and is for life. Upon his death, a new Dukar is selected. The present Dukar is Mneone Melpar, the Ninth. Although the average life span of the Merakians is four hundred years, Mneone Melpar is eight hundred and ten years old and has been ruling Merak II for the past six hundred and sixty years.

"Although the Legal Council of the Federation has not yet released its report on the constitution and laws of Merak II, it is believed that they are a law-abiding race. Their constitution is a document of more than one thousand pages and they have seven hundred and twenty-two thousand, six hundred and seventy-eight national laws, while there has not been a single case of crime during the past forty years.

"The Merakians are a primitive and childlike people—"

Manning Draco switched off the machine and went to sleep.

TWO HOURS later, as his ship braked for the atmosphere of Muphrid VIII, he awakened. He announced himself to the spaceport and switched on his landing-scanner. A scarlet pip showed up on the gray screen. He set the ship controls to follow the pip and a blue dot began chasing the scarlet one across the screen. When the two finally merged, he knew the ship was in its cradle. Contact with the cradle had automatically shut off the power. Manning waited while subtle pressures balanced themselves and then stepped out when the door opened itself.

A beam-controlled aircar was waiting for him, the name of the insurance company stenciled on its side in both English and Muphridian. This was his first trip to the planet, and he would have preferred going by surface transportation in order to see the rather large city he glimpsed as he left his ship. But it wouldn't be polite to keep the new vice-president waiting, so he entered the aircar and was whisked across the city. The car entered the top floor of a large office building where he was met by a robot and escorted to a luxurious private office.

At first glance, Manning would have sworn that the new vice-president was a human. It was only when he looked closer that he realized that here was the perfect humanoid. Every feature was human, and the only difference was so slight he almost missed it. The Muphridian's head was covered with iron-gray feathers instead of hair.

"Schmendrik Korshay," the vice-president announced himself in English, coming to meet Manning with an outstretched hand.

"Manning Draco," the investigator said. As they shook hands, he tried a swift mental probe and got the shock of his life. It was like sending his mind up against a solid wall.

"From the look of surprise on your face," Korshay said with a smile, "I presume you must have tried a telepathic thrust at me. You see, I know from Mr. Cruikshank that your telepathic abilities, both offensive and defensive, are developed more than those of any other human. I am sorry to have disappointed you."

"That's putting it mildly," said Manning. "That's the most perfect primary mind shield I've ever encountered."

"Technically, it isn't a mind shield," the vice-president explained. "You see, we Muphridians are nontelepaths—one of the few such races in the galaxy today—and the evolution which neglected us in that respect balanced it by giving us minds which cannot be read by any telepath. Incidentally, I believe the same thing is true of the Merakians. But while we're discussing that matter, would you like a drink?"

Manning Draco hesitated. The last time he had accepted a drink on a strange planet had been on Praesepe I, and it had been two days before he recovered the use of his voice.

Korshay smiled. "I realize that you are on your first visit to Muphrid and so may be wary of accepting. Let me assure you, my dear Mr. Draco, that with the exception of certain basic functions we Muphridians share human tastes as well as appearances. The drink is rather excellent brandy."

"Fine," Manning said. He was beginning to like this vice-president, a feeling he seldom had about such officers. While the brandy was being poured, he relaxed enough to relate the incident of the strange drink on Praesepe I.

"I hear there are many such traps in the galaxy," Korshay said, laughing. He handed a glass to Draco and raised his own.

"Yours has been a glamorous life, Mr. Draco. May it continue for many years."

THEY DRANK and Manning made the proper noises of appreciation over the excellence of the brandy. He relaxed even more.

"Now, then," said the vice-president, "I don't want to keep you from your assignment on Merak II. You understand, Mr. Draco, that while my position gives me a certain authority over you concerning company matters, I wouldn't presume to consider myself capable of giving you any sort of orders. This branch office is just opened and I, myself, am too new to the Greater Solarian Insurance Company."

Manning nodded. He smiled, feeling that for once the company had showed intelligence in its choice of a new executive. Up to this point, the vice-presidents of branch offices had been veritable thorns in his side.

"Therefore, the matter which I'm about to broach has been discussed with Mr. Cruikshank, and essentially it is his order although he thought it best for me to explain it to you," Korshay said.

The smile vanished from Manning Draco's face. He sat up straighter in his chair and, aware that Korshay was not telepathic, let his mind play over the more salient aspects of vice-presidents.

"Cruikshank," he said slowly, when he had exhausted the possibilities in several languages, "is a double-crossing, underhanded, illegitimate mutated offspring of a Martian wart hog. What's being pulled on me now?"

"I'm afraid you're jumping to conclusions," Korshay said, smiling, "and reacting just as he said you would. It's really very simple, Mr. Draco. This is a new office and of course lacks trained personnel. While I realize that you will handle all important investigations in this territory, there will undoubtedly be a need for minor investigations, too insignificant to warrant your making a trip. Consequently, I wish a relative of mine to go to

Merak with you and learn as much as possible about how you operate."

"A relative," Manning said with violence. He missed hearing a door in the office open. "I should have known it. I never saw a vice-president who wasn't trying to get all of his relatives on the payroll. And it's always Manning Draco who has to take the rap. Order or no order, you can damn well wait until Mercury freezes over. I am *not* going to play nursemaid to any cretinous vice-president's half-witted, monkey-faced—"

THE REST of the statement was forever lost to posterity, for Manning Draco received the second shock of his visit. A vision was moving across the room toward him. She, too, was humanoid, with a figure not only human but more so. She wore the semitransparent sport clothes which were the rage in all civilized parts of the galaxy, and she was not one of those who had to have her clothes made with concealed lights to give the illusion of curves that weren't there. Her face, with full, almost pouting lips, was framed in a halo of blue feathers, soft and swirling.

"Mr. Draco," the vice-president said dryly, "I'd like you to meet my relative—Kramu Korshay."

"Hello," the vision said, and her voice was like the music of the spheres. "I have so looked forward to meeting you, Mr. Draco. My relative has done nothing but talk of your exploits since he became associated with your company."

Manning Draco took a deep breath and tore his gaze back to the vice-president, "As I was saying," he said quickly, "I will be only too happy to cooperate with your office, Mr. Korshay."

There was only the hint of a smile on the vice-president's face. "I was sure you would," he said gravely. "I know that on your home planet there has always been a superstition that beautiful women do not possess brains, but I think you will find Kramu quite competent in all departments. Now if you'll excuse me, I'm sure you want to be heading for Merak II." He crossed the room, and kissed Kramu on both cheeks. Then he shook hands with Manning and left the office.

CHAPTER THREE

STILL DAZED by what he regarded as his good fortune, Manning led the way back to his ship. He fed the position of Merak II into the pilot and as the ship lifted into space, he turned to Kramu with a pleasant smile.

"I've heard so much about you and your ship," she said before he could even begin telling her how beautiful she was. "Won't you show me around? What do you call her?"

"*Alpha Actuary*," he said, getting up. The ship incorporated several of his own designs, and they had impressed more sophisticated. audiences than this one. The time would not be wasted. And she would be on Merak II with him until the case was finished.

"What a peculiar name," Kramu exclaimed. "Why do you call her that?"

"Because she's the first one of her kind for the *Alpha. Actuary* because in insurance an actuary is one who computes risks and probabilities, and this ship will do just that. Here, for example."

He showed her the compact little computer built into the ship above the control panel. On a small screen, the computer would flash answers in English, give mathematical formulae, and show varicolored graphs. He fed it a question about their present trip, and the time of their arrival was immediately flashed on the screen, the hour in red, the minute in blue, and the second in yellow. Then, in an impish mood, he asked the machine what would happen on his first date with Kramu. She laughed in delight when the screen flashed with all the colors then relapsed to dull gray without giving any answer.

"I've been sabotaged," Manning muttered and turned to the rest of the ship.

He showed her the audio-reader, with tapes covering almost every subject in the galaxy; he explained the demagnetizer, opening the scanners to full power so that she could see an approaching meteorite disintegrate as it approached the ship.

He demonstrated the geoscope which could select and show a three-dimensional photograph of any charted country or city in the galaxy, and let her try out the impulse-translator which would turn any language into English; he had the robosmith make her a pair of silver earrings. The latter machine, he explained, was for manufacturing trinkets when he had to land on a barbaric planet and deal with savages.

BY THE TIME he had finished showing her the ship and explaining everything, they were only thirty minutes from Merak II.

"Now, honey," Manning said as he dropped into a comfortable chair, "it'll be too late to start working tonight when we reach Merak, so we'll have dinner together and then we'll go out on the town. I don't know what they have there in the way of entertainment but if nothing else, we can always take a music cone from the ship and dance. Okay?"

"No," she said, shaking her head until the blue feathers danced, but her smile took the sting from the refusal. "We'll have dinner together and you'll explain to me the simple rules of making an investigation. Afterward, we'll either work on the case, or you will tell me of other cases so that I can learn how you work."

"Baby," Manning Draco said sadly, "if you keep that up, you're liable to find yourself the richest woman on Muphrid—but lonely. What about our date?"

"No, Manning," she said firmly. "No pleasure until after the work is finished—and then only if we finish in time."

"In time for what?"

"I have an appointment back on Muphrid which can't be put off, but if we finish on Merak in time, I see nothing wrong with celebrating our success."

"Then I'll finish it up so fast those Merakians will think they're riding the tail of a comet," he promised. "I know a swell little planetoid, not too far from Muphrid, where we can go for the weekend."

"Perhaps," she said, with a smile like a delayed promise.

"You know, honey, working with the relative of an executive

in the company was never like this before. What relation are you to Korshay anyway—a niece?"

"The degree of relationship on Muphrid is not quite the same as on your Earth, but that's close enough." She glanced at the time indicator on the panel and frowned. "But before we arrive at Merak, I'd like it if you briefed me on this case, Manning. I have been told very little about it."

"Okay, honey," he said with a sigh, "you win. When Merak II was opened for trade, a couple of our men asked for the territory and were granted it. They are Dzanku Dzanku, a Rigelian I wouldn't trust as far as I could throw his one-ton body, and Sam Warren, a Terran who is just as crooked as Dzanku but not as smart. They're high pressure boys and they've sold more than four billion credits' worth of straight life insurance since then.

"But last week about four-fifths of the insured died. That is suspicious in itself, but J. Barnaby, our boss, has since heard that some of the dead have been seen alive. Chiefly, we have to prove that there was fraud in the cases or Greater Solarian is out four billion credits—a fate far worse than death to J. Barnaby. Now..."

He continued outlining the rest of the scanty information he had gathered from J. Barnaby and from the encyclo-tape. By the time he had finished, the Merakian spaceport was looming large on the screen. He switched on his communicator, but there was no immediate answer. Cursing, he threw the ship to Manual and lifted it higher. Continuing to call the spaceport, he circled overhead. After about ten minutes, with Manning's patience growing thinner by the minute, a high, shrill voice spoke from the speaker in the ship.

"Prithee," the voice said, "who is it that comes to fair Merak?"

FOR A STARTLED MINUTE, Manning Draco stared at the speaker and wondered if he was going mad. His feelings were not helped by a giggle from Kramu, or by the swift continuation of what he had thought was an auditory hallucination.

"Answer, varlet," squeaked the voice again. "Who comes to fair Merak?"

"I come to fair Merak to bash somebody in the head," snapped Manning, "if I don't get a landing beam pretty soon. This is the spaceship *Alpha Actuary*, owned and operated by Terran Manning Draco, arriving on official business for the Greater Solarian Insurance Company, Monopolated, under a Galactic Federation Charter. Now where the hell is my landing beam?"

"Thy words are most unseemly, friend," said the voice, "but approach and be recognized. Thou wilt appreciate that the landing must needs be by hand."

"I will not appreciate it," Manning muttered angrily as a thin beam of light shot up from the ground, touching his ship. He touched the controls and sent the ship hurtling toward the ground. At the last minute, he pulled it up sharply. The ship seemed to hang a few feet above the ground, then settled down with a gentle bump.

"Come on, honey," he said, "let's see what kind of jokers these are."

As Manning started to step out of the ship, he was surprised to see an arm stretch up. A hand grasped him by the elbow and helped him from the ship. In the meantime, a second arm had stretched up to help Kramu. When he reached the ground, Manning realized that both arms were attached to a native Merakian who stood some twenty feet from the ship.

As the arms retreated to about two feet in length, two eyes suddenly appeared on the globelike body. The eyes surveyed Manning, then suddenly the legs lengthened until the Merakian's eyes were on a level with Manning's. Ears budded on the side of the globe; a mouth appeared, at least a foot below the eyes, and curved into a grin.

"Greetings, gate," the Merakian said in a shrill voice.

"What?" demanded Manning. "Is this whole planet infested with idiots? You call me gate once more and I'll swing on you. Now, tell me where we—" He broke off as he recognized two figures standing beneath a canopy near what was apparently the main building of the spaceport. "Never mind," he said to the Merakian. "We'll see you around."

"Plant me now and dig me later, kid," the Merakian said sharply. The mouth and ears smoothed out and vanished as he scurried away.

Manning, followed by Kramu, strode across to the two figures beneath the canopy. One of them was a Terran, shorter than Manning, with a tense, wary expression on his face. His companion was a Rigelian, no taller than Manning but weighing a good ton. His thick, square torso was supported by two legs like tree trunks. From the upper part of his body projected six tentacles. His face was small and expressionless, with three eyestalks raised several inches above it. Two of the eyes were surveying Manning, while the third stalk was inclined in the direction of Kramu.

"Hello, Draco," Sam Warren called as they neared. "We heard you were coming, so Dzanku and I thought we'd meet you. Sort of roll óut the welcome mat for you. Thought you were coming alone though—"

"This is Kramu Korshay from Muphrid," Manning said shortly. "She's along to learn the business. Say, what's wrong with this screwy planet anyway?"

"Many things, but to what do you refer?" asked the Rigelian. His voice had a deep, sonorous timbre—it inspired confidence in the unwary.

"I mean the way these Merakians talk," said Manning. "When we were coming in for the landing, the tower blasts out with a sentence which might have come right out of the Museum of Ancient Languages on Terra. Then when we landed there's another's butterball who had a line about 'dig me now and plant me later.' What the hell that meant I'll probably never know. It sounded like Nekkarian triple-talk translated verbatim."

"Well—ah—" Sam Warren said, "when Merak II was opened for trade, the natives, eager little fellows that they are, were quite anxious to learn English. You may remember when the Terran Historical Society had the bright idea of selling taped records of all the ancient Earth dialects.

"They used the biggest visistars to record them, but the idea never took and the Society was left with a warehouse full of tapes. Well, I believe some enterprising individuals made a rather good deal on those old tapes and then sold them to the Merakians, with a vocabulary guide sheet, at—ah—a very handsome profit."

"I see," Manning said sarcastically. "I don't suppose those enterprising individuals just happened to be named Warren and Dzanku, did they?"

The Rigelian chuckled. "Now that you mention it," he said, "I believe we did have a hand—or perhaps I should say tentacle—in it. But I assure you, Draco, that it was all quite legitimate. My dear Miss Korshay," he added, making a courtly bow, his tentacles waving gracefully, "I trust you will not be unduly influenced by Draco's un-Galactic prejudices. I assure you that fully one-third of the language courses we sold were the approved courses specifically made for Merak II."

CHAPTER FOUR

WHILE DZANKU was talking to Kramu Korshay, Manning was aware that he was making sly probes at his primary mind shield. But suddenly the full force of the Rigelian's powerful mind lashed out. It crashed through his primary shield and struck his secondary shield with a force that made him reel. But the shield held, and after the first uncertainty, he felt the strength flowing back into him. Then, abruptly, the probing force was gone.

"My congratulations," murmured Dzanku. He was unperturbed by his failure. "You are, I believe, the only Terran to ever achieve the secondary mind shield. Interesting."

Although he had no hope of penetrating the Rigelian's mind shield—something which even the professional thought-probers of Alpha Cygni couldn't do, according to Federation reports—Manning Draco struck once. It was just enough to alert Dzanku for a follow-up. Then Manning struck quickly at the mind of Sam Warren. The little Terran staggered from the force of the blow, his face paling.

As he slipped through the primary shield, Manning had access to Sam Warren's thoughts and memories. There was a clutter of unimportant thoughts, but mixed with them was a vague fear. Manning understood the vagueness when he felt the erased synapse. He withdrew quickly and looked at the Rigelian.

"Clever," he said. "You knew you couldn't protect Sam from me, so you destroyed his memory of how you actually worked the swindle."

"You overestimate my mediocre talents," murmured Dzanku. "Why should I destroy Sam's memory? He is my friend. Besides, he owes me fifteen credits from a game of Castorian Rummy which we played last night. I wouldn't want him to forget that."

"I'm putting all the cards on the table," Manning said. "I think you and Sam got a slice of the four billion credits which Greater Solarian has had to pay out on policies here. In fact, I think you two engineered the whole deal. Then you telepathed into Sam's mind and erased the synapse which carried the memory of the fraud. Since your own mind cannot be read, except by another Rigelian, you feel that you are now perfectly safe."

The Rigelian's tentacles waved with an air of innocence. "If your premise were correct, that would be true," he admitted, "but would I repay the kindness of Greater Solarian in such a fashion? Are we not, as J. Barnaby Cruikshank so eloquently expresses it, one big happy family? Isn't that true, Sam?"

"Yeah," the little Terran said, grinning. "It sure is. We wouldn't do nothing like that, Manning."

ONE OF DZANKU'S eye-stalks swiveled toward the building back of them. "Ah," he said, "you are about to be officially welcomed, Manning. I hope you appreciate that this is happening only because we have the interests of Greater Solarian at heart."

Looking up, Manning saw a Merakian hurrying toward them. The legs were extended until they were about twenty feet in length so that the Merakian was advancing with tremendous strides. Above the legs, the globular body was smooth and featureless. As the native neared them, the legs began to shorten. By the time he arrived, he was no taller than Manning or Dzanku. He came to a halt, and two eyes and a mouth appeared. An ear sprouted on top of his head, only to fade quickly and reappear on the side. Another matched it on the other side.

"So sorry," murmured the Merakian, his gaze fixed on Manning. "You Terrans are so new to us that sometimes one forgets to affix organs in the places you seem to favor."

"At least he speaks normal English," Manning said in relief.

"Of course," Dzanku said promptly. "Manning, I would like you to meet Mneone Melpar, the Ninth, most luminous and high globular Dukar of all Merak, sole ruler and arbitrator of Merak II, its satellites and bodies, its possessions and potentials. Your Dukarness, these visitors are Manning Draco from Terra, and Kramu Korshay from Muphrid VIII. They come bearing the good wishes of that great galactic family known as the Greater Solarian Insurance Company, Monopolated."

Manning was not quite sure how to greet a Dukar of Merak, but before he could make a decision an extensional arm had snapped out and he found himself shaking hands. He noticed that a second right arm had appeared and was simultaneously shaking the hand of Kramu.

"I," said Mneone Melpar shrilly, "am the eight thousand, six hundred and twenty-seventh Dukar to rule Merak, now being in my six hundred and sixtieth year of reign, and of all Dukars I am most blessed by this visit. Consider the planet of Merak II and the capital city of Tor-Melpar to be your home."

"Thank you," Manning said. "As you may know, we are here to look into the matter of insurance and the unfortunate deaths of so many of your subjects. My company believes there may have been fraud."

"All Merak shall be at your disposal," the Dukar said solmenly. "Feel free to call upon the Merakian Police Force, the Merakian Stomach-Printers—even myself. The very thought of crime nauseates me. I will not tolerate any form of law breaking. I have spoken."

"Thank you," Manning said again. "Your cooperation will be reported to the Federation. Now, my companion and I would like to go to a good hotel."

"The Mneone Plaza is already expecting you. The Emperor's Suite has been reserved for you, *Tshone* Draco, and the Empress' Suite for your companion. Both have been altered for the convenience of Terrans or those with Terran form."

"And tomorrow," Dzanku said, "when you have rested, the office will be ready to serve you in your investigation."

"Office?" asked Manning.

"We have taken the liberty," murmured Dzanku, "of establishing a local office of Greater Solarian here in the city of Tor-Melpar. Sam and I are paying for it ourselves until such time as the company wishes to take it over. Naturally, Sam and I will also be happy to help you with the investigation."

"Naturally," Manning said dryly. "Now, how do we get to this hotel?"

"One of my own cars will take you," the Dukar announced, waving a hand in the direction of a globular aircar which had come up and was hovering silently nearby. "May you die quickly, *Tshone* Draco, *Tshina* Korshay."

Manning had already started for the aircar, but with that he swung around, his gaze going suspiciously from the Dukar to Dzanku Dzanku. "What's the meaning of that crack?" he demanded.

"Now, now," Dzanku said hurriedly, "the Dukar was merely using a very old and polite Merakian form of saying good-by. It was—ah—always believed that the Merakian heaven was the most pleasant place in the galaxy and so to die quickly was soon to be happy."

"Yeah, that's it," Sam Warren said.

"Okay, may you die quickly, too," Manning said sourly. "Come on Kramu," he added, turning to the aircar. They were quickly inside and did their best to make themselves comfortable in the hollows which apparently served as seats for the Merakians. The aircar skimmed off toward the city.

ALTHOUGH THE WALLS of the aircar had seemed opaque from the outside, they discovered they were transparent from the inside. As they neared the city, Manning noticed that the architecture was all of spherical lines. Here and there, on the street, they could see Merakians strolling aimlessly. Once they noticed a new store with a line of video screens, each one tuned to a different station in the galaxy, displayed in front. There was a Merakian squatted down in the midst of the screens, his globular body girdled with alternate rows of eyes and ears so that he apparently could enjoy all the programs.

"Manning," Kramu asked as the aircar scooted above the streets, "are you sure, that Mr. Warren and Mr. Dzanku had anything to do with the insurance fraud? They seem so innocent."

"They're about as innocent as a Venusian tree-dragon that's just eaten fourteen colonists," Manning growled. "Those two characters have been getting away with murder for years, but I've never been able to prove it. I've warned J. Barnaby a dozen times, but they sell so many policies he refuses to listen."

"Why haven't you been able to prove it?" she wanted to know. "I thought you had never failed on a case. That's what my relative said."

"In a way that's true," Manning answered. He watched a group of young Merakians, arms and legs retracted, rolling down a hill. Then as the scene slipped away beneath them, he turned back to the girl. "I've never failed to find a way for Greater Solarian to recover on frauds, but every time there has been a fraud in the territory of Warren and Dzanku, I have been unable to prove who was responsible for the fraud. And each time, in probing the mind of Sam Warren I've found an erased synapse, the kind caused by a blast of mental energy. As for Dzanku, it's long been known that the mind of a Rigelian can only be telepathed by another Rigelian."

"Then why not hire a Rigelian investigator to help you?" Kramu asked.

"Look, honey, you Muphridians ought to stop being so provincial and get out in the universe a little. The Rigelians have one of the oldest cultures in the galaxy, but it's a culture based entirely on dishonesty. If there's anyone more crooked than a Rigelian, it's another Rigelian. If we hired one as an investigator, he'd probably make Dzanku cut him in, and with two of them on it, they'd probably figure out twice as many frauds.... Looks like we're at the hotel."

The aircar floated to the ground in front of a large building that was made of some sort of onyx slashed with crimson streaks. It was several stories of undulating curves and arches.

CHAPTER FIVE

IN FRONT of the hotel the aircar opened, and the Merakian equivalent of a bellboy stood waiting. Not only had the usual eyes, ears and mouth—the latter stretched in a boyish grin—appeared, but he had also managed a freckled pug-nose. He extended a hand and helped Kramu to the ground. Then he reached up for the Terran.

As Manning Draco's hand closed on the Merakian's, he yelped and left the aircar with a leap that sent him sprawling to the very edge of the hotel entrance. He sat up, rubbing the palm of his hand, and looked at the bellboy. The latter was now grinning so broadly his mouth seemed to go all the way around his globular body.

"What the hell was that?" Manning demanded. Becoming aware of Kramu's questioning look, he explained: "Something stung me in the hand, something that animated rubber ball was holding."

The Merakian extended a hand, palm upward, and the fingers opened, disclosing a small metal disk.

"A hand-buzzer, pal," he said. "The newest sensation on Terra. Some fun, huh, kid?"

"Oh, my sainted asteroid," groaned Manning, getting to his feet. "They've even dug up all the ancient practical jokes of Earth and sold these characters!" He glared down at the Merakian. "Look, Butterball, show us where we register and lay off the corny gags. They haven't been funny on Terra since the year two thousand."

"Don't be a sorehead, pal," the Merakian said. His grin adjusted itself to more formal dimensions. "Just follow me, pal." He disappeared through the door.

Manning and Kramu followed him into the lobby and looked around. Except for the rather startling color scheme, it was not too different from hotel lobbies in other parts of the galaxy. About half the furniture consisted of the raised hollows in which Merakians could rest their globular bodies. The other half was a mixture of chairs, inclined cylinders, inverted pyramids with octoidal arms, and bench lounges with tail rests, giving the hotel a cosmopolitan air.

The usual blank globe was back of the desk in the lobby, but as they neared, the surface of the globe moved and eyes, ears, and mouth appeared. By this time, Manning was getting used to the transformations and was amused to notice that the mouth appeared complete with ready-made smile.

"Welcome to Mneone Plaza," the Merakian said. He twirled the register around, although Manning couldn't see why he did since it was completely round with signatures appearing on it at all angles.

"I understand reservations were made for us," Manning said. "I am Manning Draco and this is Miss Kramu Korshay."

"Of course, of course," the clerk intoned. He whirled the register around again. "If you will but sign for yourself and for the *Tshina*."

MANNING PICKED up the pen, getting a generous smear of ink on his fingers. It was incredibly ancient, and Manning confirmed his suspicions by noting that it bore the inscription *Made in U.S.A.*, which meant that it dated back to before the Federation. Apparently it was another Warren and Dzanku sideline.

As he signed, Manning's right foot felt warm. He shifted it uncomfortably. Just as he finished writing Kramu's name, he felt a sharp burning pain in the foot. With an exclamation, he looked down. Wedged in the sole of his shoe was a burning sliver of wood. He slapped the flame out and tried to rub the foot through his shoe. A sudden thought made him look up.

The bellboy was rocking with silent laughter. His mouth was spread in a grin and, as though he wanted to impress the world with his amusement, a second grinning mouth was appearing below the first one.

"Latest Terran joke—the galactic hot foot," he gasped. "Some fun, huh, kid?"

Without stopping to think about such things as intergalactic good will, Manning Draco swept the inkwell from the desk and hurled it with the same motion. As the inkwell left his fingers, he leaped forward, swinging a haymaker.

The Merakian bellboy ducked the inkwell by the simple act of retracting his legs a few inches. He looked up with sudden fear at the charging Terran, swayed briefly, and fell to the floor. Mouths, eyes, and ears vanished. The arms and one leg retracted quickly. The second leg quivered a moment and then it, too, retreated into the body.

Manning Draco stood over the perfect round ball on the floor, a baffled look on his face.

"Get up," he shouted. "Get up or, so help me, I'll dropkick you from here to Terra."

A strange Merakian suddenly trotted up. As he arrived, one huge ear budded from his side. His legs retracted until, by leaning only slightly, he was able to place the ear against the globular body on the floor.

"Manning," Kramu Korshay said softly. There was a note of alarm in her voice. "What is happening?"

"I don't know, honey," Manning answered, still watching the newcomer. "I thought he was faking, but maybe he really fainted or something."

The newcomer extended his legs until he was on a level with Manning, the large ear reducing in size. "Permit me," he said, "to introduce myself. I am Phlag Deltone, Chief Death Certifier of all Merak. The excitement of impending bodily harm has caused the death of this young citizen on the floor."

"Wait a minute," cried Manning. "Are you sure? Why, I never touched him. He can't be dead."

The clerk had come around from behind the desk and now he grabbed Manning's hand and began to pump it up and down. "Allow me to congratulate you, my dear sir," he was saying. "You have been on our planet only a few minutes and already you have caused the death of one of us. Fortunate man!"

"But I didn't do it," Manning declared, not really understanding what the clerk was saying. "The kid must have had a bad heart or something. We'll have to straighten this out. The boy must have a family—"

"They will undoubtedly be around tomorrow," interrupted the clerk, "to shower you with gifts."

"I, myself, will notify them immediately," said the other Merakian, "so that they will have time to prepare a suitable reward."

Manning stared in perplexity at the two Merakians. "Say," he demanded, "are you characters pulling my leg?"

"A pulled leg never shortens," the clerk said promptly, and it was obvious he was quoting some local proverb. "Now, my dear sir, in view of the demise of our bellboy, permit me to escort you to your rooms."

"Wait a minute," said Manning. "Is this character dead or isn't he?"

"Oh, decidedly dead," the clerk assured him. "Now, I will

take you to your suite where you can rejoice in solitude. *Dtor Phlag* will take care of the remains."

STILL DAZED, Manning permitted himself to be hustled into the spherical elevator which shot up to the sixth floor. Opposite the elevator, the clerk flung open a door to reveal three rooms decorated in blue and gold.

"For *Tshina* Korshay," he announced. Without giving Manning a chance to make any arrangements with Kramu, he hustled the Terran along to the next door down the hall. He opened the door with a flourish, revealing another three rooms decorated in green and russet. He looked at Manning expectantly.

"Very nice," Manning said automatically.

The clerk glanced around as though to make sure that there were no eavesdroppers. He cleared his throat nervously. *"Tshone* Draco," he said, "your permission to speak upon a delicate matter?"

"What?"

"Do you—ah—always react in such a violent and exciting manner when a joke is played upon your person?"

"I certainly resent some guy's trying to set me on fire, if that's what you mean," Manning, said, "but I still never touched that boy. Something else had to kill him—if he's really dead."

"You are too modest," the clerk said. There was a strange gleam in his eyes as he backed out into the hall. "Thank you, *Tshone* Draco. I shall keep your eccentricity in mind."

The door closed and Manning was alone. He leaned against the door and stared, blankly at the wall. "Nuts," he said to himself. "Absolutely, stark, raving mad."

He was sitting in front of the televisor screen when there was a tap on the door. He hesitated, then called, "Come in."

It was Kramu. She had refreshed her make-up and brushed the blue feathers until they gleamed. As she stood framed in the doorway, Manning forgot the irritations which had beset him since arriving at Merak II.

"Work," he announced, "is a sin and a crime when there is such a beautiful doll around. Let's have dinner and spend the night in romantic idleness?"

She shook her head, smiling. "No relaxation until we finish the case," she said. "Do you think there is any connection between our reason for being here and what happened downstairs?"

Manning frowned. "I don't know, honey. But it's a cinch that either someone is trying to frame me or this is the screwiest planet this side of infinity. As far as the case is concerned, it won't make much difference which it is."

"What were you doing when I came in?" Kramu asked.

"Getting ready to contact J. Barnaby."

"Why not call him and report then? Afterward, we can have dinner and then we can go over the papers together while you explain them to me. You did bring all the papers with you?"

Manning nodded, sighing heavily. "You're a hard woman, honey," he said. He drew a small, oblong object from his pocket and began to fasten it to the sending board of the televisor screen.

"What's that?" Kramu wanted to know.

"A scrambler," Manning said. "J. Barnaby has one on his set so we can talk without anyone listening in. They scramble the voices and the images."

There was a knock on the door. Manning exchanged glances with Kramu. "It's probably that desk clerk," he said with the air of a man who has reached the limit of his patience. "He was unduly interested in finding out whether I always react the same way to a hotfoot." He took a deep breath and raised his voice. "Come in."

The door opened and a Merakian stood in the doorway, peering into the room.

Although all Merakians seemed to look alike, there was a subtle difference in the attitude of this one, just as there had been in that of the Dukar. Although already equipped with eyes, mouth, and a rather handsome Greek nose, one spot on the globular body was writhing in the manner that heralded new additions. As they watched, a fully detailed patch-pocket appeared on the side of the Merakian's body. He unbuttoned the flap and drew from the pocket a large pair of black-rimmed glasses, with curved bows. He fitted these over his eyes. The pocket vanished.

"Now I've seen everything," Manning muttered to Kramu. "Not only do they grow eyes on demand, but even weak eyes that need glasses!"

THE MERAKIAN was peering through the glasses at Manning. "Manning Draco, of the planet Terra, Galaxy One?" he asked.

"That's me," Manning said, his good humor restored by the sight of the glasses.

"I," said the Merakian, "am Dtella Zyzzcar, the Fourth, Minister of Heroics to his most globular majesty, Mneone Melpar, Dukar of Merak. I just happened to be in the hotel and learned of the sudden demise of a Merakian citizen known as Psota Lpona. I believe you were responsible."

"I'll be damned if I'm going to be framed for that," Manning said. "I never touched the idiot. I want to warn you that I am accorded full Federation police powers and if you try to frame me for murder, there'll be an investigation that'll scorch your pants—or would if you wore pants!"

"You Terrans are strange beings," the Merakian said solemnly, advancing across the room. "Not only do you inhabit bodies which are impractical, if not impossible, but you continually act as if you were insane. Still, I suppose, that is none of my business." Another pocket appeared on the Merakian as he halted in front of Manning. From it, he drew a black and silver ribbon. Suspended from it was a perfectly blank sphere, about an inch in diameter, made from some sort of scarlet metal.

"In the name of the eight thousand, six hundred and twenty-seventh Dukar of Merak—may his breath shorten—" said the Merakian, pinning the ribbon on Manning's chest, "I bestow upon you the Order of Lsita Nolpon, First Dukar of Merak, for services to Merak beyond the call of an alien's duty. Since this award is in the actual likeness of our first blessed Dukar, it is hoped that you will cherish it. In the event that you feel otherwise, however, it can be—pawned is the English word, I believe—at the Dukar's private counting house for four credits, ten units."

The Merakian gave Manning a formal smile, removed his glasses and tucked them away in the pocket which suddenly appeared. He turned and marched quickly from the room.

"I'll be damned," Manning said weakly. But for the first time in his life his vocabulary failed him beyond that point.

Following his report to J. Barnaby Cruikshank, Manning took Kramu to dinner in the hotel dining room. Aside from the fact that they seemed to be the subject of conversation of every other diner, including two young gelding-scouts from Alpha Centauri, the dinner hour was uneventful.

Although he did everything to change it, Manning's evening was as unromantic as Kramu had predicted. He spent four hours going over the insurance policies and medical reports with her. Then even his final hope was blasted when Kramu laughingly sidestepped his good-night embrace and was gone. Her similarity to human women, he reflected as he went to bed, was more than just a surface appearance.

CHAPTER SIX

NEXT MORNING, Manning Draco was up early. He had breakfast with Kramu and then, despite her protestations, left her at the hotel to deal with any adoring relatives of the dead bellboy. The first name on his list was Rtanel Selmar, holder of Solarian policy Number 42X-76940876256781102, age two hundred and thirty, eldest son of Rtanel Dneeper, deceased July 4th last.

After getting directions from two Merakians, each of whom tried to play crude practical jokes on him, Manning Draco finally arrived at the domed apartment occupied by the Rtanel family. He was greeted by four regular-sized Merakians and six smaller ones. They all immediately provided themselves with human-shaped eyes, ears, noses, and mouths. They seemed genuinely pleased when he announced who he was.

"The Greater Solarian Insurance Company," Manning said, pulling out his papers, "greatly sympathizes with you over the recent loss of a son and brother. We have received your claim for benefits, amounting to—let me see—two hundred thousand credits—and my visit here is a mere formality through which we have to go before paying out the cash. You understand that, of course."

The Merakians nodded their whole bodies to indicate they did.

Manning consulted the policy in his hand. "The name of the deceased was Rtanel Selmar?"

"Yes," they chorused.

"Which of you were the parents of the deceased?"

"We were," said three of the largest Merakians.

Manning glared at the three of them. "Okay," he said, "I'll take you one at a time." He pointed a finger at the one nearest to him. "What is your name?"

"Rtanel Dneeper, the Fifth."

"What relation were you to the deceased?"

"I was the father."

"And you?" Manning asked the second one.

"Rtanel Dnina, the Third."

"Relation to the deceased?"

"I was the mother."

"Now, you?" Manning asked the third.

"Rtanel Dnolnar, the Fourth."

"Relation to the deceased?" snapped Manning, triumph in his voice.

"I was the Other."

There was a moment of silence while Manning Draco carefully remembered that Greater Solarian and J. Barnaby were depending on him. Then he calmly turned to the fourth largest Merakian.

"What's your name?" he asked.

"Rtanel Selmar, the Second," the Merakian said promptly.

"Rtanel *Selmar*—the Second, huh?" Manning said thoughtfully. He glanced at the policy. "You look to be about the same size as the Rtanel Selmar we insured. How old are you?"

"Two hundred and thirty years."

"Same age too," Manning said softly. "Do you mind if I take your stomach print?"

"Not at all," the Merakian said.

MANNING HAD stopped that morning at a local police station and borrowed the equipment for the printing. Within a few minutes, he had inked the stomach of the Merakian and transferred the print to a piece of paper. He carefully compared it to the print attached to the policy. They were the same.

"Isn't it true," he asked, "that no two of you Merakians have the same stomach print?"

"Quite true," the ten Merakians agreed pleasantly.

"Then how," Manning demanded, "do you explain the fact that you, Rtanel Selmar, the Second, have exactly the same stomach print as the Rtanel Selmar you claim died on July fourth?"

"Oh, that's simple," exclaimed the Merakian. "You see you're confused in thinking that there were two. I bought the insurance policy when I was Rtanel Selmar. Then I died and was reincarnated as Rtanel Selmar, the Second. What's unusual about that?"

"As a rule, when we pay on an insurance policy," Manning said dryly, "you can be sure that the policy holder is not only dead but is going to stay that way. The company frowns upon the whole thought of reincarnation when it involves someone we've insured."

"Strange," murmured the Merakians.

"Perhaps," Manning agreed amiably, "but I don't think you should expect to collect on this policy."

"Then we shall sue in the Federation courts," one of the Merakians said with dignity. "We were assured by the Federation authorities that no one in the galaxy would be able to take advantage of us. We paid your company with the understanding that we would be paid if Rtanel Selmar died. It is a matter of legal record that he did die. The insurance policy said nothing about not paying if he was reincarnated."

Manning Draco had a terrible feeling that the Merakian was right in thinking that the Federation courts would uphold the claim, but he showed none of this in his expression as he gathered his papers and started to leave.

"Of course, I can't say for sure," he said. "This is a matter which will have to be settled by the president of the company. I merely report what I find."

He got as far as the door when one of the Merakians spoke. It was the one now identified as Rtanel Selmar, the Second.

"Mr. Draco," he said, "would your company have any objection to selling me another life insurance policy? This one was such a good investment."

"I'd wait a few days if I were you," Manning said dryly. "I have a feeling that J. Barnaby Cruikshank would have a heart attack if faced with that question just now."

With that, he left. During the remainder of the day, Manning Draco visited thirty families. In each case he found that the policy holder had officially died, but had been just as officially reincarnated. By the end of the day, he had experienced so much that he was completely unmoved to find his suite in the hotel almost filled with various gifts left during the day by the relatives of the bellboy who had dropped dead the night before.

"I think," he told Kramu that night at dinner, "that they've got J. Barnaby over a rocket. The only chance—whether the reincarnation is legitimate or faked—is to prove that somebody deliberately planned for it to work out this way. And that looks pretty slim at this moment. These Merakians all have automatic mind blocks that stop all telepathic probes. Sam Warren's memory of the whole thing has been erased and no Terran has ever been able to get by the mind shield of a Rigelian. The only thing to do is keep checking on policy holders and hope that someone will slip up."

FOR ALMOST two weeks, Manning and Kramu worked from early morning until late night. Even Manning became so concerned with the problem that he forgot to throw his usual passes at the beautiful Muphridian. On the evening of the thirteenth day, they had records of seven hundred and fifty reincarnated Merakians, but not one bit of evidence to prove fraud.

"I think we're licked, honey," Manning said as they dropped, exhausted, into chairs in his suite. "They can make the reincarnation gag stick legally and there's nothing in the policy to stop them."

"May I make a suggestion?" Kramu asked.

"Hell, yes. What is it?"

"Why not try to probe the mind of Dzanku Dzanku if you're so certain that he and Warren engineered this? If you learned how it worked, then surely that would be enough to cause the Federation courts to make Dzanku submit to a cybernetic reading of his mind."

"It would," Manning admitted, "but that's not much better than just wishing it had never happened in the first place. No Terran has ever succeeded in probing a Rigelian's mind."

"I know you told me that," she said, "but I also know that you're the only Terran to ever develop a secondary mind shield. If you had enough strength to resist Dzanku's attempt to probe your mind, then maybe you have enough strength to probe his."

"Maybe you've got something, honey," he said slowly. "It better work though, or they'll be carting me back to Terra in a padded rocket."

"What do you mean?" she asked.

"If I use all my power in one thrust at Dzanku's mind and fail, I'll be wide open for his thrust. He'll blast my whole mind as smooth as that one synapse in Sam Warren's mind. But if we could think of some way of getting Dzanku off guard for a minute, maybe it would work."

"I think I know how you can do it," Kramu said.

"How, baby?"

"You once accused me of being provincial," she said, "so one of the days you didn't take me with you, I went to the Merakian library and studied up on Rigelians. It seems that every Rigelian inevitably has one psychological weak spot."

"Sure, they'll steal anything they can lay a tentacle on," Manning said, "but how does that help us?"

"They have one other—gambling. According to the book I read no Rigelian can resist gambling."

"That's true," Manning admitted, "but I still don't get it."

He shook his head dubiously.

"Play some gambling game with Dzanku," Kramu said promptly. "Wait until the outcome of a game depends on a single turn of a card and in that second strike."

Manning was silent for a minute, thinking it over. Finally, he grinned.

"Honey," he said, "I think you've got it." He glanced at his chronometer. "I've just about got time to catch Dzanku and Sam at the office. Wish me luck, baby."

"I'm going with you," she said.

"Not this time, honey," Manning said. "You stay right here. If I'm not back within three hours, it'll mean that I've failed. If you're here, you can call J. Barnaby and tell him to come and scoop up the remains. So you'll have to be content with wishing me luck."

"I do, Manning," she said. To his surprise, she leaned over and kissed him lightly on the lips.

"Now, go," she said, pushing him toward the door.

CHAPTER SEVEN

D ZANKU DZANKU and Sam Warren were still in the office when Manning arrived. He noticed that the rooms were as ornately furnished as the home office in Nyork and thought it was unlikely that the two salesmen would have spent that much money if their only income had been commissions.

"Hi, Manning," Sam Warren called. "It's about time you dropped into the office. How's it going?"

The Rigelian inclined his eyestalks and waved three tentacles in a friendly fashion. "Hello, Manning," he said. "What's new with the galaxy's greatest snooper?"

"Not much," Manning said casually. He dropped into a chair. "The investigation seems to be drawing a blank, and I've been working so hard I've decided to take the night off and relax."

"Where's that cute little number you brought with you?" Sam Warren wanted to know.

"Probably reading the statistics on industrial fatalities among the Martian *Drupees*," Manning said sourly. "She may look like a beautiful doll, but she acts like a computing machine in the office of J. Barnaby."

"I hear that's the only flaw in some of those humanoid races," Dzanku said. "We'll be glad to help you relax, Manning, but there isn't too much excitement on Merak II, unless you're a Merakian. There are still no human females here, and you brought the only humanoid one. You'd probably find the local belles inadequate. There is a native intoxicating beverage, but if I can judge by Sam, it doesn't seem fit for human consumption."

"I'll say," Sam said, making a face. "The one time I tried it, I couldn't see for six hours."

"I've had about all the Merakians I can stand," Manning said, "but what about local gambling halls. If I can't spend my salary, I might as well lose it."

There was a gleam in the Rigelian's three eyes as he stared at Manning.

"Well, now," he said slowly, "maybe we can take care of that. Sam and I get a little tired of playing cards with each other. Care for a little game of Castorian Rummy?"

"What stakes?" Manning asked.

"Make it easy on yourself," the Rigelian said. His tentacles were beginning to quiver with excitement.

"Ten units a point?"

"Make it twenty," Dzanku said.

Manning hesitated, then agreed.

"Okay with you, Sam?" Dzanku asked, opening a drawer.

SAM NODDED. They cut cards for the deal, and it went to Dzanku. Using, all his tentacles, he shuffled the cards, so fast the cards could hardly be seen. Then he began dealing.

For the benefit of those readers who may live in outlying provincial planets, where they're still playing either the Gin Rummy of the Twentieth Century or the Luna Triple Rummy of the Twenty-fifth Century, Castorian Rummy is played with three decks of cards, each deck consisting of ninety-five cards— the regular seven suits of thirteen cards each and the four super-jokers, Orbit, Comet, Asteroid, Nova. Each player in the game receives thirty-nine cards on the deal and simultaneously plays three games. Since it is possible to trade cards back and forth between his three hands, it is easily seen that considerable finesse is needed to play the game well. Cards are drawn, matched, and discarded in much the same fashion as in the older games. Game is one thousand points. In the event that a single player wins all three games, with one hundred extra points for each scoring and five hundred extra for the game, his opponents' scores are not counted at all and his own score is tripled.

Manning was soon aware that Dzanku was a skillful player, but then Manning himself had held his own with the best professionals. Several times, he deliberately made blunders in order to keep the score fairly even.

Tension mounted as the game progressed. At the end of two hours, Sam Warren still had small scores, less than seven hundred, in all three games. Dzanku's scores were 915, 920, and 970. Manning's scores were 930, 935, and 965. Either Manning or the Rigelian could go out on all three games in the next hand. As Sam Warren, grumbling at his own luck, dealt the cards, Dzanku was so excited his tentacles were constantly weaving about his head.

After drawing four cards, Manning Castored on his first hand and the first game was his. He put down two double color runs on his second hand, and a triple color run plus a small numbers run on his third hand. Dzanku, during the same period, had played about the same number of cards from both hands. Each of them needed one card in each hand to go out.

Manning drew the card he needed for his second hand, but didn't put the cards down. He no longer had to pretend to be nervous and he could see that Dzanku was shaking so badly his tentacles kept slipping from the cards and he was softly cursing in Rigelian under his breath.

If Manning went out on both games, at a rough estimate it would mean winning six hundred thousand units from Dzanku alone. If Dzanku won the last two games, Manning would owe him about two hundred thousand units.

Up to this point, Manning had been slapping cards down as quickly as he saw they were not what either he or Dzanku needed. Now, he drew a card and held it just above the deck, staring thoughtfully at it. The tension was so great he could see the muscles standing out along the eyestalks of the Rigelian. At that moment, Manning Draco struck.

As the full force of his mental energy struck Dzanku's mind shield, he felt the Rigelian frantically trying to pull his defenses together, but Manning realized with an inward triumph that it was too late. The next instant he felt the shield give way and he was inside a completely alien mind.

Even much later, Manning Draco was unable to tell how long his mind remained locked with Dzanku's. He probed, feeling his own strength draining, almost recoiling from some of the things he encountered, until he found what he wanted. Then he quickly withdrew.

Manning staggered to his feet and looked down at Dzanku. The Rigelian's eyestalks drooped, and his tentacles moved in feeble spasms. He knew that it would be at least an hour before Dzanku recovered. Without bothering to look at Sam Warren, Manning walked drunkenly from the office.

Back at the hotel, where Kramu Korshay waited anxiously, Manning was too exhausted to do more than mutter: "It worked, honey. Tell you tomorrow. Got—to—sleep—now…" He dropped off to sleep even as he uttered the last word. Kramu dragged him over to the bed and made him comfortable before going back to her own suite.

EARLY THE next morning, a fully recovered Manning Draco grabbed a cup of coffee and hurried off to the palace of the Dukar. After a short wait, he was ushered into the audience room.

The Dukar of Merak was seated on a throne which looked like a gigantic scarlet pumpkin, with the top hollowed out. As Manning entered, the Dukar was already equipped with eyes and mouth, and the ears were just being formed. Manning waited politely until the ears stopped growing.

"Good morning, Dukar of Merak," he said cheerfully. "I trust I have not visited you at an unseemly hour."

"Not at all, *Tshone* Draco," the Dukar said pleasantly enough, "although I must admit that it puzzles me somewhat. My experience with un-Merakian forms of life has led me to believe that they do not make an appearance until late in the day."

"You've just been under the wrong un-Merakian influences," Manning said. "But I am here upon a most serious errand."

"I am all ears," said the Dukar, adding several to give credence to his statement.

"First, a point of information," Manning said. "Is it not true that the average full life span of a Merakian is about four hundred years, but that if a Merakian is exposed to some sudden shock or excitement he goes into a cataleptic trance which is officially pronounced death, and that upon coming out of this trance in about seven days his life has been prolonged by a hundred years? And that this can happen any number of times?"

The Dukar looked anything but happy, but his voice was the same as he answered. "Within limits," he said, "that is essentially correct. However, *Tshone* Draco, it is not a trance. Sudden shocks cause all life to stop within us, and only shocks of excitement will do this. But after seven days a spark of life is revived and, as you say, one hundred years has been added. Our final death, however, is exactly like the others and occurs either at the exact end of four hundred, years or within four hundred years after the fifteenth reincarnation."

"And after each reincarnation, you keep the same name but add a number which indicates the extension?" Manning asked.

"That is correct. I, for example, am Mneone Melpar, the Ninth, and am, at the present reckoning, eight hundred and ten years old."

Manning took a deep breath and continued. "The charge I'm about to make," he said, "is not a pretty one, especially since it concerns the ruler of a planet. But I thought if we were to discuss it here, perhaps it would not be necessary to bring the matter up before a Federation court."

"I shall be interested to hear it," the Dukar said.

"Sam Warren and Dzanku Dzanku," said Manning, "came here representing the Greater Solarian Insurance Company. They discovered the facts about Merakian reincarnation and saw a chance to make a lot of money. A deal was made with you, the Dukar of Merak, and a lot of insurance was sold, especially after the deal was explained. You then declared that Merak would celebrate the old American states' holiday, the Fourth of July, which still gets sentimental recognition on Terra. A large order of atomicworks was imported from Terra, and these were exploded unexpectedly in many public places so that millions of Merakians 'died' as a result of the excitement. This in turn made my company liable for more than four billion credits. Do you deny this plot?"

"Of course not," said the Dukar. "But how did you learn the details?"

"I read Dzanku's mind."

"What a pity," the Dukar exclaimed. "He was so proud of the fact that no Terran could read his mind. But, tell me, *Tshone Draco*, why do you rush to me so early in the morning with this story?"

"Because it's fraud," Manning said indignantly. "It's the same as stealing that much money from my company."

"This is wrong?" murmured the Dukar. "Really, you Terrans have the most amazing culture."

"Not only us, but the entire Federation," snapped Manning. "This little incident puts you and your whole planet in the criminal class."

"That sounds a bit chauvinistic is the word, I think," the Dukar said gently. "It seems to me that if there is any crime involved it lies with your company for offering us the temptation. We but did what was to be expected."

IN A LOFTY tone, Manning said, "I imagine the Federation courts will think differently," Manning said. "With what I know, we can go into a Federation court and force Dzanku Dzanku to submit to cybernetic mind-reading and the whole plot will be a matter of record. You have already become a part of the Federation and have to abide by the laws of the Federation."

"Ah, yes," murmured the Dukar, gazing up at the ceiling and rocking slightly on his throne, "but I believe that I am correct in saying that until our entrance is ratified by two-thirds of the planets belonging to the Federation, and until we agree to any national changes the Federation may demand of us, the Federation courts agree that our national laws apply, as written, to all companies and aliens attempting to do business with us."

"Even so," Manning demanded hotly, "how do you justify this bare-faced swindle in which you yourself were to receive one billion, two hundred credits if it succeeded?"

"One billion, two hundred and ten credits," corrected the Dukar. "It has succeeded, for the Federation must force your company to pay. You may check up on my wording in our Dome of Justice, but I believe that the sixty-seven thousandth article of our national by-laws reads: 'Any company, corporation, monopoly, or individual doing business, residing, or visiting within the confines of the glorious planet, Merak II, may be relieved of property or monies, or defrauded in any shape or manner, providing the reigning Dukar is given a share of the proceeds amounting to not less than thirty-four per cent.' It's really supposed to be one-third," the Dukar added, "but I do hate having to calculate fractions."

"I don't believe it," Manning said flatly. "Anyway, I'm putting Warren and Dzanku under arrest, and we'll see if you get away with this."

"That may be difficult, *Tshone* Draco. Sam Warren and Dzanku Dzanku were around two hours ago and borrowed one of my fastest ships. I was rather surprised at the hour, but then one may expect anything of aliens…. If I were you, *Tshone* Draco, I would go to the Dome of Justice and read the Merakian laws and then consult an attorney."

"I'll do just that," snapped Manning. He headed for the door but was stopped by the Dukar's voice.

"While you're there," the Merakian ruler said, "you might also glance at article one hundred and two thousand which states: 'Any company, corporation or monopoly maintaining offices within the confines of the planet Merak II which permits itself to be defrauded in any way is subject to a fine, to be paid into the Merakian treasury, equal to the amount lost by fraud."

For a minute, Manning was speechless. "But Greater Solarian doesn't maintain an office here," he protested.

"You forget," the Dukar said blandly, "that Warren and Dzanku opened an office here. It's true that they paid for it themselves, but the Merakian Senate passed a new law—late last night—which holds a company and its employees as one.... Good morning, *Tshone* Draco."

CHAPTER EIGHT

MORE THAN three hours later a red-eyed Manning Draco stumbled out of the Merakian Dome of Justice. He had not read all the Merakian laws by any means, but he had read enough.

In spite of this, he was in better humor by the time he arrived back at the hotel. Kramu Korshay was waiting in his suite, a frown on her pretty face.

"That was unfair, Manning," she cried. "You were too tired to tell me what happened last night and then you left this morning before I was up."

"Never mind, honey," Manning said. "You'll hear it all as I report to J. Barnaby. You'd better stuff your ears when he answers after hearing the first part."

He went directly to the televisor screen and attached his scrambler. Within a few minutes, the well-fed face of J. Barnaby Cruikshank was peering from the screen.

"Well, Manning," J. Barnaby said, "what's happened? You called our attorney an hour ago, but he said I would have to get the whole story from you. What is it?"

As quickly as he could, Manning related the whole story of the plot of the insurance policies. "Also," he added at the end, "they have a law here which will force you to pay a fine equal to the amount of the policies you must pay out. As of the moment, J. Barnaby, you owe the Merakian people and the Merakian government the small amount of eight billion, twelve million credits."

Although the televisor image was not in color, it was easy to see that J. Barnaby's face was turning a choleric red. The first sputters were just beginning to smooth out into understandable, and reprehensible, words when Manning interrupted.

"Hold everything, J. Barnaby," he said. "There is no way to

get out of paying the eight billion. Your own lawyer will tell you that. But I've got a way for you to make it all back and more within a short time."

"How?" J. Barnaby asked hoarsely.

"First," said Manning, "cancel all the life insurance policies still existing here. Next, appoint the Dukar as sole representative of all Greater Solarian interests on Merak, with a third cut."

"I'll see him in hell first," bellowed J. Barnaby.

"By law you have to give him a third," Manning said, "and besides it'll be worth it. Third, issue a special insurance policy for Merakians only. You might call it death insurance and you insure them against not dying. In other words, if a policy holder doesn't die, we pay off. Then we set up a subsidiary company to import and operate all kinds of excitement. We get the Dukar to declare every day a holiday and bring in lots of atomicworks. We start gambling houses on every corner, bring in horse, car and spaceship races, practical jokes like exploding cigars. Excitement makes a Merakian drop dead, so we'll give them a whole planet of excitement. Each time one drops dead, his insurance policy is canceled and he has to take out a new policy for his next reincarnation. See the possibilities, J. Barnaby?"

J. BARNABY did. His face smoothed out into his best presidential smile. "Manning, my boy," he said expansively, "you've done it again. This will mean a nice fat bonus for you. Now, hurry home. We've got a bit of a problem with some industrial policies on Pollux—"

"Put it on ice," Manning interrupted. "I'm taking a vacation." He switched off the screen, unfastened his scrambler, and turned to Kramu. "Well, honey," he said, "the business is done and now we can turn to that pleasure you've been putting off. What do you say about a weekend on one of the Pleasure Islands of Arcturus?"

"I'm sorry, Manning," she said, shaking her head so that the blue feathers danced, "but I told you that I had an important appointment back home on Muphrid. I'm due to make my first appearance before the Transverse Fission Council late this afternoon. So you'd better get me back home."

"Transverse Fission Council?" said Manning suspiciously. "What is that?"

"You should stop being so provincial," Kramu said, amusement in her eyes, "and travel around the galaxy more. Come on, let's get out to your ship."

Manning grumbled and bullied, but all to no avail. He was still alternately trying to be masterful and pitiful later when the ship touched at Muphrid.

"I'm sorry, Manning," Kramu said for the hundredth time, "but it's really better this way. I know you think I'm beautiful and I appreciate the passes you've been throwing. But you see we Muphridians are evolved from the race of Paramecia."

"What the hell is the Paramecium?" Manning demanded.

"Look it up, honey," she said laughingly. "Then if you still want a date with me, all you have to do is wait about three hundred generations. Good-by, now." She blew him a kiss and was gone. He had one glimpse of her blue-feathered head as she entered an aircar, and then he was getting orders from the tower to blast off.

When his ship was once more out in space, its nose pointed toward Terra, he began to search through the record tapes, completely ignoring the continued signaling of his televisor. Finally, at the bottom, he found a tape labeled Paramecium. He slipped it into the reader and leaned back.

"In any consideration of sexual reproduction," said the smooth voice of some librarian, "the situation noted in the Paramecium, a member of the most complex class of protozoa, the Infusoria, is most interesting—particularly since many advanced humanoid races are the descendants of this evolutionary strain. Paramecia possess a large oval nucleus and in a small depression in their sides each one possesses a tiny spherical micronucleus, reproductive in function. Commonly the elongate animal reproduces by a simple transverse fission into two. After a number of such divisions, usually several hundred, the process is interrupted ordinarily by a temporary union of two individuals during which, after disintegration of the macronucleus and elaborate preparation of the micronucleus, micronuclear material is exchanged. The animals then separate and resume reproduction by division. This process seems to hold true for all races which have evolved from the Paramecium. Regrowth is rapid and under favorable conditions, four divisions occur every twenty-four hours. Calculations show that a single Paramecium, or individual evolved from Paramecium, can thus produce two hundred and sixty-eight million offspring in one month. This—"

MANNING SHUT off the reader and stared at it numbly. Then he suddenly became aware of the insistent buzzing from his televisor. He reached over and turned it on. The angry face of J. Barnaby Cruikshank appeared on the screen.

"Where the hell have you been?" demanded J. Barnaby. "And what do you mean by saying you're going on a vacation? You can't go now. Why—"

"It's okay, J. Barnaby," Manning interrupted. "I'm coming home. I'll be there in about an hour."

"What's the matter with you?" asked J. Barnaby peering from the screen. "You look pale. Have you been slugged or something? What happened?"

"I'm not quite sure," Manning said slowly, "but I think I just barely missed being the father of two hundred and sixty-eight million children, and on what you pay me—I can't afford it."

ACT TWO / FALL 3472

THE REGAL RIGELIAN

CHAPTER ONE

ALTHOUGH IT was lunch time, the Cosmic Roof of the Mercurian-Astoria Hotel in Nyork belied the clock. Lights were dimmed to a romantic glow. The ceiling was a three-dimensional panorama of the stellar system. In the background, a Venusian stringed orchestra provided muted love music. Seated at a corner table, Manning Draco managed the difficult feat of eating Vegan pastry while reciting Martian poetry and gazing passionately at Lhana Xano.

It was now four months since Lhana Xano had gone to work as the receptionist at the Greater Solarian Insurance Company, Monopolated, and a steady campaign on the part of Manning Draco had finally produced a luncheon date. He made the proper dramatic pause before the last line of the poem, taking advantage of it to finish off the last of the pastry, then ended with lyrical passion. He leaned back in his chair and gazed at his companion.

There was no doubt that Lhana Xano was a Martian beauty. Her head fur, glistening like burnished copper, was arranged in the latest Terran style. The soft lights of the Cosmic room did wonders with her copper skin and slant eyes. She wore a green dress, caught up over one shoulder and tight-fitting, which revealed her voluptuous humanoid figure.

"You did that well," she said as he finished the poem. "I didn't know that you were so familiar with the Martian classics." A slight lisp was her only trace of Martian accent.

"There's so much you don't know about me," Manning said lightly. "You really owe it to yourself to learn *all*. I don't spend all of my time, you know, being chief investigator for Greater Solarian. For, example, I have a very fine collection of Martian *Tsigra* art—from the *Zylka* Period—in my apartment. If you'd care to see it—" He broke off as Lhana burst into laughter.

"What's so funny?" he demanded.

Lhana stifled her laughter, but there was still a glint of amusement in her three eyes.

"Since I've been working for Greater Solarian," she said, "I've been going to night school and studying Terran history."

"I don't see anything about that to make you laugh when I start talking about Martian art."

"You wouldn't," she said. "I've been studying the social history of Terra and I was thinking how funny it is that you Terrans have progressed so much in all the sciences without having improved the art of seduction."

"What do you mean?" Manning asked gruffly.

"Almost two thousand years ago, male Terrans were inviting girls up to their apartments to see their etchings. And here you are using the same technique. The only thing that's changed is that etchings have now become Martian *Tsigra* art."

MANNING DRACO grinned. He was not one to be long bothered by such counterattacks. "Well," he said, "from all I've been able to discover, we're also staggering along with only two sexes and nobody has complained yet. So we'll forget the *Tsigra* art. How about—"

This time he was interrupted by a waiter who appeared carrying a portable visiplate.

"Mr. Draco?" he asked.

"Yes," Manning said, scowling. "What is it?"

"A call for you, sir," the waiter said. He plugged the visiplate into the table socket and departed.

The angry face of J. Barnaby Cruikshank stared out from the visiplate screen. The eyes were fixed upon Manning Draco.

"Ha!" said J. Barnaby Cruikshank. It was rumored around the galaxy that the president of the Greater Solarian Insurance Company could pack more sheer malevolence into a simple "Ha!" than most people could get with the aid of two magnetiguns.

"Go away," Manning Draco said wearily. He had been too long exposed to J. Barnaby's anger to be impressed. "I'm busy and besides it's my lunch hour and you do not own me body, soul, and lunch hour."

"Your lunch hour," J. Barnaby said bitingly, "was up fifteen minutes ago. It's bad enough that I have to put up with your making passes at every female in the office, but I will not tolerate your juvenile seduetions being carried out on office time. If you're not back here within ten minutes, the name of Manning Draco will merely be an unfortunate blot on our otherwise perfect industrial relations record."

The screen faded as J. Barnaby broke contact.

"Now how did he know where to find me?" Manning mused. A sudden thought made him look at Lhana. She nodded brightly.

"I left word that we were lunching here," she said. "After all, I'm not as important a cog in the Greater Solarian scheme as you are and I could be fired for not being available."

"That's my complaint about you too," Manning said. "Between you and J. Barnaby, I might as well be a Plutonian metal termite.[2] My life is settling down to slavery and chastity."

As they got up from the table, Lhana put one hand on Manning's arm in a friendly gesture.

"Don't misunderstand, Manning," she said. "I'm really very

2 The metal termite, a native of Pluto, is a sightless, underground insect, about ten feet long and weighing close to three thousand pounds, Earth scale. It is valuable to Federation industry because it devours ore and eliminates pure metal. As a source of cheap labor, its match has not been found in the galaxy.

fond of you. Even more, I appreciate the fact that there's more to you than the wolf you show. But let's leave it like that."

"For the nonce, only," Manning said lightly. Now that they were standing he had to look up at her, for she towered a good seven inches over his six feet three. "But a Draco never gives up."

"And an Xano never gives in," she said, laughing, as they left the restaurant.

Back at the office, Manning Draco stood in front of the private office of J. Barnaby Cruikshank until the scanner recognized him. As the door swung open, he stepped inside and faced the president of the company.

"Don't tell me," Manning said lightly, "I can guess. A planet full of our insured just killed themselves off and you want me to rush out and bring them back to life. Right?"

"*You* can afford to joke about it," J. Barnaby said in a pained voice. "You draw a nice salary in return for working about once a month. You can have a quiet, leisurely luncheon, keeping a valuable employee away from her work—while I sit here staving off disaster so that you may continue to draw that nice, fat salary—"

"Spare me your tears," Manning said with a grin. He draped himself over a chair. "I've seen your income tax returns… Now, what's the problem?"

"You know the planet Alphard VI?"

Manning Draco nodded. "The only habitable planet of ten in an orbit around Alphard. Rated as a Class C planet, despite a civilization which fulfills the requirements for Class B. Reclassification has been refused because the inhabitants are considered incurably eccentric. The Alphardians are considered non-humanoid, although there is now a suit in the Supreme Galactic Court contesting this ruling."

"Right," J. Barnaby Cruikshank said. "Alphard VI was admitted to the Federation ten years ago. We sold our first insurance policy to the Emperor that same week. We continued to sell a few policies there, but made very little headway until three years ago. Then, within the space of one year, we sold policies to almost three-fourths of the population."

"Dzanku and Warren?" Manning asked with a grin.

HERE J. BARNABY winced, his face taking on a persecuted expression. "Yes," he said. "Rigelian Dzanku Dzanku and Terran Sam Warren—the two best salesmen in the galaxy, as well as the crookedest, the dirtiest, double-crossing—"

"I gather that they did something which is going to cost you money?" Manning said.

"They're doing it now!" J. Barnaby struck the top of his desk with a clenched fist. "But this time we're going to throw them in jail!"

"We?" Manning asked gently.

"We," J. Barnaby declared, glaring at his chief investigator. "You'll get the goods on them and I'll see to it that the Federation judge gives them the limit."

"That's what I call a division of labor," Manning murmured. "Okay, what are they doing?"

"As you probably know," J. Barnaby said, "the Federation Charter permits us to establish a monopoly only when the government of a planet agrees to it. Although we have been the only insurance company operating on Alphard VI, the Emperor has always refused to grant us a monopoly. Now, a new insurance company has been established on Alphard VI."

"Dzanku and Warren?"

J. Barnaby nodded. "If it were legitimate competition, I wouldn't mind," he said piously. "Here, look at this." He tossed a large handbill to Manning.

It was printed in Alphardian and in English. Although he knew some Alphardian, Manning turned to the English version and read:

YOU CAN MAKE MONEY BY DYING

We are pleased to announce that the Galaxy Insurance and Benefit Association is now establishing its main offices on the glorious planet of Alphard VI and will issue special life insurance policies to all legal citizens of this planet at one-half the cost of any life insurance policy issued by any other company now operating in Galaxy I. In addition to this great saving, all of our policies carry an automatic double indemnity clause which becomes a part of the policy when a policy-holder has been insured by us for a period of fifty years or longer. Think of the fun you can have with the money saved from premiums—think of the joy which will come to your family when you drop dead!

But that is not all! In addition to this super-colossal offer, the Galactic Insurance and Benefit Association will give you a generous trade-in allowance on your old insurance policy if you are now insured by another company. All you have to do is bring in your present policy, sign it over to us, and receive a certificate entitling you to an extra one thousand credits of insurance with us. Be insured by the Galactic Insurance and Benefit Association and be the envy of your neighbors! If you carry one of our policies, you can't afford to live!

Dzanku Dzanku, Pres.
Sam Warren, Sec. & Treas.

Manning Draco tossed the leaflet back on the desk and grinned. "The Galaxy Insurance and Benefit Association," he said. "So far as Dzanku and Warren are concerned, there'll be more benefit than insurance in that association."

"Exactly," J. Barnaby said angrily. "It's easy to see what they're going to do. Not only will they sell a lot of policies which they never intend to honor, but did you catch that business about trading in old policies? They're going to get a lot of dumb natives to sign over policies they bought from us, then they'll arrange a convenient accident for the natives and collect from us. And this time we're going to stop them before they do their dirty work."

"How?" Manning asked innocently.

"That's your job—and you'll do it or else." Abruptly, J. Barnaby softened. "You can do it, Manning, my boy. There isn't a smarter operator in the galaxy than you. Aren't you the only person on

Terra who has developed a secondary mind shield? Didn't you once get the best of Dzanku and Warren—even to reading the mind of that slippery Rigelian, something that no one is supposed to be able to do. You won't fail me in the hour of my direst need."

"The visiscreen lost a great scenery chewer when you became a monopolist, J. Barnaby," Manning said. He grinned. "I don't know when I've seen you give a greater performance."

"I've already notified the field," J. Barnaby said gruffly. "Your

ship will be ready when you get there."

"Okay. But just remember one thing, J. Barnaby—once I was lucky enough to pull a fast one on Dzanku. As a result, I was able to read his mind and that was what saved your neck on Merak II. But that was strictly a fluke. After this, Dzanku will be on his guard. My secondary mind shield keeps him from reading my mind, but I'll never be able to read his again either—and I'm not sure I'd want to even if I could."

"Okay," J. Barnaby said, confidently, "so you'll find some other way of tying a rocket to his tail. I don't care what you have to do in order to get him—but get him."

"My master's voice," Manning murmured. "What if I have to break a few Federation laws to get him?"

"Then do it," J. Barnaby snapped. "But don't tell me anything about it," he added hastily. "The less I know about such things, the better."

"That's what I like about you—your high ethical standards," Manning said. He left quickly, but not before he saw the flush of anger spreading across J. Barnaby's face.

WHEN HE reached the spaceport, Manning Draco's ship, the *Alpha Actuary*, was already on the launching level. He climbed in, fed the position of Alphard VI into the automatic pilot, and pressed the button which hooked the ship into magnetic power. The small ship raced up the launching rack and thrust itself skyward.

He was about an hour out from Terra when he decided to feed an encyclotape on Alphard VI through the audio-reader. He picked the tape from the library on the ship, but suddenly there was the shrill clangor of a bell. The automatic pilot threw the ship out of magnidrive so quickly that Manning almost fell to the floor. He left the tape there and hurried to the forward screen. The warning bell and the sudden braking meant that the ray-analyzers of the ship had spotted something ahead which was neither meteor nor another ship.

Manning leaned and glanced into the viewing screen. He

rubbed his eyes and looked again. But he still saw the same thing despite the fact that his senses refused to accept it.

There, almost dead ahead of the ship, out in open space "stood" a figure. That is, Manning thought in terms of its standing there although there was nothing but space to stand on. The body was pentahedral in shape, with a head in the form of an inverted pyramid. The legs were long and skinny and planted very firmly on nothing. The entire body was a very light purple in color and the only bit of clothing it wore was a rather silly-looking green and white cap perched on the top of the head. As though to make the entire sight even less believable, one of the creature's two arms was lifted. The hand consisted of five fingers and two thumbs, with both thumbs hooked back past his shoulder in the signal which had meant a request for a ride for more than two thousand years.

"Great Fomalhaut!" Manning muttered to himself. "Now I've seen everything!" It was true that he had often picked up people thumbing rides on Terra, but this was the first time he had ever seen anyone thumbing a ride out in space.

He took over the ship from the automatic pilot and eased it up beside the figure. He thumbed the button that opened the outer door, waited what seemed a reasonable time, then closed it and watched the gauge which indicated air pressure in the air-lock. When it equaled the interior of the ship, he thumbed open the inner door. Half expecting the whole thing to be an illusion, he watched in amazement as the purple figure strode through the door and bowed politely."

"Thank you, sir," the creature said in a rather stilted but precise English. "I was beginning to be afraid that there was little travel in this direction today."

Manning Draco took a deep breath and let it out carefully before answering. "Then you were really standing out there in space," he said accusingly.

"Of course," his visitor said.

CHAPTER TWO

A S THE first impression eased, Manning noticed that there were two slanted eyes and a V-shaped mouth on the side of the head facing him. He saw no traces of what might pass for a nose or for ears.

"I thought," Manning said, "that I had seen about everything in the galaxy—but you're a new one on me. Where are you from?"

"Not from this galaxy, which is perhaps why I seem strange to you," the visitor said. "I am Nar Oysnarn from the planet Kholem in the Coma-Virgo Galaxy. May I inquire if you are going in that direction?"

"I'm going to Alphard VI, in this galaxy."

"That will be a help," said Nar Oysnarn, nodding his triangular head. "You don't mind my riding with you?"

"I guess not," Manning muttered. He started the ship and, turned it over to the automatic pilot, then turned back to the space-hiker. "It'll be worth it just to find out how you do it."

"Do what, sir?"

"Standing out there in space—where there's nothing to stand on—where there's nothing to breathe—and where I seriously doubt if that cap provides enough warmth."

"Oh, that," Nar Oysnarn said. "It's obvious you know nothing of my race. We are indifferent to oxygen, or the lack of it, and we are not sensitive to the pressure and temperature changes which seem to mean so much to everyone in this galaxy. And we find if quite restful to stand in spots where there is no gravity pull. Too bad you can't try it."

"Thanks, but I'm sure it's just as well," Manning said. "What are you doing out here in space, if you don't mind the question?"

"Not at all," Nar said courteously. "I've been attending a university on Terra and this is a mid-term holiday so I'm on my way home for a couple of weeks. I'm at Ohio University, American Territory, Terra. A freshman." As he added the last, he indicated the cap on his head with some pride.

"I see. By the way, what do I call you—Miss or Mister—?"

"Just call me Nar. You see, we Kholemites actually have no sex such as most of the races of your galaxy have."

"No sex," Manning said in surprise. "Then how do you—or am I getting too personal?"

"Not at all. My race is the dominant one on Kholem, but we do not reproduce. We are actually the children—although we have no such word in our language—of an entirely different race. The nearest I can translate the name of our parent-race is something like The Dreaming Old Ones."

"That's another new one on me," said Manning. "Do all of your race look like you?"

"No—not exactly. You see, our parent race does nothing but project images of geometric figures, which then materialize as my race. But we are many shapes—all geometric and beautiful, if I may say so—and of all colors. It makes a pleasing variety. But I'm afraid we've talked about me so much I have failed to inquire your name."

"Sorry," Manning said. "I'm Manning Draco."

Nar Oysnarn's color changed to a deeper purple. "Not the Manning Draco who is the chief investigator for Greater Solarian?" he asked in delight. "Oh, this is a pleasure."

"Thank you," Manning said, flattered in spite of himself. "But I must confess that I don't understand why it's a pleasure."

"You're too modest," Nar exclaimed. "Why, we studied about you in Freshman Neo-Mentals. You are the only Terran who has ever developed a secondary mind shield." He hesitated and then continued rather eagerly: "You know, there is a legend on my planet—I wonder if you'd mind terribly much permitting me to try to penetrate your mind?"

Manning hesitated. He had the thought that this might be some sort of trap which had been prepared for him, but then he decided that he was being foolish. If his secondary mind shield could withstand the attack of a Rigelian it should be able to take anything this creature could dish out.

"Sure," he said. "Go ahead."

The color of Nar Oysnarn began to fluctuate rapidly, ranging from a royal amethyst to a pale lavender. Almost immediately, Manning felt the alien mind pressing against his primary shield. The pressure increased steadily, then with a sharp thrust was through and striking at his secondary shield. He felt the surge of his own power and knew that the secondary shield would hold without any trouble. But as that knowledge came to him, he received one of the worst shocks of his life. The mental force which attacked him had no chance of penetrating his mind, but on the other hand he was completely paralyzed.

IT LASTED for only a minute and then he felt the force withdraw. As it went, he could move again. He felt a tingling awareness return to all of his muscles.

"What the hell was that?" he demanded when he could talk. There was a combination of fear and anger in his voice.

"I'm sorry, sir," Nar said contritely. "I should have explained it to you, but I was so eager to try it. You see, there has always been a legend on Kholem that if one of my race tried to read the mind of a creature far enough advanced to possess a secondary mind shield the attempt would fail but the creature would be paralyzed. I was so anxious to see if it was true, I'm afraid I forgot ordinary politeness."

"I guess it's true," Manning said ruefully. "Got any idea of how it works?"

"No," Nar said. "It doesn't work, however, with creatures who possess only a primary shield. I should guess, therefore, that it involves using the very strength that supports such a secondary shield and turning it back on itself in some way."

"Sort of automatically locking all the person's energy," Manning said thoughtfully. He was silent for a minute, then looked up at his geometric companion. "Are you in any special hurry to reach your home, Nar?"

"No, but why do you ask?"

"I'll make a deal with you," Manning said. "Stop off at Alphard

VI with me for two or three days and then I'll take you all the way home. I have an idea that you can help me with the case I'm working on now. What do you say?"

"Will I!" Nar exclaimed joyfully. "You bet! Will that be an experience! You see, sir, my roommate is a conceited ass[3] from Denebola who's always bragging about his adventures. This will really bring him down a parsec or two."

"Then it's a deal," Manning said. "You got any more surprises for me?"

"I don't believe so," Nar said apologetically. "We Kholemites are really a very ordinary race."

"I can see that," Manning said dryly. "I was about to run an encyclotape on the Alphardians when I stopped to pick you up, so if you'll just sit back and listen, I'll put it through now."

"You won't need to do that, sir," Nar said eagerly. "I can tell you everything that is known about the Alphardians."

"Everything?"

"Yes, sir. I have an eidetic memory—all of my race do."

"Okay," Manning said, laughing. "Go ahead."

"Yes, sir. Alphard VI is one of ten planets in the system of Alphard. It is the only habitable planet in the system. In size and shape, atmospheric pressure, and gravity it is almost a twin to Terra—if you'd like the exact figures I can provide them—" Manning shook his head and Nar continued, "Alphard VI has seven satellites which follow its orbit so closely that they are always visible. A strange feature of these satellites is that six of the seven revolve around the seventh moon in a very tight, fast-moving orbit, and it is said that one will get dizzy watching them for any length of time.

"The race of Alphardians are evolved from the order of Scolopendromorpha, subclass of Epimorpha, being a subdivision of the distinct class Chilopoda in the phylum Arthropoda. Primitive examples of this class of life are found even upon

---

3 Nar Oysnarn was speaking literally, of course, for as everyone knows the dominant race on Denebola is descended from a variety of the subgenus Asinus.

Terra. On Alphard VI, however, while retaining many of the primitive characteristics, the race has evolved in a general humanoid direction. There is in fact a case now pending in court, Alphardians vs. Humanoid Creatures of Galaxy I, which may well result in a ruling that Alphardians are humanoid.

"Alphardians are a proud race, claiming that they are one of the oldest races in Galaxy I. This may well be true, as evidence of the existence of their race is found in early periods of many planets, such evidence being found, for example, in the Carboniferous period of the history of Terra. It is interesting to note that the Alphardians claim that it is their race which is responsible for the legend of Centaurs on Terra. One of their historians has written a rather entertaining book on the subject, in which he claims that the centaurs of Alpha Centauri are imposters and upstarts.

"The Alphardian Empire is now in the two thousandth year of the Ix Dynasty, the present ruler being Emperor Romixon. His rule is absolute, with but one exception. Anyone may challenge the emperor to a game of four-dimensional chess[4] and if

---

4 By this time, four-dimensional chess is played in every civilized part of the Galaxy. For the benefit, however, of any readers who may be from such backward systems as Enif or Beta Crucia, four-dimensional chess was invented by Horace Homer Humptafield, of Terra, in 2983. It was made possible by the now famous Humptafield Penetration Theory [178yb x (bdy - 2z)4] which he had discovered five years earlier. The Penetration Theory, of course, provided the formula for reaching the Fourth Dimension, but was thought to be impractical when it was discovered that it applied only to living protoplasm and certain rare wood fibers. In other words, it was impossible to thrust any scientific instruments into the Fourth Dimension. Small animals were thrust through, but none of them lived so it was thought unsafe for Man to stick his head through and look around. The only exploring possible, therefore, was that which could be done by thrusting an arm and hand into the other dimension. The consensus was that it would be rather silly for a bunch of scientists to stand around waggling their fingers somewhere in the Fourth Dimension, so the whole, theory was tossed out by The Science Conference of 2979. Thereafter, it was ignored until Humptafield thought of using it for chess. A duplicate of the regular three-dimensional chess board was set up in the Fourth Dimension, thus enabling a player to project his moves into infinite space. While somewhat complicated, the game proved highly successful until 3201, when Vladimir Smith lost an arm while moving R-KKt3 over ∞ for a checkmate. While making the move, Smith's arm was apparently bitten off by

the challenger wins he becomes King of Alphard VI for a period of one week. This week is known as the Festival of the Greater Little and...."

Nar Oysnarn's voice droned on, giving facts and citing figures about Alphard VI, until it must be confessed that even Manning Draco fell asleep somewhere between a description of the Alphardian mating habits and the amount of shoe imports in Galactic credits.

BY MID-MORNING of the following day, the ship was nearing Alphard VI. She had just snapped out of magnidrive and Manning was taking over the controls for the approach when the Communicator buzzed. Manning flipped the switch.

"Yes?" he said into the transmitter.

"This is the Imperial War Cruiser, *Remulden*," boomed a voice from the loudspeaker. "Identify yourself and give your destination."

"The *Alpha Actuary*," said Manning, "owned and operated by Terran Manning Draco, headed for Alphard VI on official business for the Greater Solarian Insurance Company, Monopolated. Accompanied by Nar Oysnarn, of the planet Kholem in the Coma-Virgo Galaxy."

"Proceed," said the voice. There was a click as the connection was broken.

"Now what the hell was that about?" muttered Manning. "I haven't heard of any trouble in this section of the galaxy. Why should they have a war cruiser out?"

"Perhaps a holiday or something of the sort," suggested Nar. "The Alphardians are great believers in tradition."

"I remember you said that yesterday," Manning said dryly.

He bent to the task of bringing the ship in. Once, in the

---

some animal native to the Fourth Dimension. Thereafter, the game fell into ill repute until 3315 when the great Horvosa thought of setting up the duplicate board in another room and merely calling out what would be the Fourth Dimensional move. Since then this has been known as the Horvosa Application of the Humptafield Penetration Theory.

viewing screen, he caught a glimpse of the whirling silvery moons over Alphard. When he was a few thousand feet above the planet, he contacted the landing tower and identified himself. The tower provided a landing beam and he relinquished the ship to the force. He watched the blue and scarlet pips chase across the landing scanner. When they merged the ship was in the landing cradle.

Pressures adjusted automatically and the inner and outer doors opened. There was a steady drone of noise from outside as though there were a large crowd on the landing field.

"Well, here we are," Manning said to his companion. "Let's go out and look them over."

"After you," Nar Oysnarn said politely. "It would not be seemly for a mere passenger to show himself before the master of a ship."

Manning Draco grinned, but he had long before learned not to argue with the traditional ideas of creatures from other systems. He walked through the air-lock and stepped out on the field.

For a minute he was blinded by the powerful searchlights set up on the landing field. Then he could see that from the spaceport buildings right up to the edge of his ship the field was packed with Alphardians. As he appeared, the droning noise was raised to a shout. As he waited for it to die down, Manning gazed in amazement at the crowd which was obviously greeting him.

As is known to all but the most provincial of inhabitants of Galaxy I, the Alphardians are an interesting race. Their bodies proper are very similar to the bodies of primitive centipedes, being all of six feet long, usually a mottled russet brown in color, and supported by a dozen feet on each side.[5] But where the head would normally appear on a centipede, the Alphardians have the upper trunk and head of humans, rearing up at right

---

5   Industrial statistics show that Terran shoe exports were more than doubled after Alphard VI was admitted to the Federation.

angles to the rest of the body. If one ignores the lower part of the body, Alphardian men are handsome and the women beautiful by the strictest Terran standards.

As the shouting of the crowd subsided to a murmur, one Alphardian stepped forward.

"May one inquire your name and origin?" he asked, speaking in flawless English.

"Manning Draco of Terra," Manning said. He turned to indicate Nar Oysnarn. "And this is—"

"Later," said the Alphardian, holding up a hand, "we will be pleased to learn the name of your fortunate companion. But you, Manning Draco, were the first to set foot upon Alphardian soil. Know that this is the Festival of the Greater Little, now in its third day, and you are the first alien to arrive among us."

CHAPTER THREE

SOME FAINT memory tugged at Manning's mind. He had an idea that Nar Oysnarn had told him something about the Festival of the Greater Little which he should remember, but it had been during one of the periods when he was falling asleep and he couldn't trigger it into existence.

"That's very nice," he said vaguely. "Now, if you'll excuse me—"

"You don't understand?" said the young Alphardian. "It is an Alphardian tradition, dating from the first year of the Ix Dynasty, that the first alien to land on Alphardian soil during this Festival becomes a sacred hero of our race and is known throughout the Festival as the Greater Little. It is my honor, therefore, to proclaim you, Manning Draco, a Greater Little."

"I am honored," Manning said, suppressing his annoyance. It would be just his luck to run into something like this, which might interfere with his business. "This is, however, a business trip for me and so I'm afraid that I will have to decline. Now—"

"It is not permitted to decline," the young Alphardian said

stiffly. "This is our tradition and it is sacred. May I refer you to the Federation Charter, Clause 7,693, which states that all citizens of the Federation must comply with the traditions and customs of any member planet as long as such traditions and customs are not contrary to the Federation laws."

"He's right, you know," Nar Oysnarn whispered over Manning's shoulder. "I was telling you about this last night. I doubt, however, if it will seriously interfere with your business."

"Okay," Manning said. "So I'm a Greater Little. What next?"

The young Alphardian beckoned and an Alphardian maiden stepped forward. In one hand, she carried a lei of Alphardian shell flowers. From the top of her golden blonde hair down to her waist, she was as beautiful a woman as Manning could ever remember seeing—and in the case of the lei-bearer there was nothing to prevent him from noting her beauty for, like all Alphardians, she wore no clothes on her upper body. By being careful not to look down, Manning began to enjoy himself as she slipped the lei over his head and then kissed him full on the lips.

Her kiss, in fact, almost made him forget her progenitors altogether—but then as he responded to her lips, he had a momentary vision of twenty-four sets of toes curling in ecstasy and he suppressed the more obvious of his thoughts.

"Well, that wasn't so bad," Manning said when the girl stepped back. He grinned at the young Alphardian. "Is that all?"

"Oh, no," that young worthy replied. "First, you must be greeted by His Temporary Majesty, the Festival King of Alphard, after which the ritual of the Greater Little must be observed… But here comes the king now."

As he spoke, Manning could see the assembled Alphardians squirming around, packing even closer together, as they made a lane leading to where he stood. There were more shouts and the Alphardians began inclining their heads in the traditional gesture of subservience to royalty. Then Manning's worst possible fears were realized.

Striding through the throng of admiring Alphardians, wearing the royal ermine and looking as if he had always worn it, came Dzanku Dzanku, the Rigelian. Trotting along behind him, carrying the train of the robe, was Sam Warren.

"Oh, no!" exclaimed Manning.

"Ah, what a coincidence," boomed Dzanku, and there was an expression of malicious glee in the three eye-stalks bent toward Manning. "What a pleasant surprise to find that our old friend Manning Draco is to be the Greater Little under our short but glorious reign. Isn't this nice, Sam?"

"Yeah, who would've thought it," Sam Warren said with a grin.

Being a typical Rigelian, Dzanku Dzanku weighed all of a ton, Terra scale. He was, however, no taller than Manning Draco. His thick, square torso was supported by two tree-like legs. His face was small and expressionless, the three eye-stalks raised a few inches above it. He possessed six tentacles, which just now were fluttering with uncontrollable pleasure.

Sam Warren, on the other hand, was a Terran. He was smaller than Manning, with a crafty face which revealed nothing but the slyness which was his stock in trade.

DESPITE HIS surprise, as the two intergalactic confidence men approached, Manning tried a swift mental probe at Sam Warren. He suspected it would be useless and it was. Sam Warren's mind was filled with glee over the arrival of Manning Draco, but there was nothing in his mind which would indicate what he and Dzanku were planning. That synapse had, as usual, been erased.

"Okay," Manning said, turning back to Dzanku. "What's the gag?"

"Gag?" asked Dzanku, his voice filled with mock surprise. "My dear Manning, you are entirely too suspicious. It is true that I was once somewhat annoyed with you when you tricked me so that you could read my mind, but that was a mere childish outburst of the moment. Today I am merely full of the holiday spirit."

"Sure," Manning said, believing none of it. "Then what's the idea of sticking me with this Greater Little business?"

"Sheer accident, my boy—although a fortunate one. I am the king of Alphard for one week, thanks to having bested Emperor Romixon in the small matter of a game of chess. This automatically brings on the Festival of the Greater Little and custom decrees that the first alien to arrive during the Festival becomes the Greater Little. You were fortunate enough to be that first alien. Since I know you are familiar with Terran history, I might point out that the honor is roughly equivalent to being given the key to a city."

"I'm more interested in the key you've given yourself by being king," Manning said. "How much looting are you going to be able to get away with?"

"A crude way of putting it," Dzanku said delicately. "My powers are limited—but adequate. For example, it is one of my duties to determine the sort of ritual required of the alien who becomes the Greater Little."

"So that's it," grunted Manning. "Well, you can decide all you like, but I'll have nothing to do with any ritual you set up."

"In that case," said Dzanku, "it will be my sad duty to devise a suitable punishment for you—since a refusal to participate in local traditions is contrary to Federation law. As the temporary sovereign ruler of Alphard, I may punish you as I see fit. I might add that even if the emperor should feel more kindly disposed toward you, under the law he can do nothing about correcting my acts until six months from now."

A Rigelian has never been known to grin, but for a minute Manning thought Dzanku was going to perform that impossible feat. The two of them stared at each other and slowly Manning brought his anger under control.

"Okay," he finally said. "This one is your round, Dzanku. What's the ritual?"

"That will come this evening," Dzanku said. "I believe there are a number of parades and such things involving you during the remainder of the day. But I shall see you at the palace this evening. Your guard—of honor, of course—will bring you there."

He waved his tentacles amiably and turned away. As he walked through the crowd, he spoke to Sam Warren, in tones which easily reached Manning. "Sam," he said, "don't let me forget to contact the war cruiser overhead and tell them that it's all right now to permit the other alien visitors to land. We've kept them waiting long enough."

As Dzanku had promised, there were a number of things which kept Manning busy throughout the day. With Nar Oysnarn tagging along, he was paraded through practically every street of the capital city of Ix. He was pelted with flowers, had innumerable leis strung around his neck, and was soundly bussed by dozens of young Alphardian females. He made speeches, laid cornerstones, dedicated schools, and was even a judge, complete with tape measure, of a beauty contest.

In general, there was such an air of good fellowship and the holiday spirit that Manning might have even enjoyed himself if it hadn't been for worrying about what Dzanku Dzanku and Sam Warren were up to. But every time he found himself getting into the spirit of things, he'd remember the bland countenance of the Rigelian and his pleasure would evaporate. It was growing dark when, escorted by a large band of Alphardians, Manning Draco went to the palace. He was taken directly to the roof where he found Dzanku and a retinue, which included Sam Warren, waiting.

"Good evening, Manning," Dzanku said gravely. "I trust you have been enjoying the hospitality of my loyal subjects?"

"I could do without the sound of your unctuous voice dribbling into my ears," snapped Manning. "Just get on with the dirty work."

"Tcht, tcht," Dzanku said. "You must get into the spirit of things. Besides I've been told that my voice is most pleasant—well, I suppose that is a matter of personal taste. In the meantime, shall we get on with this pleasant little custom?"

Manning nodded grimly.

"Then, if you will relax, over there...." Dzanku indicated a couch arrangement on the roof. To a Terran like Manning Draco, it seemed more arrangement than couch, since it had obviously been built to accommodate the bodies of Alphardian natives. Still it was fairly comfortable, he discovered, since the upper part was built for a humanoid body and his legs could fit into the hollow built to support centipede bodies.

As he lay down, Manning found himself staring up at the Alphardian satellites, the six bright moons chasing each other madly about the seventh one. It was, he thought, one of the high spots among the confusing aspects of the galaxy.

"Now," Dzanku was saying, "all you have to do is relax on that more than comfortable couch throughout the night and count the number of revolutions made by the moons above you."

Manning glared up at him and the Rigelian's tentacles waved with pleasure.

"Where the hell did you dig up an idea like that?" Manning asked.

"Inspired, isn't it?" Dzanku observed. "But I assure you that it is quite in keeping with the festival. Throughout the history of all planets, rituals of initiation have been to some extent tests of strength or endurance. It is true that I have also been influenced in fixing your ritual by a knowledge of the early history of your own Terra. Perhaps you are familiar with the sort of thing which was popular with Terran university organizations some two thousand years ago. Hazing, I believe it was called."

Manning could only glare his anger.

"By the way," Dzanku continued amiably, "there will be various court attendants around all night to see that you don't go to sleep on the job. And, of course, the usual festival crowd to cheer you on in your efforts. I might also add that a photo-tabulator will be turned on so that we can compare your final count with it to detect any inclination toward nonparticipation.

The penalty for such is apt to be severe—and is determined by myself, naturally. I may occasionally drop back here myself to see how you are getting along. Now, if you'd care to begin...."

MANNING PERMITTED himself the luxury of one more glare, then turned to gaze upward at the whirling moons. He exerted the rigid discipline of his mind, banished his anger, and began counting the revolutions to himself.

"It's really not bad at all," Nar Oysnarn whispered from somewhere near his head. "I could tell by the emanations from the Rigelian that he was not well disposed toward you and I feared that he might give you a tough assignment. But this is relatively easy."

Manning grunted to indicate he heard the Kholemite, wryly making a mental note to discover some time what Nar Oysnarn considered relatively difficult.

The long, slow hours of the night dragged by as Manning Draco counted the circling moons, his eyes stinging with weariness. Later, it seemed as if the moons were melting into each other and there were times when he felt that he was revolving while the moons remained still. He was vaguely aware of the distant murmur of the crowd and two or three times he thought he heard the voice or caught the thought of Dzanku Dzanku. But the moons moved so rapidly there was no time to check up on fleeting impressions.

He was completely unaware when daylight came to Alphard VI and the moons faded to silvery disks. Finally the mental retreat in which he counted, hidden from the creaking demands of his body, was penetrated by the voice of Dzanku Dzanku and he was aware that it had been repeating the same thing for some time.

"The time is up, Manning," the Rigelian was saying again. "Your trial as a sacred hero of the Festival of the Greater Little is ended."

Slowly, Manning's eyes dragged their gaze away from the moons and focused vaguely on the three eyestalks inclined toward him.

"Ah, you have done nobly," Dzanku said, when he saw that Manning was looking at him. "What was your count for the night?"

Manning sorted through the numbers in his mind until he came to the last one which had registered before he switched his gaze. "Six thousand, eight hundred and forty," he said.

One of Dzanku's eye-stalks bent to peer at a tape held in one tentacle. "Excellent," he boomed. "You astound me, my friend. You were within three of the actual count. Permit me to congratulate you."

Manning Draco stumbled to his feet and tried to get a sharper focus on the Rigelian. But he kept seeing the image of whirling moons between them.

"Drop dead," Manning muttered hoarsely. He swayed from exhaustion. It occurred to him that Dzanku may have intended to exhaust him in order to strike mentally and he braced his mind shield. But there was no attack. Dzanku continued to gaze at him with the blandness of a well-meaning Rigelian social worker.

"Okay," Manning said finally. "What do I have to do next?"

Dzanku's tentacles waved reassuringly. "Nothing at all. You are now officially the Greater Little of Alphard VI—a position of only slightly less importance than my own. For the remainder of the Festival there is nothing to do but enjoy yourself. Forget the cares of everyday existence. Be gay. You are now a full-fledged hero and anything on Alphard is yours for the asking—well, almost anything."

"Okay," grunted Manning, "give me a bed and then leave me alone."

Dzanku Dzanku turned to the crowd of Alphardians and waved his tentacles for attention. "My loyal and loving subjects," he said, "escort the honorable Greater Little to your finest hostelry and see that he is provided with a comfortable room. Being a Terran, and therefore of inferior physical endowments, he must repair his manly vigor by sleeping."

Manning Draco was too tired to resent the insult. He followed a number of Alphardians off the palace roof, dimly aware that Nar Oysnarn was still with him. A few minutes later, he scrawled his name in a hotel register and was taken up to a room. He was aware that Nar Oysnarn said something about having the room next to his and then he tumbled into bed. He slept and dreamed that he wore a halo made of spinning moons.

CHAPTER FOUR

IT WAS the middle of the afternoon when Manning Draco awoke. He was considerably more rested than he had been that morning, but there was still a layer of numbness over his body and mind. He was overly conscious of the fact that he had been on Alphard VI almost twenty-four hours and hadn't done anything for Greater Solarian.

To his surprise his luggage from the ship was in the room. He quickly changed clothes and slipped out of the hotel. Searching along the streets, he found a small restaurant which served Terran food and had his breakfast. Then he went straight to the palace.

The Alphardian who greeted him in the royal chambers was old, with a long white beard covering most of his chest. Like other Alphardians, his humanoid upper half was bare of clothing. His lower body was covered with a lavender silk garment which might have been loosely described as trousers. He wore twelve pair of shoes of gayly colored Procyon suede, made from the space-cured skins of the giant capellae-mice found on that planet.

"My name is Manning Draco," Manning said. "I want to see Dzanku."

"Dzanku?" repeated the old Alphardian, thoughtfully stroking his beard. "Dzanku? I don't believe—oh, yes! You must mean His Temporary Majesty King Dzanku. Of course. I will announce your presence at once."

The old man ambled across the room, but just before he reached the door he turned and came back, shaking his head.

"I'll have to have your name," he said. "It's the rule, you know. Have to announce everyone."

"But I told you my name. It's Manning Draco."

"Of course, you did." The old Alphardian looked at him shrewdly. "Draco, eh? You must be the new Greater Little." He surveyed Manning and shook his head. "I'm not sure but what we should abandon the custom of the Festival. We seem to be attracting more and more weird specimens.... Well, I'll announce you. His Temporary Majesty seems to see all sorts."

Once more he ambled across the room, but again turned back just before he reached the door.

"I'm sorry," he said, "but who was it you wanted to see?"

"Dzanku," Manning snapped.

"You're welcome—although I'm sure I don't know why."

"What the hell is wrong with you?" Manning exploded. "I've told you in simple Galactic English that I am Manning Draco and I want to see Dzanku Dzanku, the temporary king of Alphard VI. Can't you keep anything in your mind?"

"I'm sorry," the old Alphardian said, "but I'm rather new at this job. And then I keep thinking that perhaps if I had only moved my King's Knight's pawn to King's Knight three over four into two infinity, I might not have lost. It's an interesting problem."

"King's Knight's pawn," exclaimed Manning. "Then you must be the Emperor of Alphard."

"Not now," said the Emperor, "but I will be again in three days. You know, this is the first time I've ever been beaten. I think I'll pass a law against playing chess with strangers." He sighed heavily. "Oh, well, I suppose I might as well announce you. One of my accursed ancestors made it a rule that the Emperor must serve the temporary king. I must confess it makes me happy to remember that he broke all twenty-four legs when he was courting his seventh wife."

The old man turned away and this time he made it through the door without forgetting his errand. He returned shortly and conducted Manning into the throne room. Dzanku, practically smothered in ermine and with the royal crown perching precariously on one side of his head so as not to interfere with his eye-stalks, sat on the throne. Despite the fact that it was designed to accommodate the most royal of Alphardian bodies, Dzanku managed to sit on it with an air of having always belonged there. Sam Warren lounged in a Terran-style chair beside the throne.

"The Greater Little of Alphard, Manning Draco, my friend and yours, is always welcome," Dzanku said pompously. He turned to the old Alphardian and waved a couple of tentacles. "Go away, Romixon. I'll have no servants snooping around during audiences."

The temporarily unemployed emperor walked across the throne room, but at the door he turned back. There was a worried frown on his face.

"You make me nervous," he complained. He caught the agitation in the Rigelian's eye-stalks and added hastily, "Your Temporary Majesty. I have to admit that all the laws you've passed have been all right, but I never know what you're going to do next. After all, I've made a career of being the Emperor of Alphard and I don't like some amateur messing around in it. It would be different if you were a professional. I tell you I don't like it."

"You have a low and suspicious nature," Dzanku said blandly. "Now, begone." He waited until the old Alphardian had shuffled out of the room and then turned back to Manning. "What do you want?" he asked bluntly.

"Yeah," chimed in Sam Warren, "what're you up to, Manning?"

"Boys, you got me all wrong," Manning said. "All I want is some information."

"Any time," said Sam Warren, "that Manning Draco says that he doesn't want anything it's a lead-coated cinch there's a

Polluxian somewhere in the atom pile. Watch him, Dzanku."

"I shall, old friend," Dzanku said pleasantly. There was a wariness in his eye-stalks. "What kind of information, Manning?"

"The relationship between the Galaxy Insurance and Benefit Association and this thing of you being king," Manning said. "I don't know how you worked it to pull this festival racket just as you and Sam are starting your new business, but it's obvious that you'll squeeze every advantage out of the position. I want to know what you've done so far."

"I fail to see how this is the concern of Greater Solarian," Dzanku said.

"Easy," Manning answered with a grin. "We've been notified that a number of our policy holders will not keep up their policies in the future, but in the meantime have made you the beneficiary during the remaining time the policy is in force."

"Ah, yes, our trade-in program. A rather brilliant touch, I thought."

"But what business is it of yours?" Sam Warren added.

"We don't like to have the same person or same company," said Manning, "be the beneficiary on so many policies. You boys ought to know how such things upset J. Barnaby Cruikshank. It makes for too much temptation for fraud."

DZANKU OGLED Manning piously. "Perish the thought," he sympathized. "But everything Sam and I have done here on Alphard has been completely legitimate. In fact, you could easily learn all about it from the records so I might as well tell you. Sam and I are the sole owners of a corporation known as the Galaxy Insurance and Benefit Association. We are an Alphard-ian corporation. Since we are the first local corporation to be formed for the purpose of insurance, under local laws no other local group can go into competition with us for at least two years."

"How did you manage a local corporation since neither you nor Sam are citizens of Alphard?"

"Emperor Romixon," Dzanku said, "owns one share of stock in the corporation and is the chairman of our Board of Directors—at a generous annual stipend, I might add. Up to about a week ago, in open competition with Greater Solarian, we had sold about two thousand insurance polices due to our generous trade-in offer. But I assure you we have no intention of arranging for the—ah—demise of those policy holders. What we'd collect from Greater Solarian would only have to be paid to the heirs on our own policies."

"Uh-huh," said Manning. "That covers anything nicely up to a week ago. But four days ago you became the temporary ruler of Alphard. What has happened since then?"

"I admit the business outlook has improved," Dzahku said mildly while Sam Warren grinned. "I presume you know that the emperors of Alphard have always been great lovers of chess, thereby accounting for the tradition which permits anyone who beats the emperor to be king for one week. I enjoy the game myself in a modest way and it was by a fortunate chance that I defeated Emperor Romixon."

"I'll bet," murmured Manning.

"Since becoming king," Dzanku continued, "I have introduced a certain amount of socially minded legislation—you know I've always been interested in economics. First, in the interest of national welfare, I have passed a law which permits only Alphardian companies to sell insurance. The matter of the security of the relatives of a bereaved one should not be subject to the whims of interplanetary speculation." He paused.

"Which means cutting out Greater Solarian and all other companies of the Federation," said Manning, "and leaving your little company with a veritable insurance monopoly on Alphard VI?"

"You might put it that way," Dzanku said, "although the monopoly is good for only two years. In addition to this, I have also passed a law which makes it necessary for every Alphardian citizen to carry not less than five thousand credits' worth of life insurance. As a result, the Galaxy Insurance and Benefit Association has, during the past four days, sold two hundred and twenty million insurance policies with more orders coming in. It has, I must admit, been a most satisfactory week, so far."

"And I suppose," Manning said bitterly, "that you and Sam will put the advance premiums in your pockets and blast off a few hours before your reign is over—since the Emperor can certainly do something about those two laws once he's back on the throne."

"On the contrary," Dzanku said, "we are thinking of staying around. There will be three more days in which I can pass laws and there are untold possibilities on this little planet. I assure you that the Emperor will not rescind my laws."

"Why not?"

"He can't. No emperor, or even temporary Festival king, can pass a law which is harmful to either the people of Alphard or to the Crown. My first law, limiting the selling of insurance to only local companies, is obviously to the benefit of Alphardians and to change it would be harmful to the people. In my second law, I was thoughtful enough to include a clause which puts a special ten percent tax on all insurance benefits. This goes directly into the coffers of the Emperor. Therefore, he cannot repeal that law either."

"Of all the bare-faced robbery," began Manning.

"But legal," interrupted Dzanku. "I'm afraid, my dear Manning, that Greater Solarian is through here on Alphard and there is nothing you or J. Barnaby can do about it. You might as well close up the branch office while you're here."

Manning Draco had a suspicion that this was true. It looked very much like he and J. Barnaby had both been bested for the first time in their lives. But he wasn't admitting it yet.

"Maybe," he said. "But tell me something, Dzanku. Why did you go to all the trouble of holding other alien ships up above the planet until I arrived? Why did you want me to be elected the Greater Little?"

"I'm a generous person," said Dzanku grandly. "I knew that there was no way that Sam and I could lose and that you were making a long trip for nothing. So, in a sentimental moment, I thought it would be nice to let you share in the Festival honors."

"It also gave you a chance to make me count those damn moons until my eyes were popping out," Manning growled. "And *that* sounds more like you."

"You wound me deeply," Dzanku said. "Now, if you will excuse us—there is the small matter of some special tax exemptions I'd like to work out. You know, despite one of the oldest proverbs of which you Terrans boast, I've discovered that there is a royal road to happiness." He waved his tentacles in dismissal.

MANNING DRACO left the palace, but think as he could he was unable to detect even the slightest flaw in Dzanku's work. An hour with a leading Alphardian lawyer proved his worst fears to be justified. After leaving the attorney's office, he entered a public visibooth and put through a call to J. Barnaby Cruikshank on Terra. It was a good thing that the call was scrambled, for when the news was broken to J. Barnaby, the head of Greater Solarian ran through a string of profanity which would have made a space pirate, or a Fomalhautian pleasure queen, turn green with envy. When he finished, J. Barnaby's face was a choleric shade and he was out of breath—but he still had enough breath for a final order.

"You stay there and fix it," he said, "or don't ever show your face here again. I don't care how you do it, or what it costs, but get these two!" With that he broke the connection.

It was getting dark as Manning Draco walked along the main street of the City of Ix on Alphard VI. There was a festival air to the whole city—one which Manning did not share. The streets were filled with gay Alphardians. Many of them recognized him and two or three groups tried to carry him off to private parties. He shook them off as kindly as possible. For once in his life, Manning even failed to enjoy the fact that every few feet he was on the receiving end of feminine caresses and kisses. He submitted but his heart wasn't in it.

When a man is in the mood Manning was, there are only two things he can do—and this has not changed between the days when man drove a yoke of oxen and when he flashed from sun to sun in slim space cruisers. Since it was impossible to smash J. Barnaby in the face and there could be little satisfaction in using a visiscreen to tell him where to stuff his job, Manning Draco turned into the first bar he came to.

It was a combination bar and night club and there was a young Alphardian female on the stage singing. It was a currently popular Alphardian song and measured by Alphardian morals it was a pretty risqué number. In English, the title of the song was "Unbutton Your Shoes and I'll Be Over." Later, the song would become popular all over the galaxy, but it was considered a comedy song on most other planets. The Alphardian males were whistling and stamping their feet to show their appreciation as Manning made his way up to the bar.

The bartender caught sight of Manning and hurried over.

"We are honored," he said. "With what can we give you pleasure?"

"What's your strongest drink?" Manning wanted to know.

"A Sabikian *Prohna*," the bartender said, "distilled from the wild *Proh* which grow only on Sabik II. But it is very strong and—"

"Good," interrupted Manning. "I'll have one."

A few minutes later, the bartender set a tall glass in front of him. It was filled with a green liquor which seemed to be shot through with amber streaks. Pale smoke curled up from the top of the glass. Manning lifted it and tossed half of the contents down his throat. Then he hurriedly set the glass down and gripped the bar with both hands. He could feel the flames in his throat and there was a reeling sensation in his head which made the whole room spin. That passed quickly but it was another two minutes before he could make his throat muscles work.

"You're right about it being strong," he said hoarsely. "How much do I owe you?"

"But nothing," said the bartender. "During the Festival, no Alphardian businessman will knowingly accept money from the Greater Little. And, by Ix, I've never seen one before who could toss off half a glass of *Prohna*."

"Fools rush in," Manning muttered, more to himself than to the bartender. He gingerly tried the drink again and discovered that if he sipped it the results were not quite so explosive.

The singer was replaced by a team of Alphardian tap dancers. At first, Manning was amused, but the thudding of twenty-four pairs of feet soon began to annoy him. He finished his drink and left.

Farther down the street, he entered another bar and ordered a *Prohna*. He sipped it and turned to watch the floor-show. A sense-teaser was under the spotlight, gyrating slowly to the music. She was half beautiful—that is, her upper half was beautiful—but to anyone not educated to the Alphardian moral code her strip act was only funny. As she danced around, she would lean over and carefully remove one shoe which she then tossed to a shouting admirer at the ringside tables. Then she slowly danced out of range of the spotlight until the applause recalled her to repeat the act with another shoe.

Four barrooms and five *Prohnas* later, Manning Draco walked down the street feeling no pain. He was filled with love for the creatures of the universe, be they man or beast or a bewildering cross between. So all-embracing was this love, in fact, that he beamed with affection when he saw the royal conveyance coming along the street bearing His Temporary Majesty, King Dzanku Dzanku. He waved wildly and six tentacles returned the greeting.

"Having a wonderful time," Manning shouted. "Wish you were here."

"Peace be with you," Dzanku called and Manning thought it was rather stuffy of him. But somehow the phrase also made him feel good and he decided it called for a drink. He headed for his fifth bar.

CHAPTER FIVE

I T WAS just after he'd taken his first sip of the *Prohna* that he saw her. A Terran—an Earth girl. And so beautiful, so breathtaking, that Manning knew it was real and not the result of the Sabikian drinks. From the top of her golden red hair to the bottom of her small feet she was in every respect his dream girl. He grasped his drink firmly, moved around a number of half-drunken Alphardians, apologizing as he stepped on three feet of one of them, and slid into a place beside her at the bar.

Her name was Jadyl Genten—a name that was like music to him, although perhaps it was the voice with which she told him. She had been feeling lonely, surrounded by Alphardians, and was as happy to see another human face as he was. Over his *Prohna* and her Acruxian *Leeba* highball, they exchanged the sort of information which passes quickly between two enchanted people. She liked all the things he liked, hated the things he couldn't stand, longed for the things which were his heart's desires—and before long the glow which came from standing beside her far surpassed the smoky warmth of his drink.

They had dinner at a little place around the corner. Although its ability to provide Terran food was only passable, the fact that they ate together made the cuisine superb. They drank cool green wine, imported from Al Na'ir, and afterward they danced to the disturbing music of an Alphardian string quartet.

Later, they went up to his hotel room—mostly to get away from the fact that the Alphardians couldn't forget that he was a part of their festival. Manning Draco had dropped all of the wise mannerisms which had so long marked his presence with women and it was important that they be alone.

There, in the hotel, he sat at her feet and softly recited the great love poems of a hundred planets. And like a good Earth man, who explores the galaxy before settling down at home, he came at last to a love poem of the old Earth. As always, it was the tale of a man and a maid and when he reached the part concerning their first kiss, Jadyl leaned over and kissed him. He recited no more poetry that night.

The two days which followed were dreamlike in their ecstasy. The visicreen crackled calls and he ignored it. There were rappings at the door and once the anxious voice of Nar Oysnarn outside, but he paid no attention. Then, on the morning of the third day as he sat telling Jadyl of older dreams, while she nodded with understanding and sometimes agreement, the door opened. Into the room stepped Nar Oysnarn, a passkey dangling from his hand. His purple body was so pale it was almost white, but there was a determined look on his trianguar face.

Nar Oysnarn advanced into the room. He ignored the Terran girl and at first Manning Draco was annoyed, but then he decided that it was only the tactful politeness of one from another culture.

"You will forgive me," Nar Oysnarn said politely but firmly, "but you asked me for my help and I am here to render it."

"Your help?" Manning asked and then only vaguely remembered that he'd had some thought of using Nar's peculiar powers against Dzanku.

"Yes," Nar said firmly. "And while I realize that you have probably decided not to tackle your case until the Rigelian is no longer king, it is my belief that this is a mistake. He is most vulnerable who has the most power. And since this is the last day of the Festival, I respectfully suggest that you must act today."

While it was true that forty-eight hours earlier, Manning Draco would have happily permitted the Greater Solarian Insurance Company to go smash, and it was equally true that he hated to leave Jadyl for even one minute, he was now doubly aware of his responsibility to others.

"You're right," he told Nar. He turned to Jadyl and ran his fingers playfully through her hair. "You stay here, honey," he said, "while I go take care of some business. It won't take long and then you and I will head for Earth." Nar watched him stonily.

He went jauntily through the door, followed by Nar Oysnarn, and out of the hotel.

"What is your plan?" Nar asked when they were on the street.

It was there, with the sharp Alphardian wind blowing some of the tendrils of perfume from his mind, that Manning Draco forced himself to put all of his mind to the business of Greater Solarian. He looked at the little Kholemite in consternation. "I'll be damned if I know," he confessed. "Originally, I did have an idea whereby with your help I could tie Dzanku up in knots. But Dzanku being even the temporary king of this screwy planet makes the original plan dangerous. If only Dzanku hadn't challenged the Emperor to chess—" He broke off and stared into space.

For the first time since he'd landed on Alphard, Manning Draco's brain had begun to work. The first day had been taken up with anger and frustration and the strain of counting the revolutions of the moons. The next two days had been lost in romance. Now, all at once, he thought he saw the solution. With a sensation of guilt, he felt that it was a solution he should have seen at once.

"I think I've got it," he said to Nar. "Come on."

THEY WENT first to the Royal Alphardian Library, where Manning pored over the Constitution of Alphard VI. After that, he spent a few minutes in the general reading room of the Inter-Planetary Annex. Only a few minutes were needed, for Manning possessed an eidetic mind and when he left, the pages he'd read were firmly impressed in his memory. With Nar Oysnarn puffing to keep up, they headed for the palace.

The same old Alphardian, he who was Emperor Romixon, was in the anteroom as they entered. He seemed to have lost the vacant stare of two days before and there was a glint of recognition in his eyes as he looked at Manning.

"I suppose you want to see Dzanku?" he grumbled.

"If you please," Manning said.

"All right, but I tell you I'm pretty sick of this whole thing.

I'll be mighty glad when tomorrow comes. Why, I don't know how everyone stands it being commoners. Who's that with you?"

"Nar Oysnarn, of the planet Kholem, Coma-Virgo Galaxy. He's a friend of mine."

"You Terrans will take up with anyone," the old Alphardian sneered. He went into the throne room, but was soon back. "He'll see you," he said curtly.

They followed him into the throne room and there was Dzanku once more lolling on the throne, with Sam Warren nearby. Both of them were obviously pretty well pleased with themselves.

"You may leave, chamberlain," Dzanku said to the old Alphardian. "It's nice to see you, Manning. Where have you been keeping yourself?"

"Let Romixon stay," Manning said. "He'll be interested in what I have to say."

"Oh, very well," Dzanku said, waving a tentacle agreeably. "What's on your mind, Manning?"

"I am here," Manning announced, "to challenge you to a game of four-dimensional chess."

The Rigelian lost his amiability. "What's the gag?" he snapped.

"No gag at all," Manning said cheerfully. "You and I are going to play a game of chess, with the throne you're now occupying going to the winner. In other words, if I beat you, I become king of Alphard."

"You can't do that," declared Dzanku. "You have to challenge the Emperor—which means you'll have to wait until tomorrow."

"Wrong, Dzanku. The Constitution of Alphard merely says that anyone can challenge the *ruler* of the planet, and therefore this applies to the temporary ruler as well as to the regular one."

"Is that right, Romixon?" Dzanku demanded.

"He's right," the old Alphardian said gloomily. "But I wish all of you would stop acting as if my throne were a credit someone tossed on the dice table. It's undignified. I've got a notion to secede from the Federation and ban all Terrans and Rigelians from my planet." Suddenly his face brightened. "I just remembered something," he said, speaking to Manning. "Even if you win you won't be able to keep me from becoming Emperor again tomorrow. The Constitution says that no one Festival can last more than one week and that only one Festival is permitted in any six months period."

"That's true," Manning said, "and I had no intention of trying to keep you from resuming the throne. But if I win, I'll be king for this last day of the Festival."

"Okay, I'll play you," Dzanku said. "There hasn't been a Terran born who could beat a Rigelian in four-dimensional chess—why do you think my planet has held the Galactic Championship for the past two hundred years? And don't think you'll catch me with a cheap trick like you did the last time—it wouldn't help you any even if it were possible."

"I wouldn't think of it," Manning said.

Dzanku pushed a button on the throne and a number of footmen rushed in. He sent them after the chess board and pieces. Within a few minutes, a regulation three-dimensional chess board had been set up in the throne room. A similar board, representing the fourth dimension, was set up in another room and the two rooms were connected by audio. Dzanku generously offered to let Manning send a representative into the other room to see that the moves were made as called, but Manning just as generously declined.

Dzanku won the choice and took the white. The game started, with Sam Warren, Nar Oysnarn, and Romixon as the only audience.

FOR THE FIRST few moves, both players moved in three dimensions only. Dzanku led off with the well-known Queen's Knight Gambit developed by Tanalov in the 28th century and Manning countered with standard moves. But within a few minutes, both players were widening the scope of play to include simple moves into infinity. As they reached the middle game, Dzanku set up a pawn sacrifice on the third level of play.

Manning studied the board for a minute, then leaned back in his chair, running one hand through his hair.

"I move," he said, taking advantage of the rule which permitted a player to call the move on an infinity play, with the pieces being adjusted later, "my queen to king's rook's four; to six over queen's knight's three; to queen's bishop three over four into three infinity... I believe that's a mate."

The Emperor Romixon sighed heavily and looked at Manning Draco with considerably more respect. He was the only one to recognize it as the same daring move which in 3316 had cost the great Horvosa the championship of the galaxy.[6]

Dzanku Dzanku poised one tentacle over the board and then froze in that attitude. A close observer might have noticed that Nar Oysnarn also seemed to be unduly preoccupied.

Manning Draco turned to Romixon. "I should like to remind you," he said, "of the rule, accepted several years ago by the Galactic Chess Rules Committee, which states that any move in the fourth dimension which results in a mate must be answered by the opposing player within a time limit of two minutes. Failure to do so forfeits the game."

The old Alphardian nodded. "I'm aware of the rule," he said testily. "Thirty seconds have already elapsed."

"Hey, what goes on here," Sam Warren said. "What's the matter, Dzanku?... Dzanku!"

THE RIGELIAN gave no evidence of having heard his partner. He still crouched over the board, his three eyes fixed immovably on the pieces, one tentacle still poised in the air. Manning Draco noticed that red veins had suddenly appeared in his eyes and they looked as if they might pop out of their stalks any minute.

It was a curious tableau, lasting for the next ninety seconds.

---

6   Lest some reader who is not giving his undivided attention to this account jump to the conclusion that Manning Draco has an Übermensch psychosis, it should be made clear that this was the first game ot chess ho had ever played. He had merely memorized a number of games, so there was nothing very spectacular about his feat.

Both Dzanku and Nar Oysnarn sat as though carved from stone. Romixon kept his eyes on the chronometer fastened to one of his forelegs. Manning Draco leaned back in his chair and relaxed. Little Sam Warren became more and more agitated as he urged Dzanku to do something—*anything.*

"The two minutes are up," Romixon announced. "Manning Draco is the new temporary king of Alphard VI and may rule"— he glanced at his foreleg—"for the next twenty-one hours and thirty-six minutes."

"Permit me to be the first to congratulate Your Temporary Majesty," Nar Oysnarn suddenly said.

There was a roar of rage from Dzanku Dzanku. He leaped to his feet, tentacles waving wildly, scattering chess board and pieces in every direction.

"I've been cheated," he bellowed, his three eyes bulging with anger. "The whole thing is illegal. That creature there"— a sweeping tentacle indicated Nar Oysnarn—"did something that paralyzed me. The rules state that no special powers are permitted."

"I didn't see him do anything," Romixon said maliciously. "According to the law, Manning Draco is now king of Alphard."

For a minute, Manning thought Dzanku was going to charge all of them. The big Rigelian was so angry he was quivering like a ton of jelly.

"By the way, Romixon," Manning said casually, "what is the penalty for assaulting a ruler of Alphard?"

"Exile to the third moon," Romixon said. "It sometimes takes as long as eighteen months for a creature to die there, although the mind cracks after eight or nine months, I understand."

With a visible effort, Dzanku restrained his anger. "All right, Draco," he said hoarsely, "you win this round. But there's nothing you can do to recall the laws I've passed. And I'll get around to you when the Festival is over. Come on, Sam."

Followed by Sam Warren, Dzanku stomped from the throne room."

The old Alphardian was doubled up with laughter, the tears streaming down his face.

"Oh, dear," he said firmly, "I haven't enjoyed myself so much since the day my father, the Emperor Dumixon, broke his silly neck while playing some alien game introduced by you Terrans." He stopped laughing and glared at Manning. "But don't you start messing up my kingdom now. At least, Dzanku fixed it so that I make a tidy little profit, so don't get any ideas you're going to take it away from me."

"I wouldn't think of it," Manning said. "But there is one thing we'd better do quickly. What is the process for passing a law on this planet?"

"Why?" Romixon asked suspiciously.

"Dzanku was angry when he left here and still filled with a desire for revenge, but once he's cooled off he may decide it's better to make sure of keeping his profit. I want to stop him from leaving here with all the money he's collected so far."

"In here," Romixon said quickly, leading the way into the next room. "Hurry up! Don't let him get away with all of that beautiful cash… There—all you do is write the new law on the visiscribe and sign your name. It then appears on the public screen and in all police courts and is an established law. But hurry!"

CHAPTER SIX

MANNING STEPPED over to the visiscribe, picked up the electronic pencil, and wrote: *No alien is permitted to leave the planet Alphard VI during the Festival of the Greater Little nor may any money be sent from the planet without a special permit signed by the ruler. King Manning.*

"There," he said, turning back to Romixon, "that will keep him from leaving or sending the money out to a confederate. Tell, me, does an ex-king have any immunity from the laws of the planet?"

"No," Romixon said and it was obvious from his grin that

he was contemplating the future of more than one ex-king. "Although," he added reluctantly, "with the exception of murder or a royal assault, prison sentences for actions during Festival week cannot be for more than six months."

"Even six months in prison will do Dzanku good," Manning said cheerfully. "Well—to work."

"Wait a minute," Romixon said hastily. "Let's not go off half-shoed. You really ought to discuss everything with me before going ahead. After all, I have had more experience in this business than you have."

"Okay—but don't try to stall me, Romixon."

The Alphardian started to pout, but then changed his mind. "How did you get the best of Dzanku?" he asked curiously.

"Nar Oysnarn," Manning said, indicating his young friend. "He has a strange ability which works only with those who have secondary mind shields—as Dzanku does. If Nar tries to read such a creature's mind it causes paralysis. When I leaned back and ran my hand through my hair, Nar merely tried to read Dzanku's mind."

"Then you did cheat," Romixon said. "Maybe I could declare the whole thing illegal and take over right now...."

"Wrong," Manning said. "The rules state that a *player* may not use special powers in order to win—and I used no special powers. Nar Oysnarn was not a player and I cannot be held responsible for the fact that his curiosity made him try to read my opponent's mind."

Romixon glared at him. "What are you going to do now?" he demanded.

"Well, first, I'm going to pass a law stating that no alien is permitted to directly make a profit on any business which may involve the death of one or more Alphardians. Since insurance does involve the death of the insured, this means that no alien may profit *directly* from insurance on this planet. I think you'll agree this is a law which is good for Alphard."

"Y-yes," Romixon said uncertainly. "But that will also mean that your company, Greater Solarian, can't sell insurance here either."

"That's right," Manning said cheerfully.

Romixon scratched his beard thoughtfully. "There has to be a catch in it," he grumbled. "You Terrans don't give things away. There must be an angle somewhere."

"Maybe," Manning said. "Incidentally, I will also pass a law confiscating for the Crown all receipts and assets of any company incorporated in Alphard for the purpose of selling such insurance. Since the Galaxy Insurance and Benefit Association is the only such company, it means we will confiscate everything that Dzanku and Warren own."

"This I like," Romixon said.

"First, however, I will pass a law making it a crime for any alien to possess money which comes from the sale of anything involving the life or death of an Alphardian. Then we arrest Dzanku and Warren, throw them in jail, and then confiscate their business."

"Good," said Romixon, stamping his twenty-four feet with glee.

"Then," Manning, said, "I'm going to nationalize insurance on this planet. In other words, the laws Dzanku passed requiring all Alphardians to carry insurance will still stand, but all insurance policies will be sold by the government."

"That sounds a little like socialism," Romixon said cautiously. "I'm not sure that it's right for an emperor to have anything to do with subversive ideas."

"Not at all. It would be socialism if the government was the people, but since you are—or will be again in a few hours—the government, it'll actually be you who own the insurance company."

"That sounds logical," the Emperor agreed.

"Of course," Manning continued blandly, "it is a matter of Federation law that all insurance companies must have available assets to cover the values of policies issued. Therefore, I will have to pass a law freezing enough of the royal holdings to equal the value of the insurance policies."

"You'll have to—*what?*" screamed Romixon. He jumped up and down with rage, the sound of his twenty-four feet like thunder. "That'll tie up every cent I own! You can't do that to me! I'll declare war!"

"And fight the whole Federation?"

THE ANGER went out of Romixon. "Please," he said. "Why did you have to come here? I was so happy before. Now you're going to make a pauper out of me—I won't have a palace to my name. What will become of me in my old age?"

"There is one other way to handle it," Manning said thoughtfully.

Romixon went down on twenty-four knees, clasped his hands together. "Have pity on a poor old despot," he said. "Handle it the other way. Leave my few remaining years untouched by the dreadful pinch of penury."

"Let me get one thing straight," Manning said. "If I pass a law which benefits both you, as the Emperor, and the citizens of Alphard, that law cannot be repealed in any way—can it?"

"Absolutely not," declared the Alphardian. "And in addition, I give you my word of honor."

"Okay, we'll do it this way. We'll nationalize insurance, which makes you the insurance company of Alphard. But because an Emperor cannot become an insurance broker without the loss of a certain amount of dignity, the government will then sub-contract the Greater Solarian Insurance Company to furnish all policies, put up the necessary assets, and pay all benefits. As the original contractor, the government—which is you—will receive a regular sales commission on every policy. How's that?"

"Splendid," Romixon exclaimed, leaping to his feet. "My boy, you have saved the throne of Alphard. I will never forget you for this." But there was a gleam deep within his eyes which reminded Manning Draco that the last sentence could have more than one meaning. Mentally, he resolved to leave Alphard VI slightly in advance of the time his reign would be over.

"Then I'd better get to work," he said.

The remainder of the morning was a busy one. Manning Draco carefully checked the wording of each law with the best lawyer on the planet, then passed them. He had the police round up Dzanku and Warren. To be sure that nothing went wrong, Manning sat behind the national judge while both of them were sentenced to prison. Then he saw to the confiscation of the property, had all of the policies transferred, and made sure that the contract between the government of Alphard and Greater Solarian was without loopholes and that one copy went off to be filed in the Federation archives.

Then he called the home office on Terra. The news that Dzanku and Warren were in jail and that Greater Solarian now carried policies on every single Alphardian instead of only a few million brought an expression of sublime bliss to the face of J. Barnaby Cruikshank. In fact, he was so carried away that he rashly offered a large bonus to his chief investigator. Manning made him put it into writing and hold the signed sheet up in front of the visiscreen. Then he broke the connection.

It was lunchtime. A triumphant Manning Draco, feeling better than he had since landing, went back to the hotel to have lunch with Jadyl Genten.

She wasn't in the room. No one in the hotel recalled having seen her leave. Manning, still king, ordered out the entire Alphardian police force. Inch by inch, they searched the city, and then later the entire planet, but there was no sign of the Terran girl. The officials of the spaceport swore that not a single ship had left.

Manning was frantic, but the fact was not changed. Jadyl Genten was nowhere to be found. At first, he suspected the Emperor but he finally became convinced that the old Alphardian was telling the truth when he said that he'd never heard of the girl. Inasmuch as during the questioning, Manning had been a little rough with the Emperor, it became even more important to leave before the time came for Romixon to regain his throne.

The only other thing which seemed plausible was that Dzanku had found some way to spirit her away in revenge. Sending Nar Oysnarn on to the ship at the spaceport, Manning Draco went to Ix Prison.

For reasons not too difficult to understand, Dzanku Dzanku was still not in the best humor and the sight of Manning Draco did nothing to improve it. He gripped the bars of his cell with all six tentacles and glared until his eye-stalks quivered.

"I'm going to ask you something," Manning said grimly, "and you'd better give me the right answers."

"I wouldn't give you the fumes of an old broken-down rocket," Dzanku said just as grimly. "Why don't you go off on a long vacation with Jadyl Genten?"

"Then you do know something about her," shouted Manning. He leaned close to the bars, and Terran and Rigelian stared angrily at each other. "What did you do with her?"

"I didn't do anything with her," Dzanku said. "In fact, I wouldn't have anything to do with her under any circumstances."

"Where is she?"

"Why don't you ask that little purple monstrosity that tags around after you? He helped you to get a throne."

"I'll make you talk," Manning declared.

"How?" Dzanku said. "You can't give me any more than the six months I'm already serving."

"Then tell me where she is and I'll let you go free."

"I'd rather stay in jail and watch you go crazy," Dranku said, and for the first time he regained some of his good humor. "Go away."

STRAIGHTENING UP, Manning Draco sent the full force of his mind slashing at the Rigelian. He felt it strike the secondary shield and lock there. For a full minute, the two of them stood there, straining. The sweat poured from Manning's face and Dzanku's eyes bulged. But their strength was equal and neither shield would give way. Finally, Manning staggered and leaned wearily against the bars. Dzanku sank down on the prison stool, his eye-stalks drooping.

"Dzanku," Manning said, "be a good guy. You and I have fought each other, but we never hurt other people in the effort to get each other. Tell me where she is?"

"I'll give you some good advice," Dzanku said wearily. "It's less than an hour before Romixon becomes Emperor again. If you're still on this planet then, you'll be right here in jail with me and for a damn sight longer than six months. Beat it and forget about Jadyl. You'll never see her again. Besides, there was something wrong with her or she would have worked better."

"What do you mean?"

But Dzanku Dzanku had gone to sleep, his tentacles wrapped around his head, and Manning knew there was no use trying to awaken a Rigelian when he didn't choose to be aroused. He turned and walked from the prison, his shoulders slumping.

It lacked only twenty minutes before the end of the Festival when Manning Draco arrived at the spaceport. A number of cheering Alphardians tried to keep him from reaching his ship, but he knew this had to be the influence of Romixon at work and he shoved roughly through.

Nar Oysnarn was already within the ship and Manning didn't even bother getting a clearance from the tower. He merely switched the ship into magnetic power and the *Alpha Actuary* leaped skyward. There were still five minutes to spare when the little ship flashed beyond the atmosphere of Alphard VI.

Manning fed the position of Kholem, in the Coma-Virgo Galaxy, into the automatic pilot, threw the ship into magnidrive and relapsed into a sulky silence which lasted until they landed on Kholem. Nar Oysnarn tried to start a conversation several times, but earned only a glare for his trouble.

"Okay, kid," Manning said, setting the ship down on the planet. "Here you are. Thanks for everything and goodbye."

Looking unhappy, Nar Oysnarn started for the airlock. But

just then Manning Draco remembered something and he grabbed the Kholemite back so fast the cap flew off his head.

"I just remembered," Manning said, grimly, "when I was trying to make Dzanku tell me where Jadyl was, he wanted to know why I didn't ask you. What did he mean by that?"

"Was she that beautiful?" Nar asked softly.

"You know she was. You saw her."

Nar Oysnarn shook his head. "No," he said, "that's what I've been trying to tell you. I didn't see her. Neither did anyone else."

"What the hell do you mean?" Manning asked angrily.

"You know," Nar said, "that all over your galaxy the Alphardians have had the reputation of being eccentric—but do you know just why they are eccentric?"

"What's that got to do with it?"

"Everything. The Alphardians are eccentric because they live out their lives beneath six moons which constantly whirl around a seventh one. Those moons are always in sight. The result is that everyone on Alphard is always in a slight hypnotic trance."

"Hypnosis?"

Nar Oysnarn nodded. "That's why Dzanku Dzanku worked out that ritual of making you look at the moons all night. He put you in deep hypnosis. He was there for a long time that night and I was sure he was in telepathic communication with you, but it didn't occur to me that he was hypnotizing you until later. Then it was too late."

"Not Jadyl," Manning said violently. "You saw her when you broke into my room this morning."

"No," Nar said gently. "You were sitting there by yourself. Think back and you'll realize that no one saw her but you. The Alphardians probably paid no attention because they merely figured you were also eccentric."

Against his will, Manning thought back to that evening in the bar, on the street, and in the restaurant.

Try as he did, he couldn't remember anyone else speaking to Jadyl or even looking at her.

"I can't believe it," he said.

"She was a post-hypnotic suggestion," Nar said firmly. "I'm sure that what happened was that Dzanku gave you some key word or sentence which would trigger the image later."

Manning was remembering meeting Dzanku on the street that night and the Rigelian's strange greeting—"Peace be with you"—which was so out of character for him.

"And," continued Nar, "I think that when Dzanku was paralyzed by the contact with my mind, the hypnotic control was broken and she vanished. That's the reason why you couldn't find her afterward."

Manning Draco sat, feeling a dream fade away into nothing, and feeling a little sorry for himself.

"But how did he make her so perfect? She liked everything I liked, seemed even to anticipate my likes and dislikes."

"I think," Nar said slowly, "that the hypnotic control made you see a feminine version of yourself—and therefore her every taste would be identical with your own. I imagine that Dzanku believed this would be such a perfect vision that there would be no danger of your spoiling his plans."

"And that's what he meant in the prison when he said there was something wrong with her or she would have worked better," Manning said, believing against his will.

There was little more to be said and Manning Draco didn't feel like small talk.

He soon said goodbye to Nar Oysnarn and the *Alpha Actuary* blasted off from Kholem.

AS HE STREAKED back toward his own galaxy, Manning Draco began to remember more of the conversation he had held in the prison with Dzanku Dzanku. And the more he remembered, the greater was his anger. So great that he knew he had to do something to get even. But what could he do to one who was in prison on a planet where it was probably unsafe for him to land? Then, realizing the lusty nature of the Rigelian and the fact that he would be shut up for at least another six months, Manning had an idea.

He landed briefly at the outlaw planet of the Deneb system—Deneb XIV. There, after some shopping around among the shifty street vendors, he purchased some Rigelian postcards—enough to supply one for each day of six months. And since, as everyone knows, Rigelian postcards can't be sent through the mails, he found a method to smuggle them into the prison on Alphard VI. He was directed to a salesman who traveled for an import house, and handled a number of illegal items on the side, who would arrange it for a price.

As small as the gesture was, it made him feel better. By the time he was reaching the Solar System, his thoughts were once more centered about Lhana Xano. Manning Draco was again on course.

Back on Alphard VI, Dzanku Dzanku cursed violently in ten languages and three crustacean dialects as the first postcard turned up in his breakfast cereal. Once, in his youth, he had known the model.

THE POLLUXIAN PRETENDER

CHAPTER ONE

IT WAS approximately four o'clock Terra Standard Time, of a mid-winter afternoon in the year 3472 in Nyork. High above the city it was snowing, but the whirling flakes never got beyond the heat-belt which was being broadcast from the spires of the tallest buildings. Inside a tastefully decorated apartment, Manning Draco fussed over the arrangements he'd made. For the tenth time, he checked the menu he'd punched on the Dinners-at-Home tape. He once more made sure that the wall vents had removed every speck of dust from the apartment. He glanced in the mirror to see if he needed to use the Glo-Shav again. He might get by.

The visiphone buzzed angrily. For the past, two hours it had been signaling methodically every ten minutes. Manning continued to ignore it.

He straightened a picture on the wall and glanced for the fiftieth time at his chronograph. Never had time gone so slowly.

As anyone might have guessed, Manning Draco was expecting a dinner guest. She was Lhana Xano, the Martian receptionist at the Greater Solarian Insurance Company, Monopolated, where Manning was the star investigator. It was now all of seven months since Lhana Xano had begun to work for the insurance company, and Manning had carried on a tireless campaign of seduction. For seven months it had been fruitless, but she had finally agreed to have dinner at his apartment. She was due to arrive at five-thirty, coming directly from work.

With the insight common to all employees, Manning had known from the beginning that the persistent visiphone calls were from J. Barnaby Cruikshank, the president of Greater Solarian. Once he had switched on one of the message tapes, turning it off again at the first blast of profanity.

At a quarter past five, the door light went on. Thinking that Lhana had managed to leave early, Manning hurried to throw open the door.

His smile of welcome faded as he looked at the two men in the black uniforms of the Galactic Police.

"Manning Draco?" one of them asked heavily.

"Yes," Manning said, "but—"

"We have a warrant for your arrest," the policeman interrupted. "Will you come with us quietly or do we have to put a paralyzer on you?"

"What's the charge?" Manning asked, a suspicion already gnawing at him.

"Obstructing the industrial process," the policeman intoned, "intent to sabotage, contempt of monopolies, and attempted seduction of personnel."

Manning had suspected J. Barnaby Cruikshank of sending the policemen; the list of charges confirmed it. He cursed with feeling.

"Where are you taking me?" he asked.

"To the offices of the Greater Solarian Insurance Company, Monoplated. Inasmuch as the plaintiff requested to see you, it is possible that you can get him to drop the charges."

"Oh, sure," Manning said bitterly. "He'll drop the charges. All I have to do is put my slave collar back on."

The policemen waited stolidly while Manning Draco left a message for Lhana on the door tape and then escorted him to their squad-flyer. A few minutes later they came down on the roof of the Greater Solarian building. Manning walked between them down to the familiar door of the president's office. The door-scanner recognized them and the door swung open.

J. BARNABY CRUIKSHANK was, normally, the very picture of well, groomed urbanity. This, however, was not true of him at the moment that the two policemen escorted Draco into his office. For once, his temper seemed to be well under control, but his rumpled hair bore mute witness to his true emotional state.

"Good work," he said to the two policemen. "You may wait outside while I speak to him. If it's necessary to press the charges, I'll call you in."

The two policemen nodded respectfully and withdrew. J. Barnaby turned a baleful gaze upon his chief investigator.

"Good afternoon, Manning," he said, making it sound more like a malediction than a greeting.

Manning dropped into one of the comfortable chairs and stared at his boss. "J. Barnaby," he said, "I've always told you that someday you'd go too far. I think this is the day. I'm annoyed."

"*You're* annoyed," snorted J. Barnaby. "There hasn't been a case assigned to you in two months. For eight weeks you've done nothing but draw your salary. Then the first time I want to see you in the two months, you refuse to answer your phone. Well, you'll either go to work or I'll send you to jail."

"You're just the boy who'd do it, too," Manning said. He was already feeling better. The sight of J. Barnaby's rages always put him in good humor. He lit a cigarette and grinned. "Okay, call off your bloodhounds. I'll go to work." He waited until he saw J. Barnaby push a button on his desk. "Now, what's the problem?"

With what was obviously an effort, Cruikshank pulled himself together. He brushed back his hair, smoothed the wrinkles in his coat, and even managed a strained smile as he forced himself to lean back in his chair. "You know, Manning," he said, his tone, almost suggesting that this was a casual visit, "I was sitting around this afternoon thinking of old times. Remember the good old days when our two best salesmen were Sam Warren and that Rigelian—what was his name?"

"Dzanku Dzanku," Manning said, watching J. Barnaby with

wariness. If there anyone in the galaxy whom J. Barnaby hated above all other it was the Rigelian Dzanku Dzanku—and he knew that the president of Greater Solarian never forgot the name of someone he hated.

"Oh, yes," J. Barnaby said with false heartiness. "Dzanku Dzanku. A splendid fellow. Remember how fond we've always been of him?"

"Wait a minute," Manning said. "Have you completely blown your jets? Dzanku and Sam Warren are the characters who almost cheated you out of millions and I'm the lad you sent out to stop them. Remember?"

"Mere boyish pranks," J. Barnaby said with a wave of his hand which erased all previous sins. "We should let bygones be bygones, Manning. It ill becomes Terrans to hold such grudges."

"Okay," Manning said amiably. "Dzanku is a fine fellow. Now what?"

"He's in trouble."

"What kind of trouble?"

"As I understand it," J. Barnaby said soberly, "poor Dzanku was under the impression that he might face prosecution in Federation courts, so he went to Pollux. As you know, Pollux is a Class E planet and therefore is not a member of the Federation. Dzanku married a Polluxian female, which automatically made him a citizen of Pollux and immune to Federation arrest."

"And then he broke some Polluxian law?"

"As a matter of fact," J. Barnaby said, "he broke seven thousand, eight hundred and twenty-six of the eight thousand laws in Pollux. It would seem that Dzanku has once more become the victim of his—er—youthful spirits."

"I feel," Manning said dryly, "that you could say excessively youthful spirits without being accused of hyperbole."

"Anyway, Dzanku has been found guilty and the death sentence has been passed. The executioncis to take place within a month."

MANNING DRACO stared with suspicion at his boss. "Normally," he said, "this is a bit of news which would have been welcomed by you with joyous cries. You might have even declared a ten-minute holiday for the whole staff in celebration of the occasion. This scene of Cruikshank's turning the other cheek is touching but suspicious. What are you leading up to?"

"I was thinking," J. Barnaby said blandly, "that you might take a little run up to Pollux and rescue Dzanku." The silence that followed was long and filled with things which were better unsaid. Throughout, J. Barnaby managed to avoid looking directly at his chief investigator.

"Why?" Manning Draco asked quietly when he had considered all of the things he would have liked to have said.

"After all, my boy, Dzanku was once a member of our happy little family. It is only proper that we should stick by him in his time of travail."

"Rocket wash," Manning snapped rudely. "Somewhere in the saccharin story you've spun for me there's some sort of a joker that's going to cost J. Barnaby Cruikshank a few million credits. Either you give me the whole story or you can call your cops back and I'll go to jail. You wouldn't send me out to rescue your own mother unless she owed you money. Give."

"My boy, you wrong me," J. Barnaby said brokenly. He waited, but when Manning showed no signs of saying anything further, he decided to continue. "As a matter of fact, there is one other matter. It will cost us a few credits if Dzanku dies anytime within the next six months."

"How much?" Manning asked relentlessly.

"Well—er—to be exact, five hundred billion credits."

Manning whistled. "That's quite a piece of change. Do you have that much?"

"I have it," J. Barnaby admitted, "but if I had to pay out that much, I might have trouble staying in business. You save Dzanku and there will be a hundred thousand credit bonus for you."

"Now I know it's serious," Manning said. "What's the catch?"

"The catch," said J. Barnaby, "is that Dzanku Dzanku took out a five hundred credit insurance policy with us when he went to work for us. It was such a small policy that, through an oversight, we neglected to cancel it when we fired him."

"A five hundred credit policy?" repeated Manning. "But what kind of clause is there in the policy that can force you to pay a billion to one?"

"Not in the policy," J. Barnaby, said unhappily. "It's Pollux. There are only twenty-five families on the entire planet, although the population of Pollux is twenty-five billion. Each family consists of one billion Polluxians. So when Dzanku married a Polluxian female he immediately had one billion heirs. And there is a Polluxian law which states that every relative of a policy holder must be considered a full beneficiary and paid the amount of the insurance policy. That's one billion times five hundred credits in the case of Dzanku. That's why we never have sold insurance on Pollux. Any Federation business must conform to the local laws of a non-Federation planet if it wishes to operate there."

"And that means they'd have no trouble going into a Federation court and collecting if Dzanku dies while the policy is in force?"

J. Barnaby nodded glumly. "No trouble at all," he admitted. He eyed Manning. "My boy," he went on, "I'm sorry if my actions seemed harsh, but you're the only person who can save Greater Solarian. I knew that once you learned the facts, you wouldn't let me down. I have faith in you, Manning—"

"Spare me the dramatic act," Manning interrupted. "I'll see what I can do."

"I knew you would," J. Barnaby cried. He strode across the room and wrung Manning's hand. "My boy, you'll never regret it. My gratitude will know no limits—"

"You'll forget about it ten minutes after I've done it," Manning said. "And I'm only doing it for two reasons. The bonus and my own curiosity. Have you got an encyclotape on Pollux?"

"It's already in your ship," J. Barnaby said, still wringing Manning's hand as he gently pushed him toward the door. "And I've ordered the crew at the spaceport to have your ship ready. Bless you, my boy."

CHAPTER TWO

A T THE SPACEPORT, the *Alpha Actuary* was already on the launching level. Manning Draco climbed in, checked the position of Pollux, and fed the figures into the automatic pilot. He hooked the ship into magnetic power and it raced up the launching rack, flinging itself skyward.

When it was well above Terra's atmosphere, the ship automatically went into magnidrive. Manning found the Pollux encyclotape and fed it into the audio-reader. Then he leaned back to listen.

"Pollux," said a pleasant voice from the concealed speaker, "is a Class E planet, not yet admitted to the Federation. It is a mean distance from its sun, Pollux, of eighty-nine million miles. Its mass is 1.2 in relation to that of Terra, its volume 1.117; its density is 5.27 times that of water; its diameter, seven thousand two hundred miles; orbital velocity, 18.2 miles per second; period of rotation, twenty-seven hours, fifteen minutes; eccentricity, 0.0201—"

Manning reached over and punched a button. The tape skipped a few inches and took up its story again.

"—gravity at surface, 1.102. In many respects, Pollux is similar to Terra. Geologically, it is in a period similar to that on Terra which was known as the Jurassic, although the general level of intelligent life is much higher than it was on Terra during that period.

"The dominant race on Pollux is evolved from a race which is physically similar to the Terran Crocodilia. It has not, however, been possible for Federation scientists to make detailed examinations of Polluxians, so it is not known in what ways they differ from Crocodilia other than intelligence.

"Pollux is an empire, the present ruler being Emperor Aatobi Uu. The first two letters of his first name are silent, as is true in the case of every Polluxian, and merely indicate his social position. Only members of Emperor Uu's immediate family have names beginning with Aa. The royal family of Uu, however, consists of about one billion individuals, ranging in social status from Aa to Zz. There are only twenty-five family lines on Pollux—"

After a time Manning cut off the audio-reader and went to sleep.

It was morning when the *Alpha Actuary* cut out of magnidrive and hovered just above the atmosphere of Pollux. Manning Draco switched the ship to manual and took it down to a few thousand feet above the planet. He then contacted the small spaceport at Uuville, identified himself, gave his reason for coming to Pollux as personal, and requested landing instructions. After a few minutes' delay a landing beam was sent up.

Leaving his ship in the landing cradle, Manning went into the terminal. It was almost deserted, although there were a few Polluxians staffing it. Manning had learned from the encyclotape that Polluxians had no space travel of their own and that few Federation ships came to the planet because local laws made trading difficult, so he was not surprised by the inactivity.

This was his first look at Polluxians. They did look a lot like the alligators and crocodiles on Terra, although it was plain that they had evolved somewhat differently. They stood erect on their two hind feet and what had once been their front feet had already developed into hands. It seemed to Manning that their snouts had shortened considerably. They were all wearing Terran-style clothing.

MANNING STOPPED at a lunch counter and waited until the Polluxian looked up.

"Do you speak Terran?" he asked.

"Of course," the Polluxian said, bobbing his head. His mouth writhed in what was probably meant to be a grin, displaying long white teeth. "We are great admirers of Terra. Our one regret is that more Terrans do not visit us. May I help you?"

"Do you have a hotel that caters to Terrans?"

"Oh, yes. Uu House. Any one of the taxis out front will take you there."

"Fine," said Manning. "Perhaps you can tell me one more thing. I want to visit someone who's in prison under sentence of death. How can I best find out where he is?"

"If he has already been sentenced to death, then he will be in the Oo Correction House. A taxi will take you there."

"Thanks," Manning said. As he turned to walk out of the terminal, he became aware that he was being watched. At first, he thought the watcher was a humanoid robot, but on closer look, he saw that what looked like burnished metal was actually flesh. The figure resembled a robot in other respects too: The head was perfectly round with no features. There was a small opening in the front, not dissimilar to the speakers on robots. Above it was a larger oval opening, seemingly depthless, which was almost identical with the electronic-eye cage of a robot.

As he realized that this was not a robot, Manning stopped and stared at the figure. It seemed to be mumbling to itself and after a moment the words became clear. It was speaking Terran.

"Hmm... Terran male. Features receded enough to probably be considered attractive. Apparently of sound body...."

"Were you speaking to me?" Manning asked abruptly.

"About you," the other corrected. "You are a Terran, aren't you?"

"Yes, but what are you?"

The figure made a sound that might have been laughter. "Captain mmemmo of Andromeda Galaxy."

"Captain Mmemmo," Manning repeated. He examined the robot-like figure again. This was the first Andromedan he'd ever seen.

"No, no," the Andromedan said. "Captain mmemmo. Upper

case C, lower case m. I trust you'll pardon me..." He stepped forward and probed Manning's arm with a forefinger. "Nicely fleshed," he added.

"If," Manning said dryly, "you're looking for a steak, I'm out of season."

"Young man," Captain mmemmo said, "how would you like to have security for your old age? Travel in exotic lands—taste the fruits of the fairest flowers—surrounded by the science of the sybarite—lulled in the lap of luxury—treated to a torrent of titillation—ten thousand credits for each year of service, carefully banked in the institution of your choice?"

"What the devil are you talking about?" Manning demanded.

"A simple business transaction," Captain mmemmo said. "I am scouting your galaxy for all sorts of young males in good health for service in the Pleasure Camps of Andromeda.[7] If you don't care to go yourself, I'll be happy to buy any young male slaves you may possess."

"Sorry," Manning said with a grin, "but you've got the wrong customer. I haven't finished with the pleasures of my own galaxy yet."

"Oh, well," said the Andromedan, shrugging, "I'll be here until I get a shipload. If you should happen to change your mind—need a spot of cash or feel like a new and thrilling adventure—just look up Captain mmemmo."

Manning grinned again and walked out of the terminal. He looked around for an air-taxi and it was some minutes before he realized that the only vehicles around. were some rather peculiar ones on the ground ahead of him. But between him and

---

7 Even now, not too much is known about general conditions in the Androm-eda Galaxy. It is known, of course, that the entire galaxy is a matriarchal society and it may be assumed, from the presence of the Pleasure Camps, that it is in a stage of moral decadence. The first Andromedan slavetraders to appear in our galaxy came with the idea of stealing inmates for the Pleasure Camps, but the Federation patrols quickly changed their minds for them. Since then, like Captain mmemmo, they have bargained for slaves or for impoverished young males will-ing to gamble a few years' virility for security.

the vehicles was something more familiar. It was a picket line.

A number of young Polluxians were marching vigorously up and down in front of the spaceport with hand-lettered signs. The lettering was in Terran and in another language which Manning guessed was Polluxian. The signs were mostly on the same theme.

DOWN WITH TERRA.

POLLUX FOR POLLUXIANS, TERRA FOR TERRORISTS.

TERRANS ARE ANTI-OVIPAROUS.

DECADENT TERRANS NOT WANTED.

Trudging along at the end of the picket line was a small Polluxian bearing a sign which read:

GIVE YOUR CHILDREN A BETTER START IN LIFE AT THE OU HATCHERY.

Just beyond the picket line a Polluxian stood on an improvised box and harangued the pickets.

"Fellow Tetrapods," he was saying, "we must protect the fair plains of Pollux from these puny Terran marauders. There's one now," he cried, flinging an arm in the direction of Manning. "Look at him. Look at the ugly nose, no larger than a wart; look at the tiny mouth and teeth so small they can have no use at all. Are these the lords of the universe? Are these the creatures who would rule us finer specimens? Arise, ye prisoners of modified denticles—you have nothing to lose but your brains!"

Manning Draco grinned and walked past the speaker. The only vehicles in sight were a number of objects which looked a little like bicycles built for two. On the front seat of each one sat a Polluxian. "Taxi, sir?" asked the nearest one.

Manning nodded and, after a moment of hesitation, climbed on the rear seat. They started off, the Polluxian pedaling with his tail. Back of them, Manning could hear the speaker raising his voice once more.

"Where to, sir?" the Polluxian asked.

"The Oo Correction House," Manning said. "What's going on back there?"

"That's Pseno Ai," the driver explained. "He's the head of the Anti-Terran Political Party. He arranges a small demonstration at the spaceport every day."

"Are there so many Terrans moving in on Pollux?"

"Oh, no. You are the first Terran to come here in more than five gestations—two and a half years by your reckoning."

"Are there many Terran industries here, then?" Manning asked.

"None."

"Then why an anti-Terran party?" Manning wanted to know. "It seems a waste of time."

"Oh, no," the driver said seriously. "We look upon the activity of Pseno Ai with pride. It is a sign of progress. Besides, as Pseno Ai points out, it doesn't hurt to be prepared. Who knows, you may be the first drop in a flood of Terrans to come."

Manning grunted something between affirmation and denial. The Polluxians seemed friendly enough, but he saw no reason for arguing with individuals who sported teeth that were a good four inches long.

After a short ride through the edge of the city—and past a towering barbaric structure which the driver said was the palace—they came to a plain stone building. The bicycle stopped and its driver indicated the building. Manning dismounted and paid him.

He was interviewed by numerous officials in the prison and finally escorted back to an isolated cell. Its occupant looked up and waved a tentacle in greeting.

"HELLO, MANNING, my knight in shining armor," he said sardonically.

The Rigelian Dzanku Dzanku was no taller than Manning, but he weighed all of a ton, Terra scale. His thick, square torso was supported by two legs like tree trunks. Six weaving tentacles projected from the upper part of his body. His face was small and expressionless, with three eyestalks raised several inches above it.

"Hello, Dzanku," Manning responded. He waited until the Polluxian guard shuffled off. "I can't remember seeing you in more appropriate surroundings. This is an ideal setting for your particular sort of beauty."

"Thank you," the Rigelian said, playing it straight. "I appreciate the compliment even though I know how eager you are to release me from this durance vile. I've continually comforted myself with the thought of my two dear friends, Manning Draco and J. Barnaby Cruikshank, moving the universe in my behalf. And how is my dear pal, J. Barnaby?"

"Concerned about your welfare."

"I'll bet," said Dzanku, with the Rigelian equivalent of a grin.

"He was also," Manning said dryly, "working himself into quite a sentimental lather over the good old days when you and Sam Warren were part of the happy Cruikshank family, but he'll get over that the first time he has a chance to cancel your policy. By the way, where is Sam Warren?"

"I'm not sure," Dzanku said. "He came here with me, but didn't stay long. Although they liked him, the local feminine pulchritude didn't strike Sam's fancy. I believe he had some small business venture in mind."

"No doubt," Manning agreed. "What's the rap on you, Dzanku?"

"Almost everything," the Rigelian said. "I believe, however, the thing which tipped the scales against me was a slight error in judgment. I sold the emperor a small planet in the Acamarian system. I had no idea he'd try to claim his property so quickly."

"And you've been sentenced to death?"

"A mere trifle now that you're here," Dzanku said.

"If it's such a trifle," Manning snapped, "suppose you tell me how to get you out."

"But that's your problem, my dear Manning," Dzanku said

blandly. "Of course, if all else fails, you can fall back on the hostage law of Pollux. I'm sure that J. Barnaby will appreciate such a move."

"What is the hostage law?" Manning asked suspiciously.

"It is possible to obtain the release of any prisoner by merely putting yourself in his place. So if everything else fails you can always go to the execution chamber in my place. It will bring me great grief, but…" He made a gesture of hopelessness with his six tentacles.

Manning told him what he could do with his grief. "As far as I'm concerned," he added, "you could rot in here; it would even be worth losing the bonus J. Barnaby mentioned. But J. Barnaby wants you rescued, so I'll do my best. Do you have any other suggestions? More practical ones."

"There must be loopholes on some of their laws," Dzanku said. "That should be more in your line than mine. Or maybe you can get on the good side of the emperor and get him to release me."

"You're a big help," Manning said. "Okay, I'll see what I can do." He left, and was escorted to the exit by a guard.

ON THE STREET again, he looked around for one of the strange Polluxian taxis. There were none in sight, but there was something that looked like six bicycles fastened together in tandem. There were five Polluxians, wearing bright uniforms, seated on it. The sixth seat was empty and there was a bright red umbrella over it. As Manning drew near, one of the gayly festooned Polluxians dismounted and came to meet him.

"Do I address the Terran, Manning Draco?" he asked.

"Yes," Manning admitted.

"It is the pleasure of Aatobi Uu, most beautiful emperor of Pollux, that you present yourself at his palace as his guest."

"That's very nice of him," Manning said, "but I'm here on business, so I don't think I'd better accept—"

The Polluxian bared his huge teeth in a mirthless grin. "It is against the law to refuse any request by the emperor," he said. "The penalty is death."

"In that case," Manning said hastily, "I accept."

He climbed onto the empty seat, feeling rather silly as he sat there beneath the red umbrella, and the bicycle-built-for-six pulled away from the curb.

The palace was a huge, sprawling edifice built of stone, looking as if it had been constructed by whim rather than any plan. Manning was led through room after room, past rows of saluting guards, and finally into the royal presence. So far as Manning could see at a glance, the emperor looked just like any other alligator except for the toga-like garment wrapped around his body and the crown which sat jauntily on his head. There was one other Polluxian in the room, a female, Manning judged, from the fact that she wore a garment similar to a dress, and held a fan before her face. At frequent intervals something resembling giggles sounded from back of the fan.

"Welcome to Pollux," the emperor said after he'd waved the escort from the room. "I am honored."

"On the contrary," Manning said politely, "I am honored."

"Of course you are," agreed the emperor. "But I am also honored, as we are very fond of Terrans. You are a Terran, aren't you?"

Manning nodded.

"I thought so," the emperor said. "It did not seem likely that there could be two races in the galaxy with such brief snouts and such inadequate teeth. You know, you Terrans are very ugly by all intelligent standards, but it is an ugliness which we find appealing."

Manning nodded and smiled, thinking that nothing could be gained by telling him how Polluxians appeared to Terrans.

"I presume you come from a good family?" the Emperor said.

"Good enough," Manning said, wondering what difference it made.

The emperor indicated the other figure in the room. "This is my daughter, the Princess Aaledo Uu."

Manning Draco said hello and the princess giggled from behind her fan.

"She saw you as you passed the palace earlier," the emperor said. "It has come into her head that she would like you for a husband. I do not find it in my heart to deny her anything."

The princess giggled again, one lizardlike eye peeping over the edge of the fan.

There was a moment of strained silence as the full import of the emperor's statement impressed itself on Manning.

"I am honored," he managed finally, "but—but, unfortunately, there are obstacles. There is a Federation law forbidding the marriage of different races."

"A very foolish law," agreed the emperor. "I'm sure that in time it will be abolished. In the meantime, we need not concern ourselves too much with it. Pollux is not a member of the Federation and we have our own laws here."

"B-but," stammered Manning, "I am a citizen of the Federation and subject to its laws."

"A mere technicality," said the emperor, thumping his tail on the floor with satisfaction. "The moment the marriage ceremony is performed, you will become a Polluxian—and a member of the royal family, at that."

"But—" Manning tried again.

"No more," the emperor interrupted. "I appreciate your eagerness—the Princess Aaledo is famous for her beauty—but we must observe the conventions. Tomorrow we will discuss the details and the date of the wedding. Now it is time for us to attend the engagement banquet I have ordered."

CHAPTER THREE

FROM EVERY VIEW except Manning's, the banquet was a big success. The leading Polluxians were there. The table groaned beneath a variety of food, some of it edible even to a Terran, and there were plenty of exotic alcoholic beverages. The prospective bride was radiant, by Polluxian standards, and if the groom-to-be seemed a little pale and preoccupied it was attributed to the shock of his sudden good fortune.

As early as possible Manning Draco excused himself, pleading fatigue from his trip, and was shown to his room. He told the servant that he'd like to make a call to Terra and, since it was understandable that the Terran might want to brag a bit, a video set was brought to his room. As soon as he was alone he feverishly put in a call for J. Barnaby Cruikshank.

After a few minutes' delay the face of the president of Greater Solarian appeared on the screen.

"Well, my boy," he said heartily, "you've succeeded already?"

"No," Manning said sourly. "I'm through, J. Barnaby. As soon as everyone's asleep in this place, I'm sneaking out to the spaceport and getting out of here as fast as my ship will go."

There was a decided change in the expression of the face on the screen. "I wouldn't, if I were you," J. Barnaby said, coldly. "Those charges against you can still be renewed, and if you leave there'll be a patrol ship waiting for you just outside the Polluxian limits."

"But you don't understand," Manning said. "Look, J. Barnaby, I've never run out on a job, but this is different. These Polluxians are nothing but fancy alligators and they have a taste for Terrans—and maybe it is a *taste* at that. Anyway, the Emperor has just decided that I'm to marry his daughter. If I stay here and refuse, I'll be swinging from the gibbet next to Dzanku's."

"On the other hand," said J. Barnaby, a calculating gleam on his face, "think of the advantages of being married into the royal family of Pollux. You can probably free Dzanku with no trouble at all. Not only that, but you can then use your influence with your father-in-law to have the local laws changed so we can come into Pollux and sell insurance. Your commissions on such a deal would add up to a tidy sum, my boy."

"To hell with the commissions," Manning said roughly. "You know what you can do with them. If you think it's such a good idea, you come up here and marry the princess."

"I am already married," J. Barnaby said with dignity. "And I've always thought that marriage would be a steadying influence on you. Believe me, Manning, I have your best interests at heart."

Manning's reply made the censors on Procyon wince.

"Let me know the date of the wedding," J. Barnaby said cheerfully, "and I'll send you a handsome wedding present. It's the least I can do." He broke the connection and the screen faded.

Manning cursed until he was out of breath. Then he just sat and glared at the dead screen.

AFTER A WHILE there was a knock on the door. Manning thought of ignoring it, but when it was repeated he went and threw open the door. A Polluxian stood there, his tail impatiently thumping the floor.

"I have come," he said in a sonorous voice, "to tell you that we don't like Terrans on Pollux. If you persist in meddling with our affairs, we'll make trouble for you."

Manning recognized him now as the Polluxian who had been making a speech earlier outside the spaceport. "You'll make trouble for me," he said with a wry grin. "You might as well come in and tell me about it, but I warn you it'll be an anticlimax."

The Polluxian stepped inside and closed the door. He whipped a wallet from his pocket and flipped it open. "Federation Bureau of Investigation," he said, lowering his voice.

The card in the wallet, with picture and prints, identified him as Albert Sauri, an investigator for the Federation Bureau of Investigation.

"Now I've heard of everything," Manning said. "What are you—a Polluxian who offered to work for the Federation?"

"I'm from Terra," the investigator said proudly. "Graduate of the FBI Special Training School."

Manning Draco stared in amazement at his visitor. "I

thought," he said, "that I was pretty well aware of what went on in the Federation, but this is a new one on me. First, if you're from Terra you must be an alligator."

"Crocodile," corrected the investigator

"Crocodile, then. But to the best of my knowledge there has never been but one Terran species—Man—that had the power of speech. Parrots have it, in a limited fashion, but only in an imitative way."

The investigator rubbed his scaly jaw. "This is top priority stuff," he said, lowering his voice, "but I checked with my bureau chief and he authorized me to talk to you. The Special Training Schools were set up five hundred years ago on Terra to train non-human Terrans for jobs as undercover agents.[8] I was a member of the first graduating class of ten years ago."

"After five hundred years?" Manning asked. "It was about time you graduated."

"No, no," said Albert Sauri, "it's just that my generation was the first to have mutated sufficiently to receive the final training. Some other time, I'll be happy to give you a rundown on the whole project. It's rather interesting. In the meantime, if you'd like to check on my authority, I suggest you call my bureau chief."

"That won't be necessary," Manning said. "I know that the FBI identity cards can't be forged or stolen.[9] I don't know why the FBI has decided to interfere here, but I can tell you that it's pretty damn welcome."

"I'm afraid I don't understand."

---

8 The Special Training Schools of the FBI were, of course, more than schools. The program had started with the selection of Terran animals which were similar to various dominant species on other planets. Through controlled genetics, mutants were eventually produced who were capable of being trained as undercover agents. Albert Sauri, alias Pseno Ai, was one of the resulting mutants.

9 FBI identity cards are made of a secret plastic formula, the chief ingredient being Theocite, or ZO^2H. The only source of Theocite is the asteroid Theo, which is owned by the FBI. The identity cards will also destroy themselves if touched by anyone other than the person for whom they're made.

Manning had a moment of worry. "Aren't you here because the Emperor has decided I'm to marry his daughter?"

"Oh, yes."

"Well, that's what I meant," Manning said, relieved. "I was sitting here wondering how the hell I'd get out of it and here you are like an answer to a prayer."

THE FBI agent flipped his tail out behind him and sat down on the edge of the bed. He explored a four-inch tooth with his thumbnail and stared solemnly at Manning Draco.

"I'm afraid," he said, "that there's some slight misunderstanding, Mr. Draco. I'm not here to stop you from becoming the morganic husband of the Princess Aaledo Uu. In fact, the FBI looks upon the marriage with considerable favor."

"What?"

"That is correct," the FBI agent said. He held up a scaly hand as Manning was about to speak. "Just a minute, Mr. Draco. The Bureau believes that Pollux will eventually become a serious trouble spot of the galaxy. Since I've been assigned here I've become one of the leaders of the anti-Terran movement and I can tell you that if anything the Bureau is underestimating the danger. Unless something is done Pollux will become the nucleus of a movement which might cause Terra to lose its control of the galaxy."

"But what the devil," burst out Manning, "does that have to do with me marrying a—a Polluxian?"

"It might make all the difference between success and failure. It's not only a question of the influence you could have on your father-in-law, the emperor, but also the propaganda value of a Terran being part of the royal family. With you working closely with me, we can probably whip this planet into line within a very few years. You can be sure you'll be properly rewarded."

"Who wants it?" muttered Manning. He shook his head grimly. "I won't do it. When it comes to a thing like marriage, a man has to draw the line somewhere. Look, I got nothing personal against the saurian family—I'm quite willing to have a crocodile as my best friend—but I'll be double damned if I'll share my bed and board with an animated reptile. Especially my bed."

"It's your patriotic duty," thundered the FBI agent. He glared at Manning for a moment and then went on in a softer voice. "I'm sorry, Mr. Draco, I'd hoped that it wouldn't be necessary for me to point out certain other things to you. But if the Emperor wants you to marry his daughter there is no way of refusing. The lightest punishment you could expect would be death, and you'd be lucky to be executed. You might also face the fact that the FBI would go to almost any length to keep you from refusing. In fact, knowing how you feel about it, I shall see to it that your ship is guarded from now on. We wanted to think that you would voluntarily help your planet, your galaxy—but one way or another, sir, you're going to help her."

The FBI agent got up and strode across the room, his heavy tail stiff with dignity. "I would suggest," he said, "that you arrange for the wedding to take place as quickly as possible. The quicker you are in position to help us, the better. And we expect you to do your duty, Mr. Draco." He opened the door and stepped into the hall. He glanced both ways and then looked back into the room. His mouth stretched in what was meant to be a smile. "It really isn't as bad as you make it, Draco. I've seen the princess and she's quite a dish. I could almost go for her myself."

"Then why the hell don't you?" snapped Manning, but the door had already closed before he got it but. He was once more alone in his room.

THERE HAD BEEN LITTLE about his visitor to improve Manning Draco's morale. He brooded about it for a few minutes and then clutched at what seemed like a small chance. As he'd remarked earlier, he knew that FBI cards couldn't be forged, but then he'd suddenly remembered that crime was always progressing. Hopefully, he put through a call to a friend who worked in the Federation Bureau of Investigation. He kept the contact open while his friend checked.

"Sorry, Manning," said his friend when he reappeared on the screen. He was grinning broadly. "Albert Sauri is for real. And there's already a folder on your forthcoming marriage. It's got a top priority sticker on it and it's stuck in the Interplanetary Politics drawer, so I guess there's nothing you can do but hope she'll change her mind."

"But there's got to be some way," Manning insisted. "There must be something you can do. Talk to the guy in charge."

His friend shook his head. "Anything that falls into Interplanetary Politics is under the supervision of John Allen Stover himself, and you know what he's like. He'd put the blast on his own mother if it'd help the record of the Bureau. There's only one thing I can do for you, Manning, old boy."

"What's that?" Manning asked desperately.

"Well, I'm attached to the Special Schools—the ones that turned out Albert. When this fall is all over, I can talk to some of our students and have you made an honorary crocodile." A loud guffaw came from the screen and Manning had a vision of his friend doubled over in mirth.

"Funny fellow," he muttered bitterly as he snapped off the set. He'd barely turned it off when there was a knocking on his door. He glared suspiciously at it, but finally called out, "Come in."

The door opened and a round, burnished head appeared. It was Captain mmemmo, the raider from the Andromeda Galaxy.

"Ah, young man," he said. "Happy youth, sitting here, no doubt, anticipating your future marital bliss? Basking in the buxom beauty of the bride?"

"Go to hell," Manning said.

The Andromedan cocked his head to one side. "Do I detect a note of discontent? Perhaps a bit of reluctance to take the final plunging step? If so, then Captain mmemmo's your man."

"What do you mean?" Manning asked.

"I offer you, young sir, not only escape from the gruesome web of matrimony, but escape from the humdrum of this galaxy. Escape and exotic pleasures, plus a royal stipend."

"The Pleasure Camps?"

"The Pleasure Camps. Where a man may—"

"Get out," Manning said.

"But you will keep me in mind—" the captain began.

Manning picked up a bowl from the table and flung it. The door closed gently and the bowl shattered against it.

Manning Draco paced the floor and tried to find a hole in the trap that was slowly closing about him. It was an almost impossible task and he knew it even as he struggled with it. He walked the floor and smoked and cursed, but nothing rewarded his effort.

THERE WAS another sharp knock on the door.

Manning stopped walking and regarded the door. He almost hoped it was Captain mmemmo returning; throwing someone out of his room would at least be a definite action.

"Come in," he called.

The door opened and two Polluxians marched stiffly into the room, closing the door behind them. They stared at Manning from great bulging eyes, then bowed in his direction.

"What do you want?" Manning demanded. He was in no mood to be polite.

"This," said one of them, indicating his companion, "is Bbtula Eo."

"That's nice," Manning said. "Good-by."

"I," continued the Polluxian, "am Dsorma Io, his friend and companion. I am authorized to speak for him."

"Fine," Manning said. "Go ahead and speak for him. Only do it somewhere else."

"Perhaps you do not understand," said Dsorma Io. "Until today Bbtula Eo lived in a state of supreme happiness, for the Princess Aaledo had gazed upon him and found him fair. Then you came along and stole her love."

"It's petit larceny as far as I'm concerned," Manning snapped, "and he can have it back. In fact, the quicker he takes the princess back the better I'll like it."

The two Polluxians spoke to each other in a language, which Manning could not understand. Then the first one turned back to him.

"Bbtula Eo wishes to understand what you are saying," he explained. "Is it possible that you mean that you do not wish to marry the Princess Aaledo?"

"That's the general idea," Manning said.

"Then Bbtula Eo has been doubly insulted. Once on behalf of himself and once on the part of the fairest flower of Polluxian royalty. He demands satisfaction."

"Meaning what?" Manning demanded shortly.

"Meaning a duel. It is my duty, as Bbtula Eo's appointed spokesman, to inform you that the duel will take place tomorrow at the ninth hour after sunrise, according to the law of Pollux. Since you are an alien to Pollux, I will further point out that it is illegal to lengthen your teeth artificially, or to sharpen your teeth to a point, or to take any other dental steps which might give you an unfair advantage."

"Teeth?" said the startled Manning. He glanced at Bbtula Eo, who immediately gave him a formal smile, revealing a generous expanse of ivory. "You mean this duel is a biting contest? You can't do that."

"The duel-by-teeth," the Polluxian said, "has been the accepted method of combat for centuries. Any other form of fighting would obviously be barbarous. We shall see you tomorrow, sir."

The two Polluxians bowed stiffly and were gone.

When he could move, which was not for several minutes, Manning Draco staggered over and locked the door to his room. He felt that he'd had all the visitors he was capable of receiving. Then he went back and flopped on the bed. He was asleep almost the moment he touched the bed, and he slept soundly all night. Even his nightmares were preferable to reality.

CHAPTER FOUR

I T WAS a somewhat haggard Manning Draco who emerged the next morning and wandered through the palace. The royal court, he soon discovered, was all agog at the prospect of both a duel and a wedding.

He finally entered a room which looked as if it might be a dining room. All too late he discovered he was sharing it with a female Polluxian who giggled from behind a fan. It was the princess. In between nervous giggles she wanted to know how he slept, what he thought of Pollux, if he'd enjoyed the space trip, and a hundred other things. Manning answered in monosyllables, paying more attention to keeping his distance.

"Ah, billing and cooing already," said a new voice. The emperor had entered the room. He thumped the floor solidly with his tail and servants began serving breakfast at once. "My boy, I can't tell you how proud I am of you. I've already heard about your acceptance of the duel with Bbtula Eo."

"Acceptance," Manning said bitterly. "Was there a choice?"

"Of course," continued the emperor, "the duel can still be avoided, although I'm sure you have no desire to do so."

"How?" demanded Manning.

"Such haste would be unseemly, but we could hold the wedding before the time set for the duel. Members of the royal family are forbidden to duel."

Manning almost choked on the bit of egg he was eating. "No," he said hastily, "I wouldn't think of trying to avoid the duel."

The emperor nodded with pleasure and went on talking about various trifles. Manning barely listened, finishing his breakfast as quickly as he could. He had finally realized that there was only one small hope for him and he'd determined to pursue it. Consequently, as soon as he'd finished eating, he arose from the table.

"I have a few personal errands to run," he said, "but I'll be back by lunchtime."

"Take the royal sexcycle," said the emperor. "It is proper that one who is about to duel should straighten out his affairs. By the way, the duel will be held after lunch. If you win, we will immediately discuss the date of the wedding. If not, my daughter will observe the natural period of mourning."

Manning winced at this blunt mention of a possible outcome of the duel. He nodded and left the room, followed by the sound of girlish giggling.

Downstairs, in front of the palace, he discovered the same six-seated, six-wheeled vehicle on which he'd ridden the day before. He ordered the uniformed Polluxians to take him back to the prison. He had determined that if Dzanku Dzanku wanted to be saved he'd have to do some saving in return. He was confident that the Rigelian would have more ideas on ways to circumvent local laws than anyone else.

He was just entering the prison when he saw the burnished figure of Captain mmemmo leaving. There was no way to avoid a meeting, but to his surprise the Andromedan merely waved a greeting and strode briskly by.

ONCE AGAIN, Manning was escorted through the prison and left in front of Dzanku's cell. Manning peered in and saw the Rigelian gripping the bars with two tentacles while his entire body shook as though with the ague.

"What's the matter with you?" Manning, asked. There was no answer and he spoke more loudly. "Dzanku! What's wrong?"

Slowly, the body of the big Rigelian calmed down. Only when the shaking had completely stopped did his eyestalks straighten up and incline toward Manning. There was a note of strain in his voice when he spoke.

"That damned Andromedan," he said. "He's gone now, but we Rigelians are allergic to Andromedans. One of them any-where within two hundred yards causes havoc in our nervous systems. And he has the nerve to offer to get me to one of his Pleasure Camps. I'd much rather be here.... Well, Manning, how are we doing?"

"Not so good," Manning said. "I need your help, Dzanku. Since I left you yesterday, I've become engaged to the Emperor's daughter."

"Capital," exclaimed Dzanku. "You don't need help, my friend. I couldn't have planned it better myself. All you have to do is wait until you're married and then pardon me yourself."

"But I don't want to get married."

"A mere bagatelle," Dzanku said loftily. "Don't forget that J. Barnaby will be gravely disappointed if you don't save me. Besides, these Polluxian females make excellent wives."

"Speak for yourself," Manning said. "You see, Dzanku, if I really have to marry this royal horror, so far as I'm concerned the worst will have already happened. So I will merely let you die and let J. Barnaby go broke. In fact, those will be the only two bright spots in my life. Get it?"

"Manning, you wouldn't!" Dzanku's three eyes stared reproachfully at him.

"I will," Manning said firmly. "I don't mind pulling J. Barnaby's or your chestnuts out of the fire as long as I can do so without getting burned. But if I have to get scorched, I don't care how many blisters you get. Now, do you want to play ball?"

"There is no loyalty left in the universe," Dzanku exclaimed piously. "I suppose I have no choice. What do you want of me?"

"First," said Manning, "if there's any one who'll be up on trickery on this planet, it's you. How do I get out of fighting a duel-by-teeth? I've been challenged by a blighted suitor of the princess."

"You could get out of it by marrying the princess before the time for the duel," Dzanku suggested cheerfully.

"I know that one. But if that's the best you can do, there'll be no pardon."

"Okay, okay, let me think." Dzanku was silent for a moment, his tentacles undulating gently. "Yeah, I remember," he said finally. "I knew there was something because I once thought I was going to have to fight one of those duels and my teeth are no better than yours. Anyway, I worked out a gimmick. When you spring it on your opponent, he'll scream his head off, but it's perfectly legal so he'll have to allow it or withdraw." Dzanku chuckled in appreciation of his own cleverness.

"What is it?"

"The dueling law states that you can't artificially lengthen your own teeth, but it *doesn't* say that you have to personally bite the other guy to win. There's a record of a duel where the friend of one of the duelists got mad, jumped in the ring and glomped off the head of the opponent and it was allowed: That's where I got the idea. Also there's no rule about whether you have to ride or walk during the duel…. The princess likes you, huh?"

"Yeah," growled Manning."

"Okay, you can get her to help without knowing it. Go in a local delicacy store and buy a large Polluxian pepper. Tell the Princess that it'll bring you good luck if she can get the other guy to wear the pepper on his head. Get her to pretend that it's because she wants him to win. These Polluxians love intrigue and she'll fall for it. And if he's a suitor, he'll be a sucker for anything she wants him to do."

"HOW WILL that help? Are you counting on the pepper flopping in his eyes or something like that?" Manning demanded.

"You'll, see," Dzanku said cheerfully. "Next, when you leave here, get a taxi—"

"I've got a palace go-cart," Manning interrupted. "One of those bicycles-built-for-six, with five uniformed flunkeys."

"In style, huh?" Dzanku grunted. "Well, tell them you want to go to Xleno's Fly-Ur-Self, downtown. It's a rental palace run by Xleno Ii. He's my brother-in-law, and he'll give you a special price if you mention my name. Rent one of his best pterodactyls."

"What?" asked Manning.

"Pterodactyl," Dzanku said. He chuckled again. "That's a big lizard that can fly—but you'll think it's jet-propelled when you get on it. It's got a bigger mouth, and bigger, meaner teeth than any Polluxian. And it's crazy about Polluxian peppers."

"Are you sure it isn't crazier about Terrans?" Manning wanted to know. Suspicion of Dzanku Dzanku was an automatic reaction.

"Oh, it would take a bite out of you if it had the chance," the Rigelian said, "but it'll be saddled and bridled and there are blinkers on the bridle. As long as it can't see you it won't try to bite you. I suggest that you rent the pterodactyl as soon as you leave here. Take it to the large field back of the palace—that's where all the duels are held—and tether it there until the duel. By then it'll be good and hungry. When the duel starts, take the pterodactyl up to a good height and then just hold on. It'll do its own spotting of the pepper."

"Then what happens?"

"The pterodactyl goes for the pepper and when he takes it that boy's head is going to go right along with the pepper. The pterodactyl isn't particular how much garbage is attached to something he wants to eat. The duel will be over and you will be the hero of the day—a fit mate for the royal princess."

"That's what I'm afraid of," Manning said gloomily. "How do I get out of that? I'm perfectly willing to help you escape, Dzanku, but not at that price. If I can't get out of marrying her, the whole deal's off. What about using the pterodactyl to pull a raid on the prison here?"

Dzanku shook his head. "A lost cause, my boy," he said. "If you had a whole army of pterodactyls, you could never make a dent on this prison."

"What then?"

"It represents a problem," admitted Dzanku. "The only solution which I can see immediately is for you to marry the princess. Then the moment the ceremony is over you can free me and then I will tell you how you can have the marriage annulled before it is consummated. How's that?"

"Meaning I have to trust you to deliver after I've freed you?" Manning said. "Nothing doing. I wouldn't trust you as far as I could throw you. Tell me your idea first."

"I confess," said Dzanku, "to a similar reluctance to trust you. Nothing would please you and J. Barnaby more than to have me come to an untimely demise, providing you could avoid paying the insurance benefits required under Polluxian law."

"But we can't," Manning said. "That's why you can trust me."

"No," replied Dzanku. "At best, the insurance policy has been a shaky lever from the start. There's always the chance the company will find a loophole which will enable them to cancel the policy. That's why I like this marriage of yours. It's better insurance for me than the Greater Solarian policy. So Manning, I'm afraid you'll have to either trust me or find a way which will ensure mutual trust."

"Good old Dzanku," Manning said bitterly.

"Good old Manning," Dzanku echoed. They glared at each other through the bars for several minutes. Then, at almost the same moment, both of them laughed.

"All right, Dzanku," Manning said. "I guess I can't blame you. We'll see what we can work out after the duel. Thanks for helping on that."

"It was a pleasure," Dzanku replied.

MANNING DRACO waved to the Rigelian and left the prison. Outside, he climbed on the sexcycle and ordered the uniformed Polluxians to take him downtown.

On the way, he stopped off at a store and bought a Polluxian pepper. Then he continued on downtown.

The sign said: *Xleno's Fly-Ur-Self.* Below that, in smaller letters, was the legend: *We buy them—U fly them—Xleno Ii, Prop.* So far as Manning could see, Xleno Ii looked exactly like every other Polluxian he'd seen—like a dressed-up alligator. His manner brightened as soon as Manning mentioned Dzanku.

"A clever boy," he said. "How is he?"

"Fine," said Manning. He went on to explain that he had come to Pollux to rescue the Rigelian, without going into any of the complicating details. "And now," he finished, "I'd like to rent a pterodactyl for the afternoon."

"Suppose you tell me what you have in mind," Xleno Ii said. "You want one for a long trip or a fast number?"

"I'm not sure," said Manning. "I have to fight a duel this afternoon and Dzanku suggested that I rent the pterodactyl for that. He also suggested that I arrange to have a pepper fastened to the head of my opponent."

"Ah," said Xleno Ii. His huge mouth spread in a grin. "That Dzanku! He is a clever one. A most astute thought." He raised his voice in a shout that sent one of his helpers scurrying out of the room. "Hey, boy. Put a saddle on Mabel." He turned back to Manning in obvious enjoyment. "Mabel is just the one for you. She is as ill-tempered and bloodthirsty as a Terran—you'll excuse the expression. I very seldom rent her, for she has to be ridden with full blinkers. Oh, she'll do nicely for your purpose. All you'll have to do is slip the blinkers when the duel starts and Mabel will do the rest. Come, Mr. Draco."

He led the way out of the private office into the main part of the building. Manning followed into a large bare room where the roof opened like a door. There was a strong musty odor which reminded him of the reptile house in the Terra zoo.

"This is the mounting room," Xleno Ii explained. "The boy will bring Mabel in here. You'll like Mabel."

"Yeah, but will Mabel like me?" muttered Manning. "If she's as bloodthirsty as you say, will she bother to tell the difference between her rider and anyone else?"

"Mabel will bite only what she can see," the Polluxian explained. "Since she will not be able to see you, you will be safe. Even when you slip the blinkers, she will be able to see only straight ahead and below. Then your opponent will be wearing the pepper. If there's anything Mabel likes better than heads, it's peppers. Ah, here she comes now. Isn't she a beauty?"

"Beauty" was hardly the word which Manning would have used to describe the creature that came into the room, accompanied by the slithering sound of scaled flesh and the overpowering reptile stench. It towered above Manning and the Polluxians, a strange wedding of bird and reptile which had also once, in the dim past, been known on Terra. Its long serpentine neck ended in a monstrous head and a double row of teeth which almost made Manning feel sorry for Bbtula Eo. Its wings were folded, but they looked as if they had a good thirty-foot spread. There was a saddle nestling on its back between the wings.

The bridle was a complicated affair completely covering both its eyes.

The Polluxian prodded the creature in the ribs and shouted, and the huge body folded to the floor.

"There she is, Mr. Draco," said Xleno Ii. He repeated his earlier statement, "Isn't she a beauty?"

Manning would have liked more reassurance on the safety, but decided there was no point in asking the same question over and over. He clutched his package tightly and tried to ignore the pounding of his heart as he climbed into the saddle.

"Just pull up on the bridle when you want her to go up," Xleno Ii said. "Flick her on top of the head with the reins when you want her to go down. There's a catch on the top of her bridle to open and close the blinkers." He and his helper drew back. "Good luck, Mr. Draco," he shouted.

"I'll need it," muttered Manning. He pulled up on the bridle and felt the pterodactyl lurch up from the floor. A moment later they were through the roof and flying over the city.

For a moment he was concerned only with keeping his balance and trying not to look directly below. But after a time, he began to get his bearings and steered the pterodactyl in the direction of the royal palace, which was easy to spot from the air.

HE BROUGHT it down on the large field in back of the palace and dismounted. He tied the reins to a large post, being sure to give a wide berth to the double row of teeth. He had more confidence in distance than in the blinkers. Then he hurried toward the palace. There was just time to hunt out the princess before lunch. He finally found her in one of the rooms near the dining room, the inevitable fan before her face, the inevitable giggle sounding from behind it. This was the first time he'd ever spoken directly to her and he tried to look more like the eager bridegroom than he felt.

"Princess Aaledo," he said. "I hope you will pardon this intrusion, but I find it difficult to stay away from your charm and—er—beauty."

She lowered her fan to smile at him and he found himself wishing she'd raise it again. He fixed his gaze on the ceiling and hoped she'd think him merely bashful.

"My dear husband-to-be," the princess said, "my own eagerness is a match for yours. I've hardly rested since I first saw you yesterday."

"Of course, of course," Manning said hastily. "I was wondering if you'd do me a small favor?"

"Anything," she said breathily.

"Well," he said, "it's about the duel. Naturally I want to win it so we can be married as soon as possible. In my world there is a belief that you will have good luck in a duel if you can get your opponent to wear some little token you have bought. I'm sure, however, that Bbtula Eo would refuse if I asked him; but I thought you might, ask him to wear it for you. It's this Polluxian pepper I just bought. Would you ask him to wear it—on his head—as a favor to you?"

Princess Aaledo thought this was a little queer, but she was a well-reared princess who had been brought up with the realization that there were many odd races in the universe and one must respect even their strangest customs. So she nodded. "Of course, dear," she said.

"You're a sweetheart," Manning said. He hastily thrust the package into her hands and retreated before the conversation could get more personal. He could hear her tail thumping the floor with pleasure as he left.

Lunch was a gala affair that day. The dining room was filled with Polluxians. The lunch was quite good, but Manning found it difficult to enjoy his food, surrounded as he was by such a host of gaping jaws and flashing teeth.

Later, he saw the Princess Aaledo over in a corner talking to Bbtula Eo. The latter was looking rather startled, but he was nodding his head, so Manning relaxed.

Shortly after lunch, there were a number of speeches by various Polluxians on the history and tradition of dueling. One young Polluxian recited a long and tiresome poem concerning the adventures of one of the greatest duelists. Then it was time for the main event.

CHAPTER FIVE

WHEN THEY reached the field behind the palace it was already crowded with Polluxians who had come to watch. Manning Draco and Bbtula Eo listened to a long recitation of the rules and were then instructed to retire to opposite ends of the field and to come out on the first blast of the royal trumpets. As he walked away, Manning saw Bbtula Eo fastening the huge red pepper to the top of his head. He grinned at the sight and headed across the field to where he had tethered the pterodactyl. It was still standing in the same spot.

Manning unfastened the reins and climbed into the saddle. Up to this point, apparently, no one had paid any attention to the tethered pterodactyl or connected it with the duel. Nor did anyone glance in his direction as he waited for the trumpets. Across the field, Bbtula Eo was marching up and down, bellowing, and everyone was watching him.

Then the trumpets sounded and Manning pulled up on the reins. The pterodactyl went up in the air with the beat of its powerful wings. Manning heard an excited roar from the crowd below. He caught a glimpse of Bbtula Eo staring upward in amazement.

Manning leaned over and fumbled at the top of the bridle. He found the catch and slipped it to one side. "Well, Mabel," he said softly, "the rest is up to you."

The pterodactyl swung its head from side to side and then it seemed to catch sight of the solitary figure on the field below. He felt the creature tensing its mighty muscles.

There was a bellow which almost shattered Manning's ear drums; then the pterodactyl relaxed its giant wings and dropped earthward with a suddenness which almost threw him from the saddle. He hung on desperately tried not to look at the rapidly approaching ground. He had a brief glimpse of Bbtula Eo. The Polluxian looked as if he intended to stand his ground, but suddenly he bolted, the pepper flapping on his head as he ran.

Manning felt the pterodactyl swerve, saw the long neck snap downward. He closed his eyes and a moment later felt the mighty wings tense into action and knew they were going up again. He opened his eyes and took a quick look below. There was a sprawled figure on the ground: The pterodactyl was working its jaws rhythmically. For a moment, Manning thought he was going to be sick.

Slowly he got a grip on himself. He leaned over and pulled the blinkers back on. Then he guided the pterodactyl over the field and set it down on the ground near the post. He quickly tethered it and started across the field. He could hear the buzz from the crowd, the mixed cheering and booing.

The royal party came to meet him. When he was almost up to them, one figure detached itself from the others and ran toward him. It was the Princess Aaledo. Before Manning could

dodge, she had thrown her arms around him. He was almost crushed in the embrace. "Oh, Manning," she squealed, "you were so clever, so wonderful. You are truly my mate."

Manning dodged what was apparently meant to be a kiss on his ear, feeling that he'd probably saved an ear by so doing.

"Aaledo," the emperor snapped as he came up. "That is not the way for a princess to act."

The princess removed her arms from around Manning, to his great relief, and reverted to her fan and the giggle. He liked her better that way.

"My son," said the emperor, "you have been declared the winner of the duel. I—ah—consulted with the judges while you were bringing down your mount and they have said that you were within your rights. It was extremely clever of you." The emperor's tone was friendly, but there was a wary look in his eyes.

"Thank you," Manning said.

"They are hastening now to amend the rules so that others may not profit by your cleverness. Naturally," he added casually, "I am pleased to know that my royal family is to be enriched by the addition of one so clever. By the way, I thought I might tell you that while you will become the Royal Pretender upon your marriage to my daughter, the law would not permit you to become emperor in the event that—ah—something happened to me."

MANNING STARED at the emperor for a moment, and then realized the explanation of the wary look. He laughed aloud. "Your Highness," he said, "should realize that Terra has a long tradition of being opposed to royalty. It would make me very unhappy to think I would ever have to become an emperor."

"Oh, well, everyone to his taste," said the emperor, but he looked relieved. "Now that you have won the duel, I think we might come to the matter of your wedding. My daughter naturally wants it to take place quickly. Young blood runs hot." He managed a quite acceptable leer. "Would you prefer that we have the ceremony tonight or in the morning?"

This was a little quicker action than Manning had expected, but he'd thought out one angle. If it didn't work, he was lost unless he could make a run for it on Mabel.

"I too am anxious," he said, hoping he sounded as if he meant it, "but becoming a member of such a distinguished and royal family is a step which bears heavy responsibilities. I should like to feel that I am worthy of it. I was about to suggest that we have a long engagement while I prepare myself. After all, I am a stranger to Pollux and I should spend some time studying the wonders of your world."

"A very worthy attitude," said the emperor, nodding his head. "I, myself, favor long engagements. Very well, my son, we shall announce the official engagement this evening and the marriage will be held two weeks from today."

Two weeks was hardly Manning's idea of a long engagement, but it at least was a breathing spell. Since the business of the duel, he was feeling confident that he could either work out something or force Dzanku Dzanku to help him. So he nodded, trying not to look too joyful.

Later, at the palace, he sent a palace guard to Xleno's Fly-Ur-Self with money and a message for Xleno to pick up his pterodactyl. Manning felt that he'd gotten along fine with Mabel so far. He didn't want to push his luck.

Early the following morning Manning Draco was up and out of the palace. He'd arranged for a pass to the Royal Archives and he started wading through the laws of Pollux, hoping he could find some solution to his situation.

That first week he read from morning until night. It was dull work, especially since he found nothing which seemed to apply to him. During that week, too, as a result of his official engagement to Princess Aaledo, he was given a small palace near the large one. It was completely staffed with servants and slaves, and it would be their home after the wedding.

His first bright idea came not from the research in the archives but from the realization that he had suddenly become a slave owner. He'd paid little attention to the Polluxians who were part of his household until one night when, for the fourth time, he was telling Albert Sauri that he would not work with the FBI.

"We could, you know," said Albert, "use other pressures on you. We don't like to force Terrans to be patriotic, but this is an important mission."

"Everything's been done to me," Manning said shortly. "What else could you do?"

"Well, you're still a citizen of the Federation, and will be until you're married to the princess. There is a Federation law against a citizen's indulging in slavery even on a non-Federation planet. I could pull you in for that."

"Go ahead," Manning said. "At least it would get me out of the marriage, and that's the only thing I want."

"But the penalty for slavery," Albert Sauri said gently, "is fifty years on Jupiter."

"Oh, go to hell," snapped Manning. He threw the FBI agent out. Then he put in a call to J. Barnaby Cruikshank and told him that he'd better use his influence to call off the FBI or the whole deal would be off. J. Barnaby promised. After the call, Manning was sitting still glaring at the screen when the idea struck him.

THE NEXT DAY he went to see the Emperor, and that afternoon a number of prison guards showed up at the small palace with Dzanku Dzanku. The Rigelian was wearing a regulation slave collar and there were heavy chains on his legs which guaranteed that he could never escape.

"Well," said Manning, when they were alone, "you're out of prison."

"In a manner of speaking," said Dzanku, indicating the leg chains. "In reality, I have merely traded in my old prison for a more portable model."

"But there's no death sentence over you," Manning said. "I had the emperor commute your death sentence and you are now my property. No one else has any jurisdiction over you. All you have to do is show me how to get out of marrying the princess and I'll give you your freedom."

"Manning, old friend, you wound me," Dzanku said. "To think that you would believe that Dzanku Dzanku would fall for that gag like a callow youth."

"What's wrong?"

"If I help you, what guarantee do I have that it will do me any good? Even if you still wanted to keep your word and free me—which I seriously doubt—you'd be unable to. The minute I showed you how to get out of marrying the princess, her father would toss you out of this palace and confiscate all of your Polluxian property. I'd be right back where I was. Personally, as much as I dislike being your slave, I prefer it to the alternatives. You set me free and when I'm beyond the atmosphere of Pollux, I'll send you a message telling you how to get off the hook."

"Now who's taking who for a sucker?" rejoined Manning.

It was another standoff. Manning Draco went back to spending his days in the Royal Archives, poring over the laws. Evenings he avoided the palace social life by pretending fatigue. He and Dzanku would play four-dimensional chess or Castorian triple rummy while he tried to trick Dzanku into showing some reaction to the customs and laws of Pollux. A couple of times, when the games were close, he tried quick mental stabs at the Rigelian, hoping to read his mind. But Dzanku's shield was always up and it invariably ended with the two of them glaring at each other.

It went on like that for another week. Finally, Manning's marriage was only two days off. There were only a few laws which he hadn't yet covered and his confidence had reached a low ebb. That night, after dinner, when he went in for his usual game with Dzanku, he took along a bottle of local liquor. He'd tried it before and didn't care much for it—*Dtseea* tasted a little like fermented swamp water—but he was feeling so low that he needed some sort of crutch.

"I thought I'd like to have a drink," he explained to Dzanku. "Care to join me?"

"I think I might take one," Dzanku said. "I've just heard that my wife has presented me with a new son. The least I can do is drink a toast to her achievement."

"Congratulations," Manning said automatically. He poured two drinks and handed one to Dzanku. Then the import of what he'd heard sank in. "Wait a minute," he said. "I don't mean to be indelicate, but it seems to me that you've been in jail too long—well, you've been in jail a good many months. Or was your wife allowed to visit you in jail? I hope I'm not hurting your feelings—"

"Not at all," Dzanku said. He sampled his drink. "These Polluxians have no palate, do they?... No, Manning, my presence or lack of it has no relationship to my wife's confinement. You see, Polluxians are oviparous—I suppose you know that. The females lay self-fertilizing eggs so that the males have no function in the raising of children. It's really a very convenient arrangement on the part of nature. Better than your planet's."

"That's strange," Manning said. "You'd think in such a culture they'd never have marriage."

"Oh, marriage is a recent innovation on Pollux and, as with any contact between the sexes, is purely a social arrangement for mutual pleasure. My wife, like any other Polluxian female, started having children the moment she became adult. In fact, she brought eight fine children to our marriage."

Manning stared at the Rigelian in the excitement of growing awareness. Then he forced himself to become casual. He took a drink from his glass and brought out the cards.

"Very interesting," he said idly. "I suppose Princess Aaledo has a few fine children around too."

"Oh, sure. Four or five, I think—" Dzanku suddenly broke off and looked at Manning. There was an expression of dismay in his three eyes.

Manning laughed. It was enough to tell him he was on the right track. He started dealing out the cards, slapping them down in gay abandon.

Dzanku muttered something in Rigelian. Manning couldn't understand it, but the tone was enough to tell him that Dzanku was swearing.

"I'm right, eh?" he said softly.

Dzanku glared at him for a minute, and finally threw out his tentacles in a gesture of defeat.

"Probably," he admitted. "You caught me off guard that time."

"Don't worry," Manning said. "I'll still save your thieving life."

"I don't like the way you make it sound," muttered Dzanku.

Manning laughed again.

EARLY THE FOLLOWING morning he was at the palace, and was soon shown into the emperor's presence.

"Well," the emperor said heartily, "tomorrow's the big day, eh? There's nothing like a wedding to give a country a festive air. What's on your mind, my boy? There's nothing too good for the future Pretender of the Empire."

"A most serious matter has come to my attention," Manning said gravely. "Naturally, I came immediately to discuss it with you."

"Naturally," agreed the emperor.

"I believe," said Manning, "that this is your daughter's first marriage?"

"Oh, absolutely. If that's what's worrying you, my boy, I can reassure you. Aaledo has had a very strict upbringing. I know how fussy you Terrans are about such matters."

"I understand, however," said Manning, "that the princess has a number of children?"

"Four, I believe," said the emperor. "As any normal Polluxian female should. Surely you have no objections to your wife's having children?"

"Not as my wife. But isn't there also a law on Pollux which states that any marriage between a Polluxian and an individual from another planet or system can only take place when the moral laws and traditions of both parties are fully respected?"

"Yes, but—"

"Then," Manning interrupted firmly, "I must regretfully call off my engagement to the Princess Aaledo. The idea of a bride who is an unmarried mother of four is offensive to my background and training. I would be the laughing stock of Terra."

"Oh, dear," said the emperor. "The princess will be terribly upset. Can't we fix this up in some way?"

"I'm afraid not," Manning said. "I am heartbroken over this myself, but, after all, traditions must be respected."

"Yes. Yes, I understand. Of course, I don't mind telling you that I'm just as glad. I wouldn't think of depriving my daughter, but I don't approve of intermarriage. Nothing personal, you understand, but you're pretty short in the tooth and I find your face rather flat and uninteresting. But I suppose that's a matter of taste."

"I like you too," Manning said, grinning.

"Under the circumstances," the emperor continued, "I fear I shall have to ask you to leave the small palace and I'll have to take back the property I've given you."

"Under the law, Your Highness, that applies only to the offending party. Since in this case I am the offended one, legally I can retain everything you've given me."

"Oh, a space lawyer," snarled the emperor. His friendliness had vanished.

"However," said Manning, "I'm quite willing to return everything to you except for one slave. The Rigelian, Dzanku Dzanku, I shall keep."

"Oh, all right," the emperor said sullenly. He glared at Manning. "But you'll have to leave Pollux within twenty-four hours. I won't have my daughter's broken heart flaunted."

"I'll be glad to," Manning said.

CHAPTER SIX

H E LEFT and returned to the smaller palace where he'd been living. He went to the video set and put in a call to J. Barnaby. It was only a few minutes before the face of the Greater Solarian president appeared on the screen.

"Relax, J. Barnaby," Manning said. "Your bank account is safe—temporarily."

"That's great. I knew I could depend on— what do you mean *temporarily?*" The last was a bellow.

"Well," Manning said airily, "I've saved Dzanku from the current death sentence, but of course he's still married to a Polluxian woman and, as you know, his insurance policy is still in force."

"Well, do something!" J. Barnaby said. "Can't you trick him into doing something so the policy can be canceled? Or get the emperor to divorce him. Or something."

"I don't believe the emperor is feeling exactly friendly toward me just now," Manning said blandly. "By the way, wasn't there something about a bonus on this job for me?"

"Of course, of course. You know me, my boy. J. Barnaby Cruikshank is always willing to pay for services."

"Good. If you'll increase the bonus to two hundred and fifty thousand credits, I'll see to it that you have a way of canceling the policy."

"Two hundred and fifty thousand," howled J. Barnaby. "Are you out of your mind? I won't pay it."

"Suit yourself. Of course, you'll be taking a chance that nothing happens to Dzanku while the policy is still in force."

"But, Manning, if anything like that happened, I'd go broke."

"I'll send my condolences," Manning said coldly.

"Manning, my boy," J. Barnaby said emotionally, "how can you do this to me? After all, I've been like a father to you and—"

"Yes, you promised me a wedding present," Manning interrupted, "when it looked like I'd have to marry a Polluxian. I promised myself I'd get even and the only place to hurt you is in your bank account. So the price is two hundred and fifty thousand."

"But that was a joke, Manning." J. Barnaby managed a convincing laugh. "I wouldn't have let it happen."

"Two hundred and fifty thousand, J. Barnaby."

"Manning, my boy—"

"Two hundred and fifty thousand."

J. Barnaby knew when he was licked. "All right," he snapped. "I'll give it to you if you find a way for the policy to be canceled within the next twenty-four hours."

"You and the emperor are both in a rut with this twenty-four hour stuff," Manning said. "But it's a deal. Good-by." He broke the connection and left the building.

At the spaceport, he arranged for his ship to be checked over and then he went into the terminal. He waited until he finally caught sight of Captain mmemmo. He held a short conference with the Andromedan, at the end of which he handed over a set of keys.

He found a comfortable seat in the terminal and relaxed. It was perhaps half an hour later that there was a tremendous racket in the terminal. It was soon explained. A number of Polluxian guards appeared, literally carrying the still-shackled Dzanku Dzanku. The Rigelian was struggling for all he was worth, but he was handicapped not only by his chains but by the fact that his whole body was quivering. Captain mmemmo strode briskly along behind the guards, directing them toward the field where his ship was cradled.

Dzanku was cursing violently in fifteen languages and a few dialects, but the tempo of his curses increased considerably when he caught sight of Manning. The latter stood up and waved, grinning broadly. Then he went out to his own ship.

THE *ALPHA ACTUARY* was five hundred miles out of Pollux when Manning saw the big silver ship of Captain mmemmo pass him. He watched it go into overdrive and vanish in the direction of the Andromeda Galaxy.

Manning put his own ship into magnidrive and then sat down and called J. Barnaby Cruikshank.

"What do you want now?" snapped J. Barnaby as soon as he recognized Manning.

"Just wanted to be sure that you're ready to deposit that two hundred and fifty thousand to my account."

"I said I'd do it," J. Barnaby said angrily.

"Okay," Manning said cheerfully. "Issue a cancellation on the life insurance policy of Dzanku Dzanku and send the money over to my bank."

"What's the grounds for cancellation?"

"There's a clause in every policy," Manning said, "which permits you to cancel if the insured leaves this galaxy. Well, Dzanku just left on his way to Andromeda."

"Why?" asked the astonished J. Barnaby.

"Oh, decidedly not voluntarily," Manning said, "but all quite legal. I got Dzanku out of jail by having him made my slave. When I was ready to leave, I merely sold him to a slave raider from Andromeda. Dzanku is on his way to serve in the Pleasure Camps. Since there is something about Andromedans which makes him shake all over, I imagine he'll be quite popular. I arranged to have the price paid for him deposited to his name on Rigel. I imagine Dzanku will want a nice long vacation when he finally gets back to this galaxy."

J. Barnaby stared out of the screen at Manning and then burst out laughing. "Dzanku in an Andromedan Pleasure Camp," he said. "The thought of that is almost worth the quarter of a million you held me up for—you robber." Still chuckling, he cut the contact.

Manning Draco leaned back in his seat. He was going to take a good long nap while his ship headed for Terra. It would be the first time he'd been able to relax fully in two weeks. He expected to dream pleasantly of his fattened bank account and of the possibility of a date with Lhana Xano, the Martian receptionist—a date which he'd find some way of insuring against another interruption by J. Barnaby.

"That was really a very clever scheme, Mr. Draco," said a voice behind him.

Manning leaped out of his chair and whirled around. For a wild moment, he thought that Princess Aaledo had disguised herself and sneaked into his ship. Then he realized that it was Albert Sauri, the Terran crocodile who was an FBI agent. "What are you doing here?" he demanded.

"Returning to Terra with you," Albert said. "I hope you don't mind too much. I would have asked you in advance, but you weren't too friendly the last time we met and I thought it might be better this way."

"Are you still hounding me?" Manning asked. "If you are, you're wasting your time. I'm not marrying the princess."

"I know. Oh, that's all in the past, Mr. Draco. I hope there's no hard feeling. I was only doing my job."

"But what are you doing here?" Manning wanted to know. "What about your job on Pollux?"

"Oh, that," said Albert with a grimace. "Would you believe it, Mr. Draco—those dirty Polluxians have a species of rabbit which they trained as agents years ago and slipped into Terra. Nobody knows how many perfectly innocent-looking rabbits in our midst are really spies for Pollux. Anyway, they knew all along that I was an FBI agent. And this morning a Polluxian guard came around and ordered me off the planet, and he sent word to my bureau that the next agent would just be thrown into prison. I fear the worst, Mr. Draco. You know what rabbits are like—there may be millions of Polluxian spies on Terra by this time."[10]

"I see," said Manning. "But what are you going to do now? I don't imagine there are any other planets where the dominant

10 By now, of course, the Federation Bureau of Investigation has rounded up many of the Polluxian spies, but it is difficult to say how many of the remaining rabbits on Terra are honest rabbits and how many are spies. It's a trying situation.

race is saurian, so it'll be difficult for you to continue as an undercover agent. What will you do?"

"That's no problem," said Albert. "As soon as I knew it was over, I got busy on the visiphone. I've already got a contract for my memoirs to be published, under the title of *I Was a Spy for the FBI*—catchy, isn't it? Then I believe I've been booked for a series of lectures on the Polluxian menace. I was thinking of leading off with—"

"Don't practice your lecture on me," Manning said hastily. "I'm going to sleep."

And he did.

ACT FOUR / SPRING 3473

THE CAPHIAN CAPER

CHAPTER ONE

MANNING DRACO, whose interest in females was as varied as it was fleeting, had, with dishonorable intent, pursued Lhana Xano for almost a year. The Martian female was the receptionist in the Nyork office of the Greater Solarian Insurance Company, Monopolated, for which Manning Draco was chief investigator. She was an attractive dish, unless one was limited to the attractions of human females. Manning Draco had no such limitations. For the better of part of a year, he had taken her to lunches and dinners, danced with her, held hands in the visitheaters, and made passes whenever he could. In the vernacular of the day, he'd never gotten to the first space platform. But he had hopes—or, to be more exact, he had had hopes until that day, just before the annual Festival of Planets in the spring of 3473, when Lhana Xano announced that she was returning to Mars to marry a whelphood sweetheart.

Not that Manning Draco was in love with her. He would have been the first to admit that his interest was purely biological. For years he had taken his physical pleasures where he found them, playing a human version of the cowbird, and Lhana's resistance had become a personal challenge. By going home to be married she was removing all opportunity of turning her challenge into a victory. It wounded his vanity, destroyed his faith in women, and made him feel old at thirty.

This was the mood in which he went to the opening night

of the Festival.

The Festival of the Planets was held in Nyork each spring on the anniversary of the formings of the first planetary union. That event had followed what historians called the Seven Hundred Year War, and the first year there had been a spontaneous street celebration in which Terrans, Martians, Venusians, and Vegans had danced together and shouted with joy. Thereafter it had become an annual affair. It was always held on the first Friday in May and lasted through Sunday. Second level streets in Nyork were cleared of all traffic and turned over to the revelers. There were street musicians and thousands of little stands dispensing the confections of a hundred planets. Nearly everyone dressed in costumes and for three days they played without restraint.

Manning Draco went to the Festival merely to be surrounded by noise and unfamiliar faces. He wore no costume and had no hope of enjoying himself. He parked his aircar on the fourth level and descended glumly to the second level.

He stopped at one of the first booths and bought on Alnilam Fire-Ice[11]—which has been described by one writer on viands as "part Alnilam frozen rum, part pineapple-lime ice, and part pure explosion." He walked along with the crowd, spooning the Fire-Ice into his mouth.

Manning was edging his way around a group of street dancers when he felt someone grab his arm. He looked around, in no mood for company—and changed his mind.

She was just tall enough to come up to his shoulder. She was in a Festival costume—or, rather, out of it, for she was dressed as an Algenibian court favorite. A jeweled belt girdled her waist. From it, in front and in back, scarlet silk fell to her ankles, the inner edges being sealed to the inside of her legs. A loop of scarlet silk curved from her shoulders, with a single brilliant

---

11 Alistair Dhu, author of *Drinking Your Way Through the Galaxy*, is believed responsible for the saying: "Terran brandy for children, Rigelian Jodiper-Whiskey for men, and Alnilam Fire-Ice for heroes."

jewel knotting it between her breasts. She wore a scarlet half-mask over the upper half of her face. There were tiny bells on the toes of her scarlet crescent-slippers.

She was Terran, with a beauty that was breathtaking. Her body was perfection, and the costume made it obvious that she was using none of the pneumatic beauty aids so common among

fashionable Terran women. Her skin had the coloring of old ivory and her long hair was blue-black.

"Hello, Manning Draco," she said, thrusting her arm through his.

HE WAS FLATTERED at being recognized. He peered closer at her masked face and was certain that he'd never met her. His pulse quickened. Perhaps, he thought, this was a better answer.

Her arms would provide the solace he needed.

"Hello," he said. "Do I know you?"

"No," she answered. "But I know you. I've known you for years."

"Then you must have started while still a child, for you're not much more than that now—but enough more," he added, glancing at the loop of silk. "What's your name, honey?"

She shook her head. "You may call me Vega, but that is all," she said. She tugged on his arm. "Come."

This was his first surprise. He'd expected her to lead him away from the throng, to a private apartment. Instead she was tugging him to join the dancers. Shrugging, he followed her.

His second surprise was that he enjoyed dancing with her. Soon he found himself doing things that he hadn't done in ten years. They threw confetti from the parapets of the second level; they raced hand in hand in pursuit of a mad parade led by a giant Alpheratzian; they ate wild love-fruit from Spica and drank the spiced wines of Polaris. He found himself laughing as much as the girl, throwing himself into the Festival spirit in a way he would have scorned a few hours earlier.

At four in the morning he said good-by to her, having had no more for his pains than a light kiss a few seconds before she climbed into an aircab. But he had no feeling of failure, and she had promised to meet him the following night.

Saturday night was a repetition of the first evening. They danced, and played games, drank and laughed, and the night was filled with pleasure. Again there was a brief parting kiss and a promise to meet the following night as she left in an aircab. For the first time in his life, Manning Draco was willing to admit that he might be feeling the beginning of love.

The last night of the Festival was like the first two, but, it seemed to Manning, even more fun. It was almost five o'clock in the morning when they climbed to the fourth level, scorning the Level-Converters, and hailed an aircab for her.

"This is the last night," he said. "Why not let me take you home?"

"No, Manning," she said softly. "I'd like you to, but it's best this way. It's been a wonderful Festival. I wouldn't want it to be spoiled."

"Me neither," Manning said. Then a horrible thought struck him. "Don't tell me you're married!"

She laughed. "No."

Just then the aircab settled down beside them. She climbed in and rolled down the rear window.

"At least, tell me your name," Manning said. "I have to see you again."

"Maybe you'll change your mind when you know who I am," she said.

"Not a chance."

She spoke to the driver and the aircab lifted slowly from the street. She leaned through the open window, looked down at him.

"It's Vega Cruikshank," she said. "Good night, Manning."

The aircab shot upward and was soon out of sight.

She was gone by the time Manning got it. He didn't believe in coincidences. He knew only one other Cruikshank. Therefore, he reasoned, she must be the daughter of J. Barnaby Cruikshank, president and owner of the Greater Solarian Insurance Company, Monopolated. He could well imagine J. Barnaby's reaction when he learned that Manning Draco was interested in his daughter. He shrugged and went home.

IT WAS ALMOST TEN the following morning when Manning Draco strolled into the Greater Solarian offices. Before he could reach his own office, the mousey creature[12] who had replaced Lhana Xano at the reception desk told him that J. Barnaby wanted to see him.

Outside the private office of the president, Manning waited until the door-scanner recognized him and the door opened. He stepped inside and faced the head of the monopoly.

"About time you got here," J. Barnaby growled.

Manning dropped into the nearest chair and smiled at his boss. "The day is young yet," he murmured. "J. Barnaby, I am displeased with you."

---

12   An apt adjective since the new receptionist came from Al Suhail IV where the dominant race is definitely related to the Terran order *Cricetinae*, genus *Peromyscus*.

"Oh, you are?" J. Barnaby asked, his voice heavy with sarcasm.

"Yes. I have discovered that you are the father of one of the most beautiful girls my jaded old eyes have ever beheld and you have studiously kept this a secret from me. This is definitely a case of unfair employment practice."

J. Barnaby Cruikshank looked as if he were about to have a stroke. As Manning finished, his face slowly reddened until it achieved a royal purple. With a visible effort, he got a grip on himself.

"You," he said with controlled rage, "have the morals of a Kochabian sex dervish. If you try to get within twenty miles of my daughter, I'll make you sorry you were born."

"I've already been closer to her than twenty miles," Manning said.

"I know," J. Barnaby said grimly. "I had a talk. with Vega when she came home this morning. She admitted she'd been seeing you during the Festival. I've already given her to understand that she's never to see you again. In fact, I'm arranging for her to leave tonight for a cruise around the galaxy."

"What did Vega say to that?"

"She said," snorted J. Barnaby, "that she'd love you no matter where I sent her. But she'll get over that."

"The girl has good taste," Manning murmured. "Must have inherited it from her mother."

J. BARNABY glared at him. "In fact, I was also intending to invent a case which would take you to the other end of the galaxy. That, however, if no longer necessary."

"Meaning?"

"There *is* a case—probably the most important case we've ever had." His tone suddenly changed; it became almost wheedling. "Manning, my boy, the fate of Greater Solarian is in your hands."

"Again?" Manning murmured. "In that case, don't you think you should look more kindly upon my interest in your daughter?"

This produced another struggle within J. Barnaby. Urbanity won. "Manning," he said, "you know I look upon you as a son. If I weren't so worried, perhaps I might have felt differently about the news. Suppose we discuss it when you return from this case? Isn't that fair, my boy?"

Manning grinned. "You," he said, imitating J. Barnaby's tone, "have the morals of a space pirate. What is this case that's making you jet-happy?"

"That's my boy!" J. Barnaby said happily. The happiness quickly faded from his face. "The truth of the matter, Manning, is that I am facing the possibility of being put out of business."

"I don't believe it," Manning said. "You've one of the most successful companies in the galaxy."

"That is true." This was a rare admission for J. Barnaby to make to one of his employees. "But my statement is also true. A claim has just been filed against us with the Committee on Extraplanetary Affairs for one trillion credits. As of Friday, our financial statement shows that Greater Solarian has assets totaling one trillion, five hundred and twenty-one million, nine hundred and forty-two thousand, seven hundred and eleven credits and thirteen units."

"Remind me to ask for a raise," Manning said.

"If this claim goes through, you won't even have a job. Our cash reserves amount to only five hundred billion credits and thirteen units. That's only half the amount of the claim. If we're forced to liquidate the rest of our assets quickly, I doubt if they will bring more than another five hundred billion credits. We'd be wiped out."

"You'd still have thirteen units," Manning pointed out. "Enough to buy two good cigars."

J. BARNABY ignored him. "On the surface, there are no grounds for us to contest the claim. Unless you can find some evidence to make a settlement, we'll have to pay the full face of the policies in thirty days."

"Dzanku and Warren," Manning guessed.

J. Barnaby winced as he nodded. "They sold the policies on Caph II."

Manning could remember nothing about the Caph system. He said as much.

"There isn't much to remember," J. Barnaby said glumly. "There are two planets in a single orbit around Caph. A Federation investigator made a brief visit there fifty years ago and classified both planets as Class G, inhabited by semihumanoids. Telemeter tests were made, but mineral showings were slight. Theoretically, limited trade is permitted with Class G planets subject to the Committee's approval. A year ago Dzanku and Warren went to Caph II and sold one hundred million twenty-year-endowment policies. The premiums were—ah—slightly higher than usual, so I accepted them without an investigation. The Committee on Interplanetary Affairs approved."

"Naturally," Manning said dryly. "You probably slipped them a cut. How much higher were the premiums than normally?"

"About twice," J. Barnaby admitted. "Each policy holder paid for one year in advance. It seemed too good to miss."

"Even so," Manning said, frowning, "why are you stuck now? Didn't you say the policies were twenty-year endowment?"

J. Barnaby looked unhappy. "Yes. Each policy called for the payment of ten thousand credits in twenty years. They were sold just a year ago. Last week the Federation made a new survey of Caph II. It seems the system exists in what is known as a Time-Fracture. While one year passes in the rest of the galaxy, twenty years pass on Caph II."[13]

"You mean," Manning asked, "that the policies were sold there a year ago by our time, but that it's already been twenty years on Caph II and so the payoff is legally due?"

J. Barnaby Cruikshank nodded.

Manning Draco laughed until the tears streaked down his face.

J. Barnaby watched malevolently.

---

13   Please see the entry *Caphian Time-Fracture* in the Glossary.

"It's the funniest thing I've heard in years," Manning said finally. "If I have to lose my job, I can't imagine a more enjoyable way."

"Meaning you won't even try to do anything about it?" J. Barnaby demanded.

"Oh, I'll try. I'll give my all for dear Old Greater Solarian. But what do you expect me to do? Surely you don't have any idea that I can find some way of canceling a hundred million policies so it won't cost you a cent?"

"No," J. Barnaby admitted reluctantly, "but you should be able to find some loophole which will let us get away with a settlement for part of the face value."

"That'll mean a quick settlement. You'll have to give me sight drafts."

"I will. You'll be authorized to settle for any amount up to fifty percent of the face value." J. Barnaby peered suspiciously at his chief investigator. "That means up to the full amount of our cash reserves, but don't go getting careless with my money."

"If you're worried," Manning said, "you can always go yourself. I'll be glad to stay here and look after things."

"No, no," J. Barnaby said hurriedly. "I trust you, my boy. I merely meant that I didn't want you to rush things on this job. Take your time."

"Okay," Manning said. "Where are the papers?"

"Here they are. I've also arranged for the spaceport to have your ship ready. Have a nice trip, my boy."

"Sure. Tell Vega I'll see her when I get back." Manning laughed at J. Barnaby's struggle to keep the smile on his face. He waved and left.

CHAPTER TWO

A T THE SPACEPORT, his ship, the *Alpha Actuary*, was already on the launching rack. Since she was always kept fully stocked and supplied, all he had to do was get in and leave.

He stepped in through the airlock, then hesitated. A tiny light was gleaming on the instrument panel.

Manning Draco stepped to the panel and seemed to be checking the instruments. Actually, he was using a small built-in telemeter. When he read the results, he grinned. He switched on his port microphone.

"*Alpha Actuary* to launching tower," he said. "Delayed takeoff. Five minutes."

"Delayed takeoff granted," said a voice from his loudspeaker.

Manning left the ship and walked briskly toward the main terminal. He returned within the five minutes, humming beneath his breath as he entered the ship. He closed the outer and inner doors of the air-lock and cleared with the tower. Within a minute, his ship was racing up the launching rack.

By the time he was well above the atmosphere of Terra, his ship had worked out the coordinates of Caph II and the position had been fed into the automatic pilot. Manning switched the ship to magnidrive and relaxed.

"All right," he said loudly. "We are beyond the legal limits of Terra. You can come out now."

For a moment nothing happened. Then the door to the tiny bathroom slid to one side and Vega Cruikshahk stepped out. She was wearing nylene coveralls which did almost as much for her figure as the absence of covering in her Festival costume had accomplished. She looked annoyed. "You're so smart, Manning Draco," she said. "How did you know I was here?"

Manning grinned and pointed to the instrument panel. "The spy ray[14] told me somebody was aboard. A telemeter analysis gave me enough more to know it was a woman. I guessed it might be you. And hoped."

"You're not angry with me?" she asked.

"Are you kidding?" he said. "It's the best thing that's happened since last Friday night."

---

14   Manning Draco had the spy ray installed after he discovered a stowaway in the ship when he was returning from Pollux.

SHE WENT over and kissed him on the forehead. She danced out of reach, laughing as he tried to slip his arm around her.

"Uh-uh," she said. "I sneaked aboard your ship because I couldn't stand Daddy making like the heavy-handed father. I decided to teach him a lesson."

Manning looked at her. "Was that the only reason?" he asked.

She flushed. "No," she said softly. "But let's leave it this way for a while. I've heard all of Daddy's horrendous tales about your love affairs. It doesn't bother me, but I don't want to be another one in your life. Maybe the fun we had was all the Festival. I wanted to find out."

"Okay," Manning said—to his own surprise. "We'll just play it your way, honey."

"I like you, Mr. Draco," she said lightly. "Now tell me all about wherever we're going."

"There's practically nothing to tell you," Manning said. "It's a Class G planet, so it's not a part of the Federation and won't be unless it's reclassified. But all that means in reality is that the planet doesn't have the sort of natural resources or artifacts which we want badly enough to devise legal methods of getting them as cheaply as possible. In spite of that, however, they may be in their own way as highly advanced as we are. Or they may not be. Any classification higher than K does indicate that the dominant species is highly intelligent, though."

"That's all?"

"Your father mentioned that the Caphians are semihumanoid, so they're probably evolved from some sort of animal life. There is one other small thing. Their time rate is slightly different than ours. If we stay on Caph II for five months, say, we'll arrive back home to find that we've been gone from there only one week. It would be a convenient spot for philandering husbands."

Vega frowned. "You mean we might be gone only a week, but we'll get five months older in that time?"

Manning laughed. "I don't think it'll work exactly like that.[15] You're young enough to risk a few months anyway."

"I'm nineteen," she said indignantly.

"Okay," he said, grinning at her. "Now, since you're turning this into some sort of a companionate test, let's see how you do in the galley. It's lunchtime."

She made a face at him and went into the tiny galley set in the rear of the ship. As Manning well knew, the supplies on his ship were chosen with an eye on efficiency rather than luxury; but when she served lunch thirty minutes later it might have been something he'd ordered from the menu of the Venusian Palace Hotel in Nyork.

"Vega, my love," he said when he had cleaned up the last possible crumb, "that was a superb meal. If you're that good in every matrimonial department, I might even consent to marry you."

"Assuming," she said demurely, "that you've demonstrated your own ability as well and *I've* consented to marry you."

He laughed. "There's just one thing I'd like to know, Vega. How did you manage to duplicate Izaran pastry on the supplies I carry?"

"Oh, it was easy," she said airily. She eyed his grin steadily; then broke down and giggled. "In fact, the whole meal was easy. I merely ordered the frozen specialty from Daddy's luncheon club and brought it with me when I came aboard."

"Charging it to J. Barnaby's account, I trust?"

She nodded.

"Smart, too," Manning said. "J. Barnaby should be glad to

---

15 Manning's guess was a good one. As Hansel Pupik later proved, in what is now known as the Third Law of Pupik, the time coordinates of Caph II, Caph I, and the rest of the galaxy act upon one another in such a manner that the visitor to Caph II ages according to the time of his point of origin. Thus a visitor from Terra could spend ten months on Caph II and would be only two weeks older since that would be the amount of Terra-Time consumed. The proof of this is so simple anyone can work it out for himself. Take the prime of the Caphian Time-Fracture (see Glossary), multiply by the radical of the spatial coordinates of Caph carried to the nth power of a and subtract 2.

get rid of you, instead of looking like an exploding star when I mentioned your name."

"It's all right, Manning?"

"Sure, kitten," he said. "Who wants a cook for his best girl? We can always scare up the price of a sandwich—even if we have to borrow it from your father."

Together they carried the dirty dishes into the galley and dumped them into the dry-wash. Then he took her around the small ship, showing her all of its special features. He was justly proud of the *Alpha Actuary*, having designed most of it himself, and she was properly appreciative.

A FEW HOURS later, the ship flashed out of magnidrive and hovered five hundred miles above Caph II. Manning and Vega bent over the viewing screen and looked at the planet below. Bathed in the bright light of Caph, it looked like a huge spinning ball. Most of what they could see was a deep blue, with here and there patches of pink. The viewing screen magnified considerably, so that they could tell the pink spots were the lakes and rivers. Despite the magnification, however, they could see nothing that resembled a city.

"That's strange," Manning muttered. He went to his communications system and switched it on. He sent out a call to the planet below, but there was no answer. He tried several languages, in addition to Terran, and finally the intergalactic sound code. There was still no answer.

"Don't tell me this is another Atik," he exclaimed.

"Atik?" Vega asked. "What's that?"

"A star system in Preseus," Manning said. "It's probably the dullest planet in the galaxy. Even the Atikans are bored all the time.[16] But I mentioned it because the Atikans reproduce by

---

16 The Atikans reproduce by the simplest form of fission, which takes place once a year and lasts about two weeks, all of the race reproducing at the same time. It can be said, therefore, that once a year every Atikan literally falls apart. During that time all business is at a standstill, resulting in the now well-worn joke about the store that is "closed for the duration of the fission season." As to the

transverse fission and during such periods everything is closed, even the spaceport."

He went back to the viewing screen and began an instrument check of the planet. After a moment, he grunted.

"It moves around its sun so that the same side is always toward it," he said. "We're on the light side, now, so I guess we'd better try the dark side. Although I don't know why anyone would live on the dark side of a planet."

"Maybe it's too hot on this side," Vega suggested.

He shook his head. "I just tested it. The temperature is only seventy-five. According to that, it must be pretty damn cold on the other side." He sent the ship hurtling toward the other side of the planet. Since they weren't using magnidrive, the trip took almost an hour. When the ship once more stopped and they went to the viewing screen there was nothing to see. They were enveloped in darkness, without even a moon to brighten the surface of the planet below. Manning increased the power of the viewing screen and they could see tiny rows of lights.

"Looks like that might be lights in buildings," Manning said. "Let's see." He went to the communicating set and switched it on. *Alpha Actuary* to the planet Caph II," he said. "Terran Manning Draco and passenger requesting permission to land."

This time he got an answer. "Okay, chum," a voice said from the loudspeaker. "Bring her in and set her down." The voice spoke excellent Terran, although there was a rather squeaky quality to the voice itself.

"How about a landing beam?" Manning asked.

"No got, sweetheart. You'll have to fly her down by the seat of your pants. Aim for longitude seventy-five, latitude twenty-one. Roger."

boredom of the Atikans, many authorities attribute this to the fact that they have never discovered sex. This is probably true, but there was a period in Terran history when Atikans were the favorite heroes of certain fiction for just this reason. As one ardent fan of the time so aptly put it: "Who wants to read a boy-gets-girl story? Everybody knows what happens when he gets her. Who wants a nice action story all loused up with that stuff? Huh?"

His choice of language, Manning noted, was a bit archaic.

MANNING DRACO was a good pilot, although it was not often that he had to demonstrate it. Space flights were all handled by automatic pilots, and practically all launchings and landings were controlled by a launching tower beam. But Manning took the ship down on instruments and landed her exactly where he'd been told to. A scarlet pip flashed on the landing screen as they touched ground.

Vega Cruikshank was still standing by the viewing screen, staring intently into it.

"Still nothing in sight," she said. "Even the tiny lights we could see from above have vanished."

"Maybe they forgot to turn on the field lights," Manning said. He was busy at the instrument panel. He rechecked the contents of the air outside. The variation from Terra was slight. Then he made a temperature check.

"That's funny," he said. "It's seventy-five degrees here, too. By rights, it should be extremely cold. Well, honey, let's go out and see what we've drawn."

He pressed a button and they stepped to the air-lock as the doors opened. Then they were at the very exit of the ship—and could still see nothing.

They were surrounded by a darkness so complete that it was like a black curtain before their eyes.

"Manning," Vega said, speaking in almost a whisper, "Do—do you think it's all right?"

"Sure, honey," he said softly. He didn't feel as much confidence as he put in his voice. He was certain that Dzanku Dzanku was not there; but it was many months since he'd heard anything about Sam Warren, and this could be a trap. But he didn't want to frighten Vega. "Maybe we've run across a race that has no sight. That would explain it."

"Welcome, Manning Draco," a voice boomed somewhere in front of them. "Welcome to Optville of Opt. We feared that you would not get here in time."

Manning got the last remark, but he ignored it for the moment.

"Where are you?" he asked. "Also, where in hell are the lights?"

"We are most sorry," the same voice said. "We have few visitors from other planets—this is only the fourth visit by Terrans—and we have never installed any exterior lights. But I am right here."

Manning felt his hand grabbed and pumped up and down. The hand in his clasp seemed similar to that of humans, although he got the impression that the fingers were unusually long.

"I note," the voice continued, "that your companion is a Terran female. She is most attractive."

"How can he tell?" Vega whispered.

"Maybe they can see in the dark," Manning answered.

"Oh, no," the voice said. "We do have vision, but we cannot see in the dark. We can, however, easily perceive your structures through the emission of high-frequency sound, the echoes of which inform us as to the nearness and shape of objects. I believe it is similar to something which you Terrans call sonar."

"Very interesting," Manning said. "Please excuse us a moment. We forgot something." He drew Vega with him back into the ship. He opened a locker in the control room and drew out an energy torch. He also slipped another small object into his pocket. They went back through the air-lock.

"I hope," he said, addressing his remarks to the general darkness, "that you won't mind if we use a light?"

"Not at all," the voice said politely from the darkness.

Manning pressed the switch on the torch and a swath of light fanned out from the ship.

They got their first glimpse of a Caphian.

CHAPTER THREE

H E STOOD directly in front of them. He was perhaps a little more than five feet in height. His general outlines were humanoid. The hands were shaped like those of a human, although the fingers were elongated and there were small webs between the fingers. His face was small, rather pointed, with a broad nose and tiny eyes. Light brown hair covered most of his face. The most surprising feature were the ears. They stood up from his head like two huge paddles, being fully twice as long as the face.

The Caphian wore the pants and coat of a full dress suit, but these were his only clothing. Beyond him stood a number of other Caphians, all differently attired. There was one wearing an old-fashioned bathing suit. Some wore a pair of pants or a coat, though none wore both. One wore only a vest, while another was attired only in a pair of yellow shoes.

Manning heard Vega suppress a giggle, but he paid no attention. He turned back to the Caphian who stood nearest.

"Thank you for the welcome," he said gravely. "I presume you know my name from the fact that I announced it to your spaceport, but may I know yours?"

"Of course. I am Phyllos Stopter, official welcomer to you, Manning Draco."

"I'm happy to meet you," Manning said. "My companion is Vega Cruikshank."

"We are also welcoming her—although she was not predicted."

"She *is* a bit unpredictable," Manning said dryly, "but just what do you mean? While you're at it, you might also explain why you were afraid I wouldn't get here in time."

"Of course," Phyllis Stopter said amiably. "Twenty years ago it was predicted that you would come to visit us. It was decreed that twenty years and seven days from the founding of our new government we would hold an election and that you would arrive before the election was held. Today is the seventh day and we were afraid that you might not arrive. But we should have had more faith in the words of our Great Gray Father."

"So it was predicted that I'd come," Manning said slowly. "As if I didn't know, what was the name of this Great Gray Father of yours who made this prediction?"

"The Great Gray Father called himself Dzanku Dzanku, before he felt himself called upon to lead us to the true life."

"I thought so," Manning. "Did he make any other predictions?"

"Oh, many. But they will all be reviewed at our election meeting tonight and you can hear them. The Great Gray Father will be there and perhaps he will make new predictions."

"I'm afraid he may disappoint you by not being available," Manning said. Manning felt safe in assuming that Dzanku Dzanku was out of circulation for some time to come. It was only four months since he'd arranged for a slave raider to take Dzanku to Andromeda to serve in the Pleasure Camps of that galaxy. Escape is practically impossible from the Camps, so he felt sure that Dzanku would be there for his full five years.

"The Great Gray Father will never disappoint us," the Caphian said firmly. "Now, if you're ready, we will take you to your hotel.

As soon as you know where you're to stay, we can go on to the election meeting." He hesitated. "Since your companion was not mentioned in the prediction, we did not make a reservation for her. Will she share your bed or do you wish other arrangements? You will forgive the question ... the sex habits of you Terrans are strange to me."

"Sometimes they're even strange to us," Manning said with a grin. "Miss Cruikshank would like separate rooms."

"It will be done," the Caphian said. "Come."

PHYLLOS STOPTER, Vega Cruikshank, and Manning Draco walked across the field, with Manning flashing the torch ahead of them. The remaining Caphians walked closely behind them.

After a short walk, they came to a long, wheeled vehicle. The driver's section was entirely open, with the rest of it enclosed. Inside there were a good fifteen seats arranged in a circle. Manning and Vega took seats inside and the Caphians crowded in after them. As the vehicle started, Manning snapped off the torch. He would have preferred leaving it on, but he thought it might bother them at such close range.

"I suppose," he said, "that Dzanku is responsible for the fact that you speak Terran?"

"Oh, yes," Phyllos Stopter said out of the darkness. "The Great Gray Father was kind enough to introduce us to many of the latest things from the rest of the galaxy."

"The clothes, too?"

"Yes. In our ignorance, we never wore clothes until he pointed out to us that it was done everywhere else. So then we ordered the latest fashion. I have noticed that your own clothes are somewhat more elaborate than ours. I suppose fashions do change somewhat in twenty years."

"Somewhat," Manning said, smothering a desire to laugh. "What else did your Great Gray Father palm off on you?"

"We bought a number of something called films which show the way you Terrans run your government and the way you live your everyday lives. Very interesting. We have adopted some of the practices, but not all. There were, of course, the language courses. And any number of small trifles."

"I'll bet," Manning said dryly. Dzanku was always the one for turning a profit any way he could. "Are these the sum total of his blessings?"

"The most important of all was that he showed us the most pleasurable practice of what you call a twenty-year-endowment policy. And, of course, taxes."

"Of course, taxes," Manning said. "You mean that Dzanku also intended to take a cut of your money on the policies?"

"Only the tax of fifty percent—which we know is an honorable tribute paid to the head of the government in your part of the galaxy. A most fair arrangement, we felt. After all, we each invested only one thousand credits, your money, in order to receive ten thousand credits, now. But all of this must seem very ordinary to you since it is done everywhere."

"At least everywhere that Dzanku can find enough suckers," Manning said. "But right now, Phyllos Stopter, I am more interested in you Caphians. I don't believe I've ever encountered any race exactly like yours. I'd like to know more about it."

Manning was genuinely interested, but he also wanted to keep his mind off the fact that the vehicle was apparently racing along at a terrific speed, guided only by some primitive form of sonar.

"We know little ourselves," the Caphian confessed. "But according to the Great Gray Father, we are evolved from a race which you on Terra know as the Chiroptera.[17] I believe that he

17 As it was later discovered, the Caphians were evolved from a race closely related to the order *Chiroptera*, genus *Euderma maculata*, more commonly known on Terra as the Spotted Bat. Physically, however the Caphians had progressed almost as far along the evolutionary scale as we have from our origins. They had completely lost their wings, the only reminder being tiny webbing between their fingers. Their faces still somewhat resembled those of the *Euderma maculata*, but were considerably more refined. The only feature that was relatively unchanged was the huge ears, with the complicated structure known as antitragi, or "false ears." The Caphians also shared one trait with their more primitive kind on Terra: As Manning was to discover, they were all especially secretive about where they lived. For hundreds of years, the Spotted Bat on Terra was never traced to its rest-

also mentioned that they are sometimes called bats. A most intelligent race, he said."

"Mmmm," Manning said, hoping it would be taken for an affirmative. "When we arrived, we came out of magnidrive over the bright side of your planet. There was no answer to my signals. Do all of you live in the dark?"

"Doesn't everyone?" the Caphian asked in some surprise.

"Only figuratively," Manning said dryly. "I gather that means you do all live on this side of the planet?"

"Yes. I believe we always have. Occasionally, it's true, we go hunting on the bright side. But actually to live there would be... quite unthinkable."

"Another thing," Manning said. "I noticed that the temperature here is almost the same as on the other side. Actually, it should be colder."

"I believe there may have been a time when our ancestors liked a colder climate, but for more years than I know we have had underground furnaces heating this side of the planet."

The conversation was stopped from going farther by their arrival at the hotel.

"We were told that you wouldn't mind if we made a reservation for you," Phyllos Stopter said anxiously, "so we did. But if it does disturb you, we will go on and you can pick out a different one when we're away."

"This is fine," Manning said.

Phyllos Stopter and the welcoming committee left, promising to return soon to escort them to the election meeting. The clerk in the hotel showed them to their rooms, which were on the same floor and near to each other.

THE ROOMS weren't bad, despite being far below the better standards of the galaxy. The beds seemed rather crude affairs, but were quite soft and comfortable. Manning left Vega in her room and went on to his own.

---

ing place; like the Spotted Bat, the Caphians were also wholly nocturnal.

Another thing for which he was thankful was that the interior of the hotel was equipped with lights. They were set in the walls and gave off a very pale glow, but even the dimness was a relief after the solid wall of blackness outside.

There was a passable bath and Manning took a quick shower. Then he used his Glo-Shav, although it was difficult to see properly in the pale light from the walls. He changed clothes and was about to go along to knock on Vega's door when she came to his.

She had changed into a blue semi-evening frock and, if it were possible, looked twice as beautiful as she had in coveralls.

"I know it isn't evening," she said, indicating her dress, "but it's dark enough so we can pretend it is."

Manning found her so attractive he was willing to pretend anything. Especially after she gave him a lingering kiss.

Within a few more minutes there was a knock on the door. When Manning opened the door it was Phyllos Stopter.

"I am most sorry," he said, "but I discover that there was also a prediction concerning the possible lateness of our Great Gray Father. Since he has not yet arrived, the elections will be delayed until he gets here. It should be soon, however."

"I told you he wouldn't be available," Manning said. "I'm sure that you'll be able to hold your elections anyway. In the meantime. I'd like to arrange a meeting with your leaders, or important citizens, to discuss this matter of your insurance policies. You know that I represent the insurance company?"

Phyllos nodded. "Oh, yes. The Great Gray Father said that we would be paid shortly after you came. So we knew that your arrival was a good sign."

"It may not be so good," Manning said. "I want to talk to you about it. Since it is obviously impossible for me to speak to each one of a hundred million policy holders, I'd like to get together with your authorities."

"I am sorry," the Caphian said, "but this is impossible. We cannot discuss it with you at all until the Great Gray Father is here."

"Why?"

"Because it was all predicted and we must not deviate from it. The predictions are sacred."

"But it can't hurt for me to talk with your authorities," Manning persisted.

"It is impossible," the Caphian said firmly. "Even if there weren't the predictions, it would be impossible. We have no authorities. All are elected for twenty years—except, of course, the Great Gray Father, who remains our superior—and their terms of office have expired. We will have no authorities until the election is held. Now, I'm sure that you will find everything very comfortable. We will notify you the minute the elections are to be held."

He bowed and quickly left the room.

Manning muttered under his breath, then grinned at Vega. "And there," he said, "you have a good example of the romance of interplanetary existence. Oh, well, we might as well start looking around. Maybe we can pick up something that will give me an advantage when these characters finally get around to admitting that Dzanku isn't coming. Let's do the town, honey."

CHAPTER FOUR

MANNING DRACO soon found that his thought had been overly optimistic. Nowhere in the large city of Optville could they find a single individual who would talk to them about the insurance policies—or about anything else of recent date. The Caphians, he discovered, had built a calendar around the first appearance of Dzanku. The present was, therefore, the year 20 A.G.G.F. (After the Great Gray Father) and everything that happened earlier was B.G.G.F. They were all quite willing to discuss B.G.G.F. events with him, but he could learn nothing about the past twenty years. Not even the form of political government they had.

It was difficult to think of time in terms of days where everything outdoors was always black night and indoors was a pale glow barely enough to see by. But it was obvious that days were slipping by.

The food on Caph II was slightly exotic but not unpalatable, and they soon came to enjoy it after a fashion. Their rooms were comfortable. Except for their own company, there was practically no entertainment. Early in their visit, there was some sort of festival in one large building which they found by accident. But it turned out to have for a climax the execution of a Caphian. The only thing they could learn about the execution was that the victim was described as *the* Public Enemy.

There were a number of buildings where they could see old Terran motion pictures. These were not documentaries, as Manning had thought from Phyllos Stopter's description, but old comedies, Westerns, and mysteries from around the twentieth century on Terra. Many of them Manning and Vega had seen in the Ancient Terra Museum in Nyork, and these prints were especially bad, so they didn't enjoy sitting through a squawking soundtrack.

As for the rest, there just was no entertainment. There were a few public restaurants, but they served nothing but food. The Caphians apparently played no games and had no regular social gatherings.

In general, the Caphians seemed a strange mixture of advancement and primitiveness. On the one hand, there was the matter of their underground furnaces which kept half a planet at even temperature—an advanced engineering project. There was also a fairly complicated vehicle which could travel on the ground and was capable of short flights. But their engineering seemed to stop there.

As far as Manning could learn, they'd had no government of any sort before the appearance of Dzanku. With the realization that Dzanku had apparently set up their government, Manning, began to have nightmares about what it would be like.

DESPITE THE EVIDENCE of the execution of a public enemy, Manning could find no record of crime. That didn't mean it hadn't existed, for the Caphians had no written language and therefore had no records of any sort. And, in keeping with this, they were completely lacking in the traditions which played such an important part in most cultures throughout the galaxies. This made it far more difficult to judge what they might do in any situation.

Their architecture—from what he could see of it in torch-light—was interesting in a somewhat mad fashion. This was the result, he later realized, of building in terms of sound reflection rather than sight. None of the buildings possessed numbers, nor were the streets named. But there was enough variation so that the Caphians could recognize a street or a building from the way their supersonic sound emissions bounced back.

If it hadn't been for a growing interest in each other, Vega and Manning would have soon been bored. As it was, a couple of weeks slipped quickly by. They slept when they were sleepy, ate when hungry, and spent all of their waking time getting to know each other better.

Then Phyllos Stopter showed up again.

"I have come to take you to the election meeting," he said.

"You mean Dzanku Dzanku is here?" Manning asked.

"No, but he will arrive soon," the Caphian said.

He led them to a large building in the center of the city. There were probably five thousand Caphians gathered there. Like all of the other buildings, this one was dimly lighted.

"This will not be exactly an election," he explained. "It is what I believe you call a nominating meeting. The election will be held tomorrow, but since we will nominate only one individual for each office, it makes little difference."

He led them up to a platform in front, where a number of Caphians were already seated. They were introduced to Macro Moptad, Vespe Troptyl, Eptes Boptsie, Pipis Loptmor, Lasion Coptna, and Nycter Memoptera, in that order.

"It is they," Phyllos explained as he guided them to seats on the platform, "who will make the actual nominations. They are known as the Committee Which Lives But to Serve the Great Gray Father."

"Very smooth," Manning admitted. "With this setup, Dzanku doesn't even need to stuff ballot boxes. Tell me, when will it be possible to learn something about this mysterious government of yours?"

He was beginning to be genuinely curious about it. During the delay, he'd even tried to probe the minds of the Caphians, but they proved to be nontelepaths with natural mind shields which were impenetrable.

"Right now," Phyllos Stopter said promptly. "As soon as it is officially election day, the matters may be discussed. What would you like to know?"

"First, what sort of government do you have?"

"I believe the Great Gray Father called it a democracy."

"I'll bet," Manning said dryly. "What is Dzanku's function in all this?"

"He assists in our elections and advises us on all matters. In return for this, he collects all the taxes. Naturally, we accept his advice on all matters since he is far wiser than we are. At our first election, in return for all the things he has done for us, we confirmed the fact that he is our Great Gray Father in perpetuity. All other officers are elected every twenty years. In the few offices where vacancies occur rather often, substitutes are appointed as needed."

"Who is your top officer—after the Great Gray Father, of course?" Manning asked.

"The Private Eye."

MANNING LOOKED at him in amazement. Then he got it, and quickly rubbed a hand over his face to hide his grin. He glanced at Vega who seemed to be busily stuffing her handkerchief in her mouth.

"Very interesting," Manning said gravely. "How did you happen to pick on that particular office to head your government?"

"It seemed the obvious choice," Phyllos said. "In so many of the films showing the way of life on Terra, the Private Eye was the most respected authority of all, even though you apparently refused to recognize this officially. In patterning ourselves after you, we have corrected this oversight."

"I see," Manning said. He wondered how much extra profit Dzanku had made from the old films by passing them off as authentic pictures of Terran life.

The Caphian glanced around the platform, then lowered his voice. "I have, however, a confession to make," he said.

"Yes?" Manning said helpfully.

"At our first election we were unable to find a suitable candidate to become the Private Eye, so our highest office was unfilled during the past twenty years. Since none of us is fitted to be the Private Eye, the Great Gray Father promised to bring us a candidate—perhaps for this election. Isn't that thrilling?"

"Very," Manning said. "But why aren't any of you capable of being the Private Eye?"

"Why, it's obvious," exclaimed the Caphian. He pointed to his own face. "Our eyes are so public."

"I should have guessed it," Manning said apologetically. "Who ruled, then, in the absence of both the Great Gray Father and a Private Eye?"

"The Private Eye's consort and the other officials made out as best they could."

"And they are—?"

"The Private Eye's consort is the Naked Blonde. Then there's the Cop, the Dick, the D.A., the Stern Old Judge, the Cowboy, the Old Rancher, the Virtuous Maiden, the Kindly Old Doctor, and John's Other Wife. Of course, we also elect a Public Enemy and a Rustler."

There were choking sounds from Manning's left. He kicked Vega gently on the shins.

"Miss Cruikshank occasionally has mild choking attacks," he explained to the Caphian. "You were saying?"

"I mentioned that we also elect a Public Enemy and a Rustler. While their capture is really the responsibility of the officers, I must say that our entire population joins enthusiastically in the pursuit. It's really great fun. Of course, when they're finally caught, we appoint another Public Enemy or Rustler."

MANNING SUDDENLY remembered the execution he and Vega had witnessed. "Wait a minute," he said. "You mean you really go through with it all the way? You elect them, then chase them down and execute them?"

"Of course," Phyllos Stopter said with dignity. "Crime Does Not Pay."

"It still seems to me that you're carrying it pretty far for a game," Manning said. "How do the victims feel about it?"

"They fully realize that it's an Honor and a Privilege to be Strung Up or Put in the Hot Seat, according to the ritual." The Caphian frowned. "We've had only one spoil-sport in the twenty years. He went, to the light side of our planet, which is, of course, out of bounds. I believe he starved to death there. It served him right."

"Who makes your laws?" Manning wanted to know.

"We elect two groups. The first group passes our more formal laws. They are known as the Seven Deadly Sins. The second group take matters into their own hands when the first group fails to act promptly. They are known as the Vigilantes."

"Tell me," Manning said, "does the other planet in this system operate the same way?"

"I don't know," Phyllos Stopter said. "We never go there. One of our ancestors built a ship which would make the trip to our first planet, but when he returned the ship was destroyed. By his reckoning he had spent one week there, but here a hundred years had passed."[18]

---

18   As Prof. Fignewton proved, Caph II was the focal point of the Time-Fracture with the time-distortion being reversed as you traveled away from the planet in any direction. This process was, however, immensely speeded up in the direction of the sun of the Caph system. Whereas the ratio between Caph II and Terra was 20 to 1, between Caph II and Caph I it was 5200 to 1. Therefore, while a

"All of this is very interesting," Manning said. "But now, how about getting down to my reason for being here? Since this is some sort of an official body, perhaps I can discuss the insurance policies with them before the election starts."

The Caphian shook his head. "We cannot discuss it when the Great Gray Father is not present; although I suppose that if you are prepared to make the payments on the policies now, we could accept that."

"That is what I would like to discuss," Manning said grimly. "There is at least one glaring irregularity about the policies—I mean that Dzanku sold you the policies with an agreement that he was to get half of what you collected. As a matter of fact, this whole business smacks of fraud. We might, as a gesture of good will, pay something on each policy, but certainly not the face value."

The Caphian was gazing at him with an expression which seemed to indicate delight. Even his paddle-shaped ears were quivering. "This is wonderful," he exclaimed. "The Great Gray Father not only predicted that you would arrive here, but he also predicted that you would speak just as you have. Is this not a miracle?"

"Not so much a miracle," Manning said sourly. "Dzanku knew what he was doing so well that it was easy to predict what we'd think. Well, if you won't discuss it, we might as well leave. I think you've told me enough so we can throw it into court."

"I'm sorry," Phyllos Stopter said. "It was predicted that you might try to leave, and it was agreed that it could not be permitted. You'll have to stay here, until the Great Gray Father arrives."

"That's out of the question," Manning snapped. "In the first place, your Great Gray Father isn't coming—"

He was interrupted by a roar from the crowd.

"You are quite wrong," Phyllos Stopter said happily. "Here he comes now."

---

week passed on Caph I a hundred years passed on Caph II and five years passed on Terra.

CHAPTER FIVE

IT WAS TRUE. Manning could only gape at the three figures who were walking toward the platform. The one in the lead was a Rigelian and was certainly Dzanku Dzanku. Directly behind the Rigelian strode a Terran. He was short and thin. His face, which usually wore a tense, wary expression, was split in a broad grin of triumph.

The third member of the trio was a stranger to Manning Draco. He was a native of the Sabikian System. He stood only about four feet high; his body was slender and round from top to bottom. The upper half of his body and all of his head were completely covered with straight platinum blond hair, all of which grew from the top of his head and fell downward so that he resembled an upturned mop. A pair of tentacles protruded from the hair, but that was all that managed to penetrate the growth. His two feet were more like short flippers, but he seemed to have no trouble keeping up with the Rigelian and the Terran.[19]

The three of them marched up on the platform and over to Manning Draco. Sam Warren and the Sabikian halted just back of Dzanku Dzanku.

"My dear Manning," Dzanku said. "What a pleasure to see you again. And who, may I ask, is your charming companion?"

"Miss Vega Cruikshank," Manning said. He turned to the girl. "Vega, this is the celebrated Dzanku Dzanku. The rather skinny little runt behind him is Sam Warren. I'm afraid I'm not acquainted with the small fugitive from a barber shop."

"May I present Pisha-Paisha," Dzanku said. "A colleague of mine from Sabik."

---

19   Sabikians are unrelated to any life form known on Terra. They are a sightless race; thus it makes little difference that their hair covers the face. Like the Caphians, they are naturally equipped with a sort of sonar. This, plus acute hearing and minor telepathic powers, enables them to do just as well without sight. Although extremely intelligent and highly advanced, the Sabikians are an aggressive, antisocial race. While the rest of the galaxy carries on considerable trade with the Sabikians, every merchant ship going to the system of Sabik has to be accompanied by a patrol ship.

"Hello," boomed the Sabikian, his deep bass voice issuing from somewhere back of the blond hair.

"Hey," Sam Warren said in tones of admiration. "She's some dish. That Manning always was a picker, eh?"

"Decidedly," Dzanku said. He gave a courtly bow to Vega. "Miss Cruikshank, it is a pleasure to meet the charming daughter of such a brilliant father. I trust that you will not permit yourself to be prejudiced toward me by the opinions of your father and Manning. They are so persistent."

While Dzanku was speaking to Vega, Manning Draco made his first move—an attempt to learn what the Rigelian planned. He tried a fast mental probe of Sam Warren. The little Terran winced under the impact, but Manning learned nothing. As usual, the important synapses had been erased clean by Dzanku. Manning switched and struck at the Sabikian. He was met with such a blast of malevolence that he withdrew in self-defense.

"Vicious little character, isn't he?" Dzanku asked, having missed none of the byplay.

EXPECTING NOTHING, but feeling the need for some action, Manning slashed a probe at the Rigelian, but the latter's shield stopped it. Purely out of reflex action, Dzanku struck back. Manning felt the surge of mental power against his own secondary shield; then it withdrew.

"We are worthy foes," Dzanku said. "Of all those whom I've fought, you are the one I most respect, Manning. The only Terran who has ever developed a secondary mind shield—the only non-Rigelian who has ever penetrated my shield, even though you did it the once by trickery. Yes, I shall regret your final defeat."

"It won't come from you," Manning said. "How did you get out of Andromeda?"

"It was relatively simple," Dzanku said. "I merely found a rich patroness who took me out of the Pleasure Camp for use in her own private harem. I invaded her mind and took possession of it. She told everyone that she and I were going away for the weekend and she then piloted me to Rigel IV. I've written a little something[20] about it and I would have brought you an autographed copy, but they weren't ready yet."

"I am desolated," Manning said. "This is some sweet little setup you have here, Dzanku."

"I like it," Dzanku said.

"You don't really expect to get away with it, do you?" Manning went on. "The fraud is pretty obvious. As soon as I report the situation to the Committee on Extraplanetary Affairs, they'll certainly cut the claims in half—if they don't throw the whole thing out."

"Ah, but I do expect to get away with it," Dzanku said. "The Committee has already given J. Barnaby thirty days in which to pay off. This will stand as long as they have no evidence to make them reverse their decision. You, my dear Manning, are not going to make your report before those thirty days are up—if at all. Incidentally, there are guards posted at the spaceport, so I'm afraid you can't make a run for it."

"What are you going to do?" Manning asked.

"You'll soon see," Dzanku promised. If Rigelians were capable of smiling, Manning was sure that Dzanku would have been smiling as he turned and walked to the center of the platform. He held up three tentacles and the murmur of voices died down.

"My dear ones," he said, "I, your Great Gray Father, have returned even as I promised you I would. As was predicted in my Epistle to the Caphians, I was somewhat delayed, but I bring good news which will more than make up for the delay of the elections. After twenty years of being without a proper head for your government, I bring you one who is perfectly equipped to serve as your Private Eye. Never have you seen one whose eyes were more private. I give you your friend and mine—Pisha-Paisha."

---

20 *I Was a Love Slave,* the uninhibited memoirs of a victim of the Andromedan sex practices, by Dzanku Dzanku. Published by Doublelightyear & Company, $2.25. Available at all galactic bookstores. (Adv.)

There was a roar from the crowd as the Sabikian stepped forward.

"Good Chiroptera," Pisha-Paisha said in his booming bass voice. "I come before you wearing no man's collar, dedicated to no program save that of your welfare and amusement. If elected, I promise—"

"Pipe down," Dzanku said, covering his mouth with a tentacle. "I make all the speeches here. Besides, it's in the bag."

THE SABIKIAN withdrew to the back of the platform. It was impossible to tell if he was disappointed.

Dzanku said, "I, therefore, nominate Pisha-Paisha as your Private Eye, to serve for the next twenty years."

There was a roar of approval from the crowd.

"Now for the other nominations," Dzanku continued. "For the office of the Naked Blonde, I nominate Coryno Preoptsis." There was another roar of approval. Such roars continued to go up after each name was mentioned: "For the Cop, Dasyp Throptsora; for the Dick, Euder Zopta; for D.A., Nycti Wonopter; Myo Cranoptsa as the Stern Old Judge; Mega Optopta as the Cowboy; Molossid Choroptsyl as the Old Rancher; for the Virtuous Maiden, Antroz Anoptical; the Kindly Old Doctor, Nycter Memoptera; Lasion Coptna as John's Other Wife."

Everybody was obviously nominated unanimously. The same applied to the seven names Dzanku rattled off for the Seven Deadly Sins and for the twenty names he mentioned for the Vigilantes. Then he paused, and there was an atmosphere of expectation in the room.

"Now," Dzanku said, "I wish to nominate our good friend, Eptes Boptsie, as the Rustler." There was a burst of applause. "And as Public Enemy, I present a man whom you will come to love as much as I do—Manning Draco."

The applause and shouting were deafening. Manning Draco was too stunned to do anything but stare.

"And now a special treat," Dzanku said. "This year we are creating a new office which should increase our future pleasure.

To serve simultaneously with the new Public Enemy, we are electing a Gangster's Moll. For this responsible position, we are nominating Miss Vega Cruikshank."

Applause and huzzas.

This time, Manning was on his feet by the time the sound had died down.

"Dzanku," he said, "you must have blown your jets. You can't get away with this bare-faced plan to murder Vega and myself. You know what will happen if you succeed in killing us. Not only will there be no payment of any kind, but J. Barnaby swings enough influence in galactic affairs to have this whole planet de-energized right out of existence by the patrol."

"The—ah—accident," Dzanku said, "will not be discovered until after we've collected the money. If you and Miss Cruikshank prove especially agile, it may not even *happen* before then. When it does, however, everyone will be quite upset about it. All sorts of apologies will go forth. I will feel quite badly myself, although I fear I won't be able to take part in the apologies and explanation. Pressing business will demand my presence elsewhere."

"So that's how it'll be," Manning said. He turned to face the crowd. "Caphians, don't you realize that Dzanku Dzanku is a famous galactic criminal? There are warrants out for his arrest on a dozen planets. He is now planning something which may cause your entire planet to be destroyed—but he will not be here to die with you."

There was a low murmur of anger from the crowd.

"Please," Dzanku said. "You are speaking of the Great Gray Father of Caph. You are making my friends angry."

MANNING HAD first thought that the tone he'd heard was directed against the Rigelian, but now he realized that the Caphians were glaring at him.

"Okay," he said to Dzanku, "you win that round. But at least let Miss Cruikshank leave the planet. She's done nothing against you."

"I want to stay with you, Manning," Vega said firmly.

"A proper sentiment," Dzanku said. "Besides, my dear Manning, although the question about Miss Cruikshank concerns not what she may have done against me in the past but rather of what she might do in the future, I still wouldn't think of interfering with such local matters. My dear Pisha-Paisha— as the new Private Eye, would you consider granting an amnesty to Miss Cruikshank?"

"No," boomed the Sabikian. "Justice must prevail. These people represent an element which must be wiped out to the last man—er—and the last woman. If I am elected—"

"I told you it was in the bag," Dzanku snapped rudely. He turned back to Manning before the latter could say anything. "I would suggest, my dear Manning, that you waste no more time in foolish argument. You see, on this planet, officers assume the mantle of their office before they are elected. Therefore, you have about an hour before the greatest manhunt—and womanhunt—in the history of Caph will begin. Out of a spirit of friendship, I suggest that you make use of that hour."

"Don't knock yourself out trying to do us a favor," Manning said. "Come on, Vega."

He took Vega's hand and they walked down through the crowd, which was now definitely unfriendly. Outside, he switched on his torch and hurried her down the street.

"Manning, what will we do?" Vega asked anxiously. "What can we do in only an hour? We haven't got a chance in this darkness...."

"Yes, we do," Manning said. They were already a couple of blocks away from the election building. "I took one precaution which Dzanku knows nothing about. We can't get off the planet, but we can get away from this part of it. Here, hold the torch."

She took it and Manning pulled something from his pocket. It was a small square box with two tiny knobs set into its face. Manning began manipulating the knobs.

"What's that?" Vega asked.

"Remote control, tuned to the life raft on the *Alpha Actuary.*

This will bring it to us. It'll be gone before the guards around the ship know what is happening. The raft doesn't have enough power to leave the planet, but it'll outfly any of the cracker-boxes these characters have. Keep the light up, so I don't bring it down on our heads."

In a few moments, the small life raft suddenly appeared out of the darkness. Manning moved the controls and it drifted slowly down to the ground beside them. They both climbed aboard. In the light of the torch, Manning set the controls of the raft. Then he clicked off the torch.

The raft rose swiftly above the dark city.

CHAPTER SIX

WITHIN THREE hours the blackness had turned to a murky gray. Only a few more minutes and the view was similar to that of a sunrise on Terra. The great sun of Caph appeared just over the horizon ahead of them. It was the first sight of sunlight they'd had in two weeks and they blinked in the bright glare.

He continued to fly for another hour over the bright side of Caph II. Then he brought the raft lower and searched for a landing place. He finally found one that suited him and brought the raft down on a stretch of blue soil near one of the little pink lakes. It was a spot slightly higher than the surrounding land, giving them a good view in every direction. And there was a cluster of towering purple trees which offered partial conceal-ment for them.

"Now what do we do?" Vega asked as they stepped out on the ground. "I must confess that I feel better just because there's some sunshine."

"Me, too," Manning said. "Although after a while it may become as tiring as the perpetual darkness. I guess the first thing to do is fix a place to live for the time being and then— I'm hungry. How about you?"

"I am—but what do we do about it? Do you suppose there's some game around? And will it be safe to eat it if there is?"

"Don't worry about game," Manning said. "This raft is meant to take care of the shipwrecked spaceman. I guess we fall into that category." He opened the rear of the raft and took out a tiny-square package. "This, believe it or not, is a very fine tent."

He opened valves on the package and they greedily sucked in air, filling the walls of the tent. When the walls were rigid, he set it beneath the purple trees. It made a snug little shack, eight feet long and six feet wide, with air-filled walls and an air-cushioned floor. Vermin-proof and insect-proof.

"Home was never like this," Manning said as they surveyed it. "Now, for that dinner." He took a small telemeter from the raft and twisted the controls, watching the dials. "We have a choice of a number of dehydrated morsels, which the Spacemen's Service guarantees to give us the proper diet. They say nothing about the taste, so I think I'd rather have a steak. How about you?"

"A steak?" Vega said. "You're kidding."

"Never," he said seriously. He was busily dragging small items from the raft. "Steak, I think, *and* a tossed green salad, with perhaps a raw egg added to the dressing." A small piece of metal unfolded into a cooking plate. Other pieces buckled together and mysteriously became a servomotor. Manning set the controls on it and then stood back with a gesture. The servomotor hummed pleasantly.

There were hazy lines on the platform of the servomotor. They coalesced and became a steak, juicy and red. Manning removed it and waited for a second one.

"Manning," Vega exclaimed. "You're wonderful."

"Not me," he said modestly. "Science. It plucks protein and iron and calcium, and all the little things the Spacemen's Service struggle so hard to dehydrate, from the air and makes a steak." He pulled the second one from the platform and shut off the servomotor. "How would you like yours, honey?"

"Medium rare," she said. "You're making me feel ever so much better, Manning. I was feeling very isolated and pioneering and despairing, but we're going to be all right—aren't we?"

"Maybe," Manning grunted. He slipped the two steaks on the cooking plate and set its controls. He pulled some tiny packages from the raft and selected one. "You might as well know the best and the worst, honey. Thanks to the raft, we'll have a reasonably comfortable place to sleep. We have enough food or means of getting food to last us for almost two years if necessary. We have a small energy gun which will hold off any direct attacks—especially since I don't think the Caphians have much in the way of weapons and the *Alpha Actuary* is locked so they can't use her. Water can't represent a very serious problem. We even have a small emergency communication set which will reach out about a thousand miles—enough if someone comes looking for us. I don't think Dzanku Dzanku can do very much about dislodging us. On the other hand, we can't do much but sit here unless someone comes after us."

He was fiddling, with the servomotor again.

"You'll think of something," Vega said confidently.

MANNING WINCED. "For a moment, you sounded exactly like your father—but I'll overlook it," he said magnanimously. He turned on the servomotor and it upended and began burrowing into the ground. It quickly disappeared, sending a stream of blue sand spurting up behind it.

They watched it without speaking. After a while the servomotor climbed up out of the small, round hole it had made in the ground. Manning turned it off and opened a container in it. There, was a small amount of pink fluid in it. He examined it with the telemeter.

"Well, aside from the color," he said, "it's very like Terran water, so I guess we can drink it. Maybe the color will grow on us." He took a short, thin section of pipe from the raft. He pulled on the ends. It telescoped out. He thrust it down into the hole made by the servomotor. He held a cup near the top of the pipe and pressed the plunger-button. A pink stream shot out into the cup.

Manning tried it. "Hey, not bad," he said. He passed the cup over to Vega.

"Wonderful," Vega said When she'd tasted it. "It tastes more like wine!"

"The telemeter still says it's water, and it never lies," he said. He took a small amount of the water and the small packages he'd selected earlier. A moment later he had a bowlful of bright green salad. Another tiny package and the water produced the salad dressing for the greens. Then Manning again changed the controls on the servomotor and switched it on. The motor hummed and substance shimmered on the platform.

"You know," Manning said, watching it. "Centuries ago our ancestors used to titillate themselves with the question of which came first, the chicken or the egg. Now, if they'd had a servomotor, they could have answered the question." He reached out and picked up the egg from the platform. He broke it over the salad.

By this time the steaks were ready. They sat on the ground in front of the tent and ate.

"Sorry there's no coffee," Manning said when they'd finished. "I guess they decided that wrecked spacemen can get along without it. The servometer's coffee tastes too much like dishwater."

"I don't mind," Vega said. She'd stretched out on the ground and was sipping some of the pink water. "You know, I'm going to find it hard to realize that time is passing when the sun is always in the same place in the sky."

"It's passing, all right. Unless I've gotten twisted up, we just, had a fashionably late dinner."

"And a very good one, too. I've never met anyone who could cook so well out of thin air. You'd be a blessing to a thrifty housewife."

"I like you, too," Manning said. "In fact, I just polled myself a few minutes ago, and I've voted you the girl I'd most like to be stranded with on Caph II."

Vega laughed. "Why, thank you. Although I must say it sounds like a far-fetched possibility." She glanced at the tent. "Our new house looks quite nice. Tell me, does your magic raft also supply beds?"

"Bed," Manning said succinctly. He got up and walked over to the raft. When he returned he was carrying a small machine and a coil of wire. He sat on the ground and inserted the wire into the machine.

"Music, too?" Vega asked.

"Not exactly," Manning said. "I've been meaning to ask you something, Vega. Will you marry me?"

SHE STARED at him, wide-eyed. "I hadn't exactly thought of asking you in these particular surroundings," Manning, went on, "but I see no reason for letting Dzanku interfere with *everything*. Will you?"

She looked at him for a long moment, then nodded almost shyly. He leaned over to kiss her.

"You mean when we get back to Terra, don't you?" she asked later.

He shook his head, grinning. "No, I meant right now. I told you I'd been meaning to ask you."

"I don't understand," she said.

"Back on Terra," he said, "when the spy-ray told me there was someone already in my ship, I used a telemeter. The analysis of the perfume and cosmetics agreed with what you'd been wearing during the Festival. So I was pretty sure it was you. Remember that I requested a five-minute delay from the launching tower?"

She nodded.

"Well, I went into the terminal and applied for a wedding license to marry Vega Cruikshank. I also arranged for a remote ceremony. It's recorded on this magniwire. This machine can simultaneously record and play, so all we have to do is turn it on and answer in the proper places. The machine itself will automatically record the date. When we return we'll deposit the spool of wire with the Bureau of Records."

"I never knew science was so wonderful," Vega said.

"Oh, sure," Manning said. "At least, J. Barnaby can't question my intentions on this trip."

"It'll never occur to him." She giggled. "You know, Daddy had planned to send me on a trip with an old family retainer. Before I went to stow away on your ship, I bribed the servant to leave, so I'm sure Daddy thinks I'm safely touring the galaxy and recovering from a schoolgirl's infatuation. So if that's the only reason you're doing this, you can still change your mind."

"A Draco never takes a backward step," Manning declared.

He switched on the machine. A moment later, they were responding to the voice that came from the loudspeaker.

When it was over, Manning picked up Vega and carried her into the tent.

"Under the circumstances," he said, "I think we can just ignore the Caphian sun and declare night to be any time we want it. But, first, a very important item…"

He hurried out of the tent. When he returned he was holding both hands behind him. "It didn't turn out exactly right," he said. "I'm afraid that the servomotor couldn't find enough sugar in the Caphian atmosphere, so the icing tastes a little like cotton." He brought one hand into view. It was holding a reasonable facsimile of a wedding cake. Then he produced the other hand. In it was two cups of Caphian water. "Pink Champagne," he said.

Vega laughed and came into his arms. The wedding cake and the "pink champagne" dropped to the floor unnoticed.

It was much later before either of them spoke.

"It was very thoughtful of the Spacemen's Service," Vega said sleepily, "to provide only one bed."

CHAPTER SEVEN

B Y MANNING DRACO'S reckoning a week passed without any sign of Dzanku Dzanku or the Caphians. Except for the necessity of keeping a lookout, it might have been a pleasant honeymoon. Then, shortly after their eighth breakfast, one of the peculiar-looking Caphian vehicles came into sight, flying slowly toward them. Its course left no doubt that the campers had been spotted. Manning held the energy gun and waited.

The vehicle descended to the ground just out of firing range. The figure that climbed out was easily recognized as that of the Rigelian. He turned to face them, but made no move to draw closer.

Manning. It was a thought inside Manning's head. He recognized it as coming from Dzanku. The distance was too great for conversation, so the Rigelian was resorting to telepathy.

What took you so long? Manning thought.

My Caphians are still badly trained in the art of intrigue. Dzanku's thought was tinged with embarrassment. *It was only about an hour ago that they discovered the life raft was gone from your ship. Until then it was believed that you were hiding somewhere on the dark side. The penalty of inadequate help.*

"What's going on?" Vega asked.

"I'll tell you later, honey," Manning said.

Are you armed? came Dzanku's thought.

Yes.

I was afraid so. Unfortunately, the Caphians have very inferior weapons and I neglected to bring any with me. You see, I am being perfectly frank with you, my dear Manning.

Nice of you, Manning thought ironically.

Not at all. Due to a blunder you have been permitted to gain a temporary stalemate. I'd rather not have to sit it out. So if you and Miss Cruikshank would care to surrender, I will merely hold you as prisoners until the insurance policies are paid, and then you can go home.

You mean the Great Gray Father will take us under his wing. Dryly.

Yes. I can guarantee your eventual freedom even though the Caphians are disturbed by the turn of events. They think it was very unsporting of you.

So sorry to disappoint them, Manning thought. *And you. But I'm afraid we rather like it here. So we'll have to turn down your kind offer.*

Why? I know your raft is incapable of taking you off Caph. I also know that you can't get a message out. We both know that J. Barnaby will not let loose of one trillion credits until the last possible minute. That's thirty days Terran time—which is more than a year and a half on Caph.

We have enough food for two years. And before the time is up J. Barnaby will ask the patrol to investigate why he hasn't heard from me.

You refuse to surrender, then?

Yes.

Dzanku turned and re-entered the Caphian ship. A moment later it lifted into the air and moved leisurely away.

"Now will you tell me what that was about?" Vega demanded. "The two of you standing a mile apart and glaring at each other!"

Manning repeated the telephathic messages and explained his own special abilities along that line. If he exaggerated a trifle, it can be blamed on the fact that Vega was beautiful and that they had been married only a week. And if she seemed to believe even more than he said, it was because matters have always stood in this fashion between a man and woman in love.

"I don't think I like that," she said, frowning. "Imagine being married to a man who can read your mind. It's positively indecent."

"Your mind?"

"No, silly. It's an invasion of privacy. They shouldn't permit people like you to just wander around."

"*We* have ethics," Manning said loftily. "Besides, you could always have me arrested for wife-peeping." He put his arm around her and drew her closer.

DURING THE NEXT three weeks there were four attempts made on them. Three times the Caphians came by air, and once on foot. They were armed with primitive combustion weapons which were no match for Manning's energy gun. All four raids ended in a complete defeat for the Caphians, without Manning and Vega even being in danger.

"We ought to be due for another visit from Dzanku," Manning said after the fourth try. "I think it's about time to switch tactics."

"How?"

"If we just stay on the defensive, Dzanku is liable to come up with something that's too much for us. He's plenty smart and he does have enough time. I doubt if your father will get worried enough to have the patrol sent for about three weeks—which is sixty weeks Caphian time."

"But what can we do?"

"I think we have one chance," Manning said slowly. "Rigelians are great gamblers. In fact, they can't resist any sort of gambling. I've used this gambit against Dzanku before, so it'll have to be something special. I think I will challenge Dzanku to a game of *Tzitsa*." [21]

"That's a game?" Vega asked.

"It's a game," Manning said. "You might call it a sort of cosmic and deadly crossword-puzzle game. It's limited to two

---

21   *Tzitsa* was invented by Tzitsakele Tzitsakele, a famous gamester of the 12th Dynasty on Rigel IV, after whom it is named. It was an immediate success with the Rigelians and has always remained the most popular game on that planet. Tzitsa is directly responsible for keeping the Rigelian population at low level, it being estimated that there are around one billion *Tzitsa* fatalities on Rigel IV each year. Emanuel Chotnik, the well-known Terran philosopher, contends that *Tzitsa* is the greatest boon the galaxy has ever known; that without it as a check on the Rigelian population, Rigel IV would have long ago attempted to conquer the galaxy. The fatalities also explain why the game has never been taken up, except in a modified and more peaceful form, by other telepathic races.

players. Dzanku certainly gets few chances to indulge in it. He could play it with Pisha-Paisha, since the Sabikian is telepathic; but he needs him, so that would take the pleasure out of it. You see, *Tzitsa* is continued day after day, never ending until one of the two players is either dead or a drooling idiot. Dzanku will jump at the chance to play with me."

"But it's dangerous," Vega protested.

"No more so than sitting here," Manning said. "This way, Dzanku can keep trying out new ideas until he hits on one that works. It he's playing *Tzitsa* with me, he'll have no time to be working out other schemes. I can hold my own with him mentally, and maybe I can trick him into a position where I can win."

"But how can you trust him?" Vega wanted to know. "If we go back to the dark side, he'll have us where he wants us."

"Normally, that would be true, honey. Judged by our standards, Rigelians are amoral. To them, lying, stealing, and getting the best of anyone in any way is socially acceptable. If Dzanku can cheat me when we're playing, he will. But if he were to kill us or imprison us when we've gone there specifically to play *Tzitsa*, that would be tantamount to running out on a gambling challenge. That would disgrace Dzanku for life. The fact that I'm a Terran would make it worse. So Dzanku's pride will force him to keep his word."

AS MANNING predicted, within twenty-four hours one of the Caphian ships appeared and settled to the ground just out of the range of an energy gun. The Rigelian appeared and faced toward them.

Are you ready to surrender, Manning?

We're very comfortable, Manning thought in response.

Don't let your small success go to your head. The only reason you're still alive is that the Caphians have always considered this half of their planet out of bounds. Except for very brief hunting forays after a certain insect which they like, they have had a deep prejudice against coming here. But I am overcoming this, and when they are finally convinced, I will have one hundred million Caphians, all of whom are expendable. What chance do you think your puny little energy gun will have then?

Manning Draco carefully kept his secondary shield drawn over any deeper thoughts as he projected his answer. *We'll worry about that when you get them convinced. Our only problem here is one of boredom when there are no Caphians to shoot. The next time you drop out, you might bring along a small Tzitsa board, if you have one.*

He caught the flash of excitement in Dzanku's mind before the Rigelian blocked it out. *You play Tzitsa?*

Didn't you know? Manning thought, with just the proper amount of surprise. *I learned from Sbita Sbita. Three or four years ago.*

Sbita Sbita vanished four years ago.

I know. He made a mistake on his four thousand and second horizontal.

Sbita Sbita was a good player. No more thoughts followed it. Manning knew that back of his secondary shield, Dzanku was wrestling with temptation.

"I think I've got him," Manning said softly to Vega.

I don't have a small Tzitsa board, came the Rigelian's thought finally, *but I have had the Caphians build a regulation board in one of the buildings in Optville. It's as fine as any board on Rigel. I've been having a few practice games with Pisha-Paisha, but Sabikians have no flair for games. If you'd care to come into the city...*

And have you grab us the minute we crossed into the darkness? Manning thought scornfully.

No. Upon my gambling honor, you and Miss Cruikshank will not be molested in any way. The only restriction is that your ship will still be guarded and you will not be permitted near your communications.

Manning let a sense of excitement and temptation flash across the surface of his thoughts, and then he apparently clamped down on them as though to conceal an eagerness to play. *There would have to be conditions.*

What?

We are no longer to be known by those ridiculous appellations, the Public Enemy and the Gangster's Moll. If you must have them, elect new ones. The scope of the Tzitsa *must be limited to Ancient Terra. And it must be announced at the beginning that if I win, I take over all of your powers on this planet.*

Dzanku hesitated only a minute.

Agreed. I will return for you soon. As he turned toward his ship, the Rigelian's thoughts were heavy with arrogance and triumph. He didn't bother to try to conceal the amusement he felt at the thought that a Terran dared to challenge him at *Tzitsa.*

Manning and Vega watched the ship leave.

"Well?" Vega asked.

"He fell for it," Manning said. "He's so sure of himself that he even agreed to limiting the game to Ancient Terra. He might have scorned playing with me, but I convinced him that I'm good."

"How?"

"I told him that I learned to play from Sbita Sbita and that I finally defeated him. Sbita was a Rigelian who finally pulled one trick too many and was killed on Deimos four years ago. But practically no one knows how he was killed, so Dzanku was willing to believe me. He's coming back for us."

"Manning," Vega asked uncertainly, "are you sure we should go? We're safe here."

"It's better this way, honey," he said. He put his arm around her and drew her close. "Don't worry. We'll pull through."

CHAPTER EIGHT

A FEW HOURS later, Dzanku was back. Manning and Vega got in the life raft and followed him back into the darkness of the other side of the planet. Manning started using his torch as soon as they left the sunlight.

They set the ships down near a large building and went inside. It was by far the largest building they'd seen on Caph. Its ceiling was a good twenty stories above the floor. One entire wall and the ceiling were covered with closely fitted blocks about a foot square.

Sam Warren was there, grinning nervously as they came in. There were a small handful of Caphians present, but that was all.

"Where are all your little friends?" Manning asked, looking around.

"We elected a new Public Enemy and and a new Gangster's Moll," Dzanku said, "so they're all out hunting them. There's nothing they love more than a good exciting chase. Playful little rascals, aren't they?"

"Oh, very," Manning said dryly.

"I shall miss them when I've retired with my half-a-trillion credits," Dzanku said.

"*If* you retire," Manning responded. "You want to talk all day, or shall we play *Tzitsa?*"

"By all means, we shall play," Dzanku said. His three eyes were alight with excitement. "It's too bad you never mentioned this talent of yours before, Manning, old friend. Come on."

He led the way to one end of the room. There were two large, comfortable chairs facing each other. Near them were smaller chairs.

"Miss Cruikshank and Sam can be observers," Dzanku said. "I've trained a number of Caphians to work the switchboard, so everything is in readiness."

"Manning," Vega said, as she walked with him to his chair, "how does this work?"

"Simple," Manning said. "It's much like a crossword puzzle. Let us say that Dzanku goes first. He has to give me the definition of a word and the number of letters in it. But only one of these does he give me vocally. The other I have to pick out of his mind. It's only a thought. Then I can either work out what the word is or try to pull the word itself out of his mind from behind his secondary shield. While I'm doing that my mental defenses must be let down to some degree and he will then try to strike with enough mental force to kill me. As the game progresses, it becomes more complicated because each new word must fit into the overall pattern up there." He pointed to the squares on the wall and the ceiling.

"As each word is given," he continued, "it is put up there. Lights back of the blocks spell it out. As the game progresses, we must try to form the pattern of words into a recognizable design. And we take turns. First, Dzanku will feed a definition and try to kill me while I'm getting the word; then I will give him a definition and try to kill him while he's getting it. And this goes on until one of us wins." He grinned reassuringly at her.

"Are you ready?" Dzanku asked. Manning nodded.

"Horizontal, twenty-one," the Rigelian said.

"A Vtiga gambit,"[22] Manning muttered.

"Five letters," Dzanku announced.

MANNING DRACO warded off the probing strength of the Rigelian's mind and fished for the thought. He got it almost immediately: *Agalloch wood.*

"Garoo," he announced. A second later, the word flashed into existence on the wall.

The first few rounds, Manning knew, would be easy. Neither he nor Dzanku would be anxious to futilely waste mental strength, so they'd both make only tentative stabs for a while.

"What happens," Vega whispered to him, "if you get a word

22 Although a *Tzitsa* game may last for months or even years if the opponents are evenly matched in mental strength and skill, which means hundreds of thousands of horizontal and vertical strings of words, the Regelian rules provide for the players to proceed in blocks of one hundred words each way. The players may skip around within the framework of the hundred words across and the hundred words down, but the final square must still fit together. The Rigelian who started this rule was Vtiga Vtiga. Therefore, the player who chose to start with any position other than Horizontal One, or Vertical One, was said to be using a Vtiga gambit.

that fits the definition and the spaces but wasn't the one he was thinking of?"

"It counts," Manning said. He turned his attention back to the Rigelian. "Vertical fifty. Sour ale." He thought: *six letters,* and felt Dzanku nibbling at his mind. He lashed out and his strength bounced off Dzanku's shield.

"Alegar," the Rigelian said, and the word flashed on the wall. Dzanku continued: "Vertical one. Six letters." *Boastful air.*

"Parado," Manning said as he caught the thought. "Horizontal one. Seven letters." *Bowstring hemp.*

"Pangane," Dzanku answered.

It was, Manning thought, almost like fencing; but with mental energy instead of foils. It was parry and thrust, parry and thrust, only there was no pinking; a careless guard would be fatal.

"Vertical thirty-five. Grivet."

Four letters.

"Waag.... Horizontal seventy-two. Seven letters."

Green cheese.

"Sapsago.... Horizontal fourteen. Not to be escaped."

Eleven letters.

"Ineluctable.... Vertical ten. Starvation."

Six letters.

"Inedia.... Horizontal ninety-three. Two letters."

Whirlwind.

"Oe.... Horizontal forty. Spade-shaped."

Nine letters.

"Palaceous.... Vertical eighty-one. Synthetic rubber."

Nine letters.

"Elastomer.... Vertical forty-two. Sponge spicule."

And so it went. Placement, definition, number of letters. Parry and thrust. Answer. Manning Draco and Dzanku Dzanku crouched in the two chairs facing each other, their voices falling into buzzing monotones, their faces occasionally straining with effort. A small section of the wall lighted up with words.

Twice they stopped to eat and take a short rest; then they were back at the deadly game. In the beginning, they took no more than a minute for each word, but the time slowly lengthened. Halfway through the day they were up to about five minutes for each word, and this proved to be about their average. Sometimes they took longer, when one or the other would make a surprise thrust and their mental energies would be locked for several suspense-filled seconds.

THEY'D BEEN AT IT for twelve hours when they finally halted for the day. They were to meet in the same place twelve hours from now. Manning was gray with tiredness. Dzanku's eyestalks drooped with fatigue.

After that, so far as Manning was concerned, all time became a refined torture. For twelve hours each day he and Dzanku played *Tzitsta*, battering at each other's mind's. Then he would stagger to his hotel, with Vega helping him, and fall into deep sleep. When he would awaken, they'd be at it again. There was only darkness, the dim lights of the Caphian buildings, and the endless parries and thrusts of mental energy. Hours and days all melted into each other, and fatigue gripped him until he wondered if he'd be able to meet Dzanku again. But somehow he always found the strength, and they'd be at it again.

"To think," Manning said to Vega, "Rigelians do this for *fun*. No wonder we think they're a little crazy."

At first, Manning tried to keep a more accurate track of time by marking each session on the wall. But there were a few occasions when he was too tired to make even a mark, and soon his record was thrown off. Although he wasn't certain, he felt that too much time had passed and that he'd better make an attempt to end it.

The session that ended with Vertical twenty-five thousand, two hundred and eighty[23] was the one in which he decided that

---

23 This may seem like a long-playing game, and in terms of Terran games it was. Many games of *Tzitsa*, however, run this long on Rigel IV. The Rigelian record ended on Horizontal 627,453. It was a game of *Tzitsa* between Bloota Bloota and

he'd have to make his supreme effort the following day.

He'd tried a number of tricks, as had Dzanku, but none of them had worked. He had, however, worked out a new tactic which he thought might turn the trick.

The session that day was starting with a brand new block somewhere near the center of the ceiling. For the first time since they'd started playing, Manning Draco made no attempt to strike at Dzanku. He kept his own shield as securely locked as he could and concentrated on developing a special pattern of words on the ceiling.

The lack of attack made the Rigelian cautious, but as the hours went by with no trick in sight he recovered his vigor, lashing viciously at Manning. But he was still curious enough so that it was obvious that the new tactic had him worried.

The most immediate result of this was that Dzanku was the more exhausted of the two as they went into the final stretch of the session. Throughout nine hours, Manning had carefully fed words to Dzanku in such a manner that in the center of the ceiling there was a fairly solid block of words with the exception of a smaller block. Focal point of this smaller block was Horizontal twenty-five thousand, three hundred and forty-one. The words around it had limited it to eight letters. Vertical words had supplied four of the letters, so that it looked like this: A-A-A-A.

"Abigeat," Manning said, supplying the word for the last definition Dzanku had given. "Horizontal twenty-five thousand, three hundred and forty-one. Eight letters."

Calmness.

Manning turned to look at Vega and laughed.

Dzanku fumbled for the word. For once, he was slightly off balance. His tentacles were undulating nervously. He was becom-

---

Zhunfa Zhunfa held on Rigel IV In 2946. When it ended in the defeat of Zhunfa, Bloota was himself so exhausted that he was unable to kill Zhunfa, although he did erase nearly all the latter's synapses. The winning word, incidentally, was *Zzxzzzy*—a phonetic spelling of an obsolete Spican word meaning "So what?"

ing more and more worried by the fact that Manning had not struck at him once all day. The sight of Manning's carelessness, in the face of his own inability to immediately think of the word, made him try to snatch the answer from Manning's mind. He felt the Terran's shield give slightly and then stiffen. The Rigelian put all his strength into trying to find the concealed word.

He felt triumphant as he caught a fleeting suggestion of a word that seemed to be *ataraxia*. Of course, he thought—

AT THAT MOMENT, Manning Draco struck with all his force. The strength which he had carefully marshaled throughout the day exploded against Dzanku's shield. There was a split second when the wily Rigelian struggled to repair his defense, but then Manning was through the shield. At the last moment, he softened the blow. He steeled himself against the impact of that alien mind and stayed there.

Dzanku Dzanku struggled futilely against the possession, something akin to panic in his three eyes. Finally, he subsided. His skin was ashen.

"Finish it," he gasped.

"No," Manning said. His voice was hoarse with strain, but he didn't dare use any of his strength to project thoughts, so he spoke. "I'll give you a chance to live. Did you announce that I would succeed you here if I won?"

"Yes," the Rigelian said.

Manning could tell this was the truth. "Tell Sam," he said, "to go get your Sabikian friend and bring him here. And you'd better tell him to warn the Sabikian to behave himself when he gets here."

"Go ahead, Sam," Dzanku said weakly. "You heard him."

The frightened little Terran scuttled from the building.

In a few minutes, he returned with Pisha-Paisha, and the two of them stood waiting for further orders.

"I'm letting you escape," Manning said with effort, "on one condition. I'll let you go to Caph I, but nowhere else. In fact,

I'll see to it that you have no way of returning without finding a fuel there. And since you liked selling twenty-year-endowment policies so well, you can represent J. Barnaby on that one planet and for that one type of policy only. As long as you stay on Caph I and sell those policies, you'll be all right. But I'll arrange to have the patrol throw a blockade around the Time-Fracture so if you ever leave you'll be nabbed. Do you accept that?"

"Yes," Dzanku said.

"Sam and Pisha-Paisha?"

"Whatever Dzanku says," Sam Warren mumbled.

"Yes," the Sabikian said in his booming voice.

"Okay," Manning said. He exerted a twisting force, then withdrew from the Rigelian's mind. There was a cry of pain from Dzanku and he slumped to the floor, unconscious.

While Sam Warren and Pisha-Paisha were still staring at Dzanku, Manning Draco struck again. This time at the Sabikian. The shield was a slight one and the Sabikian dropped to the floor beside the Rigelian.

"All right, Sam," Manning said. "I guess I can take care of you. So I'll help you start your trip." He turned to look at Vega. He saw how tired she looked and the lines of pain on her face. He shouted to the few Caphians in the building.

"Your Great Gray Father has resigned," he told them, nodding toward the recumbent Rigelian. "I am now your Great White Father. My wife doesn't feel well. Take her to our hotel and assist her in any way you can." He kissed Vega. "I'll be with you as soon as I can, honey. Take care."

He hurried out with Sam Warren. It took them no more than an hour to convert one of the Caphian ships into something that would be able to fly to Caph I. In converting it, Manning was careful to cripple the ship which had brought Dzanku to Caph II. When the patched-up Caphian ship was ready, Manning saw to it that it was fueled enough to take it to the other planet and no more. Then he had the Caphians carry Dzanku Dzanku and Pisha-Paisha into the ship.

"They'll recover in two or three hours," he told Sam Warren. "It's been nice seeing you, Sam."

Sam Warren gave a sickly grin and went into the ship. A moment later it rose in the darkness and headed for Caph I. Manning Draco hurried back to his hotel.

CHAPTER NINE

THE DRACO family spent another week on Caph II. As Manning explained to Vega, he could have used his power to make the Caphians settle for the return of their premiums, but he wanted to be fair with them. She agreed. So he spent several days coming to an agreement with them about their policies. Then he spent a few more days with them on purely personal business. When he was through, the Caphians were happily engaged in a new pastime.

Manning and Vega made the trip from the surface of Caph II to the outer rim of its atmosphere in several hours, going slowly so that sunlight would not burst too quickly upon eyes unaccustomed to light. Then he threw the *Alpha Actuary* into magnidrive.

There was one more brief stop before going on home. Manning spent two hours with the dignified members of the Committee on Interplanetary Affairs. His connection with J. Barnaby Cruikshank was enough to get him admitted, but after that he was on his own. When he left, the senatorial faces were wreathed in happy smiles.

It was not much later that Manning Draco strode into the Nyork offices of the Greater Solarian Insurance Company, Monopolated. The mousy receptionist looked up from a magazine, her eighth finger on the right hand marking her place.

"Oh, Mr. Draco," she said brightly. "Shall I tell Mr. Cruikshank you're here?"

"Don't bother," Manning said. He started to walk by when her plaintive voice stopped him.

"Mr. Draco—I wonder if you could tell me a four-letter word meaning *no more?*"

Manning stopped in mid-stride. He slowly reached over and took the magazine from her hands. "In this case, it would be *torn*," he said evenly. He ripped the magazine into shreds.

He went on down the corridor. The door scanner recognized him and swung open. J. Barnaby Cruikshank, looking more disheveled than usual, turned away from the big video screen which showed him everything that went on in the outer office.

"What was the meaning of that little display of temper?" he demanded.

"I," Manning said, "have just spent eight months doing crossword puzzles. Twelve hours a day. Two thousand eight hundred and eighty hours. One hundred and seventy-two thousand—"

"Never mind," J. Barnaby said hastily. "How did you make out?"

Manning grinned. "I settled with the Caphians for fifty percent of the face value."

Relief and despair intermingled on J. Barnaby's face. "I'm a ruined man," he said in a melancholy voice. "That leaves me with a cash reserve of only thirteen units. Who can run a business on that?"

"You can," Manning said. "You'll have more money coming in. Besides, you'll more than make it up. Dzanku and Sam Warren are working for you."

"*What?*"

Manning nodded. "I've limited them to Caph I, however, and they are to sell only twenty-year-endowment policies. Those will be policies you'll never have to pay off on."

"What do you mean?"

"Twenty years on Caph I are fifty-two hundred years on Terra. So the policies will be due in 8673." Manning chuckled. "I think it also rids us of Dzanku and Sam Warren. By the time they can find a fuel and get away, at least a hundred years will pass here."

For the first time, J. Barnaby looked happier. Manning could almost see him adding up the premiums on the policies that might be sold on Caph I. "But what will I do for cash in the meantime? Manning, my boy, I may be late with your salary due to your rashness."

"That's all right," Manning said airily. "I'm quitting anyway."

"What?" For the second time, J. Barnaby was startled.

"As of now," Manning said, nodding, "I'm going into business for myself. I've made an arrangement with the Caphians, and I've been granted a monopoly by the Committee on Interplanetary Affairs—although I had to give the robbers ten percent."

"What business?"

"The Draco Vacation Service. Vacations on sunny Caph. It's just the thing for most of the population. Take a little overworked secretary who gets only a two-week vacation. By dealing with me, she can spend her vacation on Caph, which means she'll have ten months of rest and yet will be gone only two weeks. It'll mean that everyone can work eleven and a half months and rest ten months out of every twelve months. I'll put every other vacation spot out of business."

"That's—er—very nice," J. Barnaby said dully. He hated to hear of anyone else making money. "But you've certainly put me in a spot, Manning."

"You're just overtired, J. Barnaby," Manning said. "Why don't you take a week off and run up to Caph II? The five months' rest will make you feel like a new man. I'll tell you what—it's on the house. Won't cost you a cent."

"That's very nice of you, Manning," J. Barnaby said uncertainly.

"Why not come home with me now for dinner," Manning said. "You can relax and we'll talk about it. I got married while I was gone, you see."

"You did?" It was J. Barnaby's third surprise. "Well, that was unexpected. A Caphian female?"

Manning shook his head. "A Terran girl."

"Oh?"

"This wench," Manning said, "stowed away on my ship, and I discovered her after I was out in space. She turned out to be pretty, so I decided to marry her."

"Well—I'm very glad to hear it, Manning. Just what you needed, my boy. I'm delighted."

"I'm glad you're delighted," Manning said gravely. "How about it? Want to come home to dinner with me?"

"I believe I will," J. Barnaby said. He'd decided it wouldn't hurt to cultivate Manning now that Manning was becoming a monopolist himself. "Stowed away on your ship, eh? I guess I wouldn't know her then…."

"As a matter of fact, you do," Manning said. "Her name is—or was—Vega Cruikshank."

There was a long silence as J. Barnaby's face threatened to turn purple again. But at the last second he remembered that Manning Draco, the monopolist, was a different son-in-law than Manning Draco, the investigator.

"Well," he said weakly. "Married, huh? Er—congratulations."

"Thank you," Manning said. "Let's go now. I'd like you to see your grandson before he's put to bed. Incidentally, we've named him Barnaby Draco."

"Grandson!" yelped J. Barnaby Cruikshank. "Grandson? But that's impossible! You were gone only two weeks, and you said yourself that you met Vega only three days before you left."

"True. But while we were gone from, here only two weeks, we were on Caph II for ten full months." Manning slapped J. Barnaby on the shoulder. "Come on, Grandpop!"

GLOSSARY

Aircar. A vehicle which moves through the air instead of being confined to one plane of operation by gravity. Propelled in various ways, including jet, isoprene, carbon, magnetic, and hand propulsion. Latter method not recommended by the Academy of Space Flight.

Alnilam. The only contribution of the Alnilamese culture has been Fire-Ice, probably one of the strongest intoxicants in the galaxy. It is the opinion of the historian Gybor that the Alnilamese might have conquered the universe with Fire-Ice if they had only started soon enough.

Alphard. A second-magnitude star in the center of the constellation known as Hydra. Also called Alpha Hydrae.

Alphardian morals. Morals in this system seem to confuse Terrans, perhaps because the Alphardians consider feet secondary sexual characteristics. This explains the rather unfortunate occurrence of three years ago when a group of Terran women wore open-toed shoes on the streets of an Alphardian city.

Atik. Very little is known about Atikians except that they reproduce by the most primitive form of fission and have no sex life. It is believed that Atikians get very little fun out of life.

Bloota Bloota. Galactic champion *Tzitsa* player from 2902 to 2947. (As is the case with all Rigelians, Bloota's name is here spelled phonetically. There is no known Terran sound for the Rigelian obligative-guttural.)

Caphian Time-Fracture. For the benefit of those interested in the mechanics of Caph time as related to the rest of the galaxy, we offer the explanation of Vladimir Q. Fignewton, the federation astrophysicist. Since we are dealing with time coordinates, as well as spatial-coordinates, we shall denote the time of the event "now" by O. Thus $t = O$ denotes that the time of the event is now in terms of Terra and the rest of the galaxy, and in a similar manner that the event takes place "here" by O. But in referring to Caph II, we would say that $t = O \times 20$. In other words, on Caph II, the past has negative $\times 20$ ($N \times 20$) time coordinates, the present has zero $\times 20$ ($Z \times 20$) time coordinates, and the future has positive $\times 20$ ($P \times 20$) time coordinates. Now, to explain the Caphian Time-Fracture: We find that Caph (the sun), whose mass is M, exerts a pull on Caph II (sometimes called the planet Opt) with a force

$$f = M \times \frac{4\pi^2 K}{R^2}$$

(Here K depends on the nature of Caph II, and R is the radius of the orbit of Caph II.) Since neither Caph II nor its sun falls on one another, we may assume that the two forces f and F are equal,

$$M \times \frac{4\pi^2 K}{R^2} = m \times \frac{4\pi^2 K}{R^2}$$

or:

$$Mk = mK$$

From this we have:

$$K/M = k/m$$

which signifies that these ratios are the same for Caph as for Caph II. Let us denote the ratio

$$K/M \text{ (or } m/k) \text{ by } c/4\pi^2$$

We have then

$$K/M = c/4\pi^2, \text{ or } 4\pi^2 K = cM$$

and

$$k/m = c/4\pi^2, \text{ or } 4\pi^2 k = cm$$

Then the expression

$$f = M \times \frac{4\pi^2 k}{R^2},$$

after 4π2k is replaced by cm, becomes

$$f = c \times \frac{(mM)}{(R^2)}$$

This expression is the mathematical statement of Fignewton's law of general Time-Fracture. The more mathematically alert readers will instantly notice that the $Z \times 20$ coordinates appear nowhere in the Fignewton Law. This is because Fignewton has proved that the event cannot possibly take place "here" by O (ref. the beginning of this definition) since, due to the Time-Fracture, Caph II is neither "here" nor "there"; therefore, postulates Fignewton, the $Z \times 20$ coordinates have no place in any theory which attempts to prove the existence of the Time-Fracture. This has led certain short-sighted critics to label the Fignewton Law "The Theory of the Excluded O." In rebuttal, however, it should be noted that Fignewton's assertion can be proved by

$$s = \frac{v^2 \sin 2A}{g}$$

Castorian rummy. Readers are warned against playing this game with strangers. Be especially wary of playing with any form of life which has tentacles.

Chess, four-dimensional. Invented by Horace Homer Humptafield in 2983. Beginners are recommended to start with Humptafield Parchesi in order to get used to thinking about infinity before moving on to chess.

Coma-Virgo Galaxy. Although a few individuals from this galaxy, such as Nar Oysnarn, have recently visited our universe, we still know very little about this near (only ten million light-years away!) neighbor. We understand, however, that the Federation's Committee on Expanding Frontiers has government psychologists studying the mentality of the weird life forms found there.

Committee on Interplanetary Affairs. A ranking committee of the Galactic Congress. It passes on all business transactions throughout the galaxy and grants all monopoly charters. By coincidence, six of the seven members are Terrans.

Credit. Cash. A credit is worth approximately $1.75, Terran Old Currency.

Cybernetic mind-reading. A patented method of electronically recording the innermost thoughts of any intelligent being. We are told that the exact details have never been released because the process is so simple that anyone could build his own C.M.R. out of odds and ends.

Demagnetizer. An inverse magnetic action which completely erases all magnetic flux in any object which is the focal point of the action. With all magnetism gone, the object falls apart. Used to destroy approaching meteors and (occasionally) a favorite uncle who has just made out his will.

Door-scanner. A method by which a door, using a variation of a platinum-iridium Sponge, can "remember" the structure of a regular visitor and "recognize" him on a return trip. Generally speaking, this is a fairly successful gadget, but we have heard reports of such a door, on being faced by identical twins, short circuiting and quickly making an ash of itself.

Doppler effect. To an observer approaching the source of any wave motion, the frequency appears greater than to an observer moving away. This explains why waiters never see you beckon them.

Dtseea. An alcoholic beverage popular on Pollux. The reason it tasted like fermented swamp water to Manning Draco was because it *is* fermented swamp water.

FBI. Federation Bureau of Investigation.

FBI Special Training School. A place for developing certain species which otherwise might be classified as inferior animals.

Fignewton, Vladimir Q. Terran mathematician, 3420-3486. Famous for founding fignometry, a branch of calculus used for measuring voids.

Fission. A method of reproduction used by life forms who haven't learned any better.

Galactic Federation. A political union of 107 planetary republics.

Galaxy. The Milky Way, containing several billion star systems.

Gelding scout. Alpha Centauri's version of a boy scout. On Centauri, however, the young scouts are gelded so that nothing can interfere with their pursuit of woodsy lore.

Glo-Shav. A method of removing facial hair by means of light, or electromagnetic waves at the wavelength of approximately 8×10^{-5} cm.

Humanoid. Nonhuman life which has evolved along similar lines to humans.

Humptafield, Horace Homer. Inventor of four-dimensional chess and Humptafield Parchesi.

Hydroponics. A method of growing plant life without benefit of soil. Known by early Terran Southern sharecroppers.

Infinity. Slightly more than a *googol.*

Jupiter. The largest planet in the solar system. Used as a penal colony after 2876.

Light-year. Astronomical measure of distance, the distance traveled by light in one year. Approximately six trillion miles.

Lorentz-Fitzgerald Contraction. The theory that a moving body contracts in length along its line of motion, ultimately reaching zero length at the speed of light—making it impossible for any ship to exceed 186,326 miles per second. The Terran scientist Glomb was in the middle of finally proving this theory when a Terran pilot succeeded in traveling 377,424 miles per second. Glomb later became assistant janitor at the Terran Space Academy.

Mind shield. A mental force field which prevents a telepath from mind-reading.

Monopolist. One who has obtained a charter from the government giving him a monopoly throughout a certain area of the Federation.

Nyork. Phonetic spelling of New York (Terra), accepted as standard in 2375.

Other. The name of the third parent (father and mother being the first two) on Merak. It is believed that two of the parents take active part in conceiving the child while the third parent bears and rears it. Merakians being somewhat modest, however, there has never been any proof of this.

Parallax. The angle between the direction of two bodies, as seen from two different points of view. Example: A man about to enter the apartment of his mistress suddenly realizes his wife is standing in the hallway. The resulting viewpoints would constitute a parallax.

Parsec. Approximately 3.3 light-years. A unit of measure seldom needed by the average man.

Praesepe. A misty patch in the center of the constellation Cancer. Manning Draco's mistake there was in not realizing that something called limeade was actually made from lime and not limes.

Rigel. A star system approximately 542 light-years from Terra. The fourth planet is the only one inhabited. No extensive studies have been made, but it is known that Rigel has a completely criminal culture. Also, Rigel and Sabik are the only two known systems in our galaxy where the life form is completely alien to anything known on Terra.

Seven Hundred Year War. The interplanetary war lasting from 2306 to 3014.

Sex. (Censored.)

Sexcycle. A six-wheeled vehicle on Pollux, having nothing to do with the popular Terran sport despite the suggestive name.

Smith, Vladimir. A mediocre chess player until he lost his arm in the fourth dimension in 3201. Thereafter he made a fortune by writing his memoirs.

Spaceport. A landing and launching field for spaceships.

Telepathy. Sometimes known as E.S.P. It was soon discovered that the universe was about equally divided between telepathic and nontelepathic races. The latter invariably had natural mind blocks so their minds could not be invaded by telepaths. The only exception to this was Terrans (Manning Draco was the only Terran with any degree of telepathic ability) and their minds could be invaded by anyone—but no one wanted to.

Terra. See Prolog.

Terrans. Those inhabitants of Terra who are loosely classified as Man.

Thought-probers. Professional mindreaders of Alpha Cygni. They did a brisk trade with Terran businessmen.

Transverse Fission Council. The birth-control body on Muphrid. Considering the procreative potential of the Muphridians, something of the sort was necessary or they would have overrun the galaxy.

Tzitsa. A lethal form of crossword puzzle.

Tzitsakele, Tzitsakele. A Rigelian of the 12th Dynasty (about 1950) who invented *Tzitsa.*

Unit. Small cash. The equivalent of 17½ cents, Terran Old Currency. One hundred units equal one credit.

Venusian tree-dragon. A protein-breathing dragon, resembling a slippery elm tree in appearance, native to Venus. Unwary tourists are often trapped when they stop to rest beneath what they think is a tree, only to be quickly breathed in.

ABOUT THE AUTHOR

KENDELL FOSTER CROSSEN (1910–1981) was raised in Ohio and South Dakota, and worked in the Upson steel mills, in the Fisher Body Corporation, and as an insurance investigator. In 1937 he became associate editor at the old Munsey Company, where he edited a variety of magazines, including mystery, adventure, cheesecake, movie fan, and comics.

He began writing fiction in 1939. Under the pseudonyms Ken Crossen, Richard Foster, Bennett Barlay, and Kent Richards, he sold about two million words of mystery and adventure stories. In addition, he wrote radio scripts for *Suspense, Mystery Theatre, The Kate Smith Show,* and *The Saint.* His pulp character the Green Lama appeared under the name Richard Foster in *Double Detective* magazine as well as a series of comic books. His science fiction books include the futuristic novels *Once Upon a Star* (1953), *Year of Consent* (1954), and *The Rest Must Die* (1959), as well as two edited anthologies, *Adventures in Tomorrow* (1951) and *Future Tense* (1952). In the 1950s–1970s, under the names M.E. Chaber and Christopher Monig, Ken Crossen wrote a series of insurance detective and spy novels, notably those featuring the globe-trotting Milo March.

Made in the USA
Lexington, KY
30 May 2017